Enjoy the book
let me know what you think

MDThrillers@AOL.com

MD RD

# POINT SOURCE

# POINT SOURCE

### Richard G. Pellegrino
### M.D., Ph.D.

MOMENTS OF DISCOVERY PRESS™
Hot Springs, Arkansas
YourMovieProject.com

Moments of Discovery™ Press
P.O. Box 20230
Hot Springs, Arkansas, 71903
YourMovieProject.com™
1-866-storyline


ISBN  0-9748396-0-4

Cover by Joe A. Correia Photography, Hot Springs, Arkansas, based on a design by Josh Cannon. Typeset by Hall Printers, Hot Springs, Arkansas.

*This book is dedicated to my wife, Rita,
the author of my own personal true love story
since she was sweet sixteen.*

# ACKNOWLEDGMENTS

I'd like to begin by thanking all the women in my life, without whose criticism, I would not be the man I am today. In particular I'd like to thank Nancy Gratton, my editor, for her patience and diligence in seeing this project through to fruition. Her advice and counsel were invaluable. I'd also like to thank Mike Politis, Ph.D., DVM, my creative collaborator, for the many hours of work he put into the project. The editorial comments of my wife, Rita Pellegrino, were instrumental in shaping this book.

The manuscript was read by Silvia Frank, Penny Thornton, Carol Jeffers, Carla Thibodeaux, Nina and Gus Pellegrino, Lellie-Beth Rhodes and Beth Williams, and their thoughtful comments are greatly appreciated. Carla has also spent countless hours helping with the production aspects of this book. I'd also like to thank my colleague, Dr. Padmini, and my staff: Pam Ames, Mary Melinda Davis, Diana McAlister, Jan McRaven, Lisa Perry, Judy Rone, and Sandy Spalding for holding down the fort when I had to concentrate on writing. Thanks also to Josh Cannon who created the original cover design. I'd also like to thank Jesse Elliott, Staff Sgt. Michael J. Avila, USMC, Geoffrey Wolf, R. J. Dunn, Janet Welch, Cathern Kinsey, Katherine Rowe, Bob Pellegrino and James Talbert, all of whom provided technical information that went a long way to lending credibility to some of my descriptions and plot twists. My brother Ron and his wife Ann helped a great deal with legal and business matters. I would also like to acknowledge my patients and especially those who participated in YourMovieProject.com and were kind enough to give me insight into their lives. On this score, I would like to particularly thank Su Jolley, Jacque Fondren, and Danna Fordyce. Of course, I could not have done this without the understanding of my wife and children, who have shown great patience while I devoted untold hours that should have been spent with them to the writing of this book.

A very special thanks goes to my parents and grandparents, whose lives illustrated the American dream, and to my children, Richard and Rachael, whose job it is to keep that dream alive.

# FOREWORD

*Point Source* is a real page-turner; a medical thriller that begins with a rare cluster of a debilitating neurological disease in a small Arkansas town and develops into a bioterrorist plot with international implications. Previously healthy people are suddenly becoming frighteningly ill, and their symptoms are alarmingly similar to those that characterize multiple sclerosis (MS). First to learn of the danger is an ordinary citizen—ordinary except for the fact that she has spent years living with MS. She enlists the aid of an intrepid neurologist with a taste for puzzle solving. The doctor, Angela Donatelli, takes charge, and leads a band of unlikely heroes against a terrifyingly remote but deadly enemy.

The book combines a chilling plot with a thrilling conclusion. Evil forces are matched against scientific ingenuity, compassion, persistence, and common sense. The story is as complex as the real life mystery of viruses and MS.

The author, Dr. Richard Pellegrino, is a neurologist in Hot Springs, Arkansas, renowned for his work in clinical research and his expertise on multiple sclerosis. He brings together his medical training and a profound appreciation of rural Arkansas and its people. His characters are well drawn, his plotting is fast-paced, and his portrayal of the disease of MS and its impact on patients and the people who love them is insightful.

And this is important, because Dr. Pellegrino wants to do more than tell a good story. He is a man with a mission—to enrich the public's understanding of the disease of MS. It is this aspect of his tale that means the most to me, for I too am a neurologist specializing in the treatment of MS. I identified with Dr. Pellegrino's accurate description of MS symptoms and the special bond that forms between people with MS and their friends and families. I admire the principal heroine, Dr. Donatelli, because she embodies the best of my breed: a very caring physician/scientist who is trying to balance her personal life with the urgent medical needs of her patients. Her commitment and determination to pursue her scientific instincts in solving the mystery are, in the end, the only weapons she can bring to her quest to save countless lives.

Jack Burks, M.D.
Chief Medical Officer
Multiple Sclerosis Association of America

*November 23, 2002 — 8:30 am*
*Yun Luck Restaurant, Hammerstone, Arkansas*

The message crawled along the bottom of the TV screen as
the talking heads blathered on, "South Korean statesman Bo Li
Yeung has set the date for his U.S. visit." Pulling back from the
set, Fred Kim snorted derisively. "Statesman! Ha!" To both
Charlie and Fred Kim—and to their ruler back in Pyongyang—
Bo Li was a treacherous fool, and a very real threat. More
immediately, he was their target. Because of him, they had
come to this small, unimportant Arkansas town and created
small, unimportant lives for themselves. To the ignorant people
of Hammerstone (pop. 2,227—could a town *be* any smaller,
Fred wondered), Fred and Charlie were just a couple of
Chinese waiters. But the local folks were mistaken. Fred and
Charlie were soldiers in Kim Il Sung's clandestine army, members of a small North Korean terror cell, set here in Arkansas
with a specific task in hand.

In the tiny room above the Yun Luck Restaurant, Charlie
Kim leaned back from the rickety card table at which he sat.
This was it, thought Charlie. Their prey was finally going to
walk into the trap. He wasn't set to come for another month,
but his arrival would finally justify their long, boring stay in
this miserable town. The time was drawing near when they

would strike their blow for The Beloved Ruler. After that, who knew? Perhaps they would die in the attempt. The thought made Charlie shudder, but he regained his composure and got to work. Time to make sure the weapon would be ready. He picked up the phone.

Fred, on the other hand, took his mortality fatalistically. For President Kim Il Sung and the glory of his homeland, Fred believed no sacrifice was too great. Whether they lived or died was irrelevant. The mission, to strike a blow against the enemies of The Beloved Ruler, was paramount.

They'd arrived little more than a year ago, taking over from two others who had initiated the project back in the late 1990s. They knew very little about the details of the mission—only that their predecessors had been educated men, whose mission had been to set up some kind of biological weapons manufacturing plant out in the hills beyond town. Once they'd made certain that the man tasked with creating the weapon was fully operational, their phase of the job had wound down. Control over the project passed to the military, and that's when Fred and Charlie had been ordered here to take over.

Fred turned with a start as he heard Charlie slam the phone down. That's the second time he'd failed to get through—Dr. Burns wasn't answering the phone. Their scientist was misbehaving again, Fred thought. This was surely not the glamorous duty they had imagined back in the homeland. They were just glorified babysitters, keeping watch on their pet weapons engineer. For months on end, there'd been nothing to do except perfect their cover stories in town, work in the restaurant, watch the news broadcasts, and periodically check in on the internet in the so-far vain hope that new orders would come through.

Charlie tried again and finally reached Burns on the other end of the line. "Dammit, where you been?" he shouted into the phone. He listened impatiently for a few seconds and then quickly cut in. "Today. It must be ready today!" Charlie listened a moment, then again rudely interrupted. "They'll pick it up at three o'clock. No later. And have the papers ready then, too." He slammed the phone down without waiting for a reply.

"Can you believe it?" Charlie's incredulousness was extreme enough to be apparent on his usually expressionless face. "He was out taking a walk! A walk! In those ruined hills. I don't see how he was ever trusted to do such important work."

Fred shook his head. "Trust was never a part of this," he observed. "We need only his brain, his skills. Once we've gotten what we need from those, we're done with Burns entirely." He grinned, and the feral glint in his eye would have given a lesser man a year of bad dreams.

*November 23, 2002 — 3:00 pm*
*Hammerstone, Arkansas*

Jennifer Richmond knelt at the edge of her garden plot, relentlessly clearing away the post-harvest detritus of her summer vegetable garden. Every now and then she rocked back on her heels to work the kinks out of her back. As she straightened up and stretched, her eyes were drawn up the forest-clad hills of Arrowhead Mountain, looming large over her little abode. The mountain had run wild now, although only a few short years ago there had been a thriving community nestled up there among the trees.

Jenn returned to her work, feeling a little like a school kid playing hooky. It wasn't often that she got to spend an afternoon at home, what with the demands of the antique shop she owned in town. Today, however, she'd left her partner in charge, giving her the perfect excuse to stay at home and play in her garden.

As she put a little muscle into pulling up some particularly stubborn roots, the peaceful silence of the day was broken by the rough cough of an old truck approaching Arrowhead Mountain from the direction of town. Once again, Jenn leaned back from her work, one hand brushing her hair from her eyes so she could get a better look. There had been a little more traffic than usual because of the high school bake sale, but this was the first vehicle she'd seen heading up towards the mountain. Looking closer, she recognized the beat-up old Dodge pick-up moving up the road. That told her all she needed to know, even from this distance. It had to be the Yancy boys, off on one of their odd jobs.

Luke and Jesse Yancy had been a year behind her in school, always in the same grade together, even though they'd been born a year apart. Jesse, the younger one, was a wise guy. Back then he seemed to spend half his life tinkering under the hood of a car. The other half was spent getting into fights, usually in defense of his brother Luke. Luke was strong and good natured, but really didn't have sense enough to come in out of the rain, and Jesse just knew that the world would chew him up and spit him out if he were left to face it alone. In the cruel world of the schoolyard, Luke was picked on relentlessly.

The boys had grown up a few miles out of town. Most folks thought it was a shame that the boys grew up motherless—Vera Yancy had run off not long after Jesse was born—but they seemed to have grown like weeds under the careless eye of their father, Leroy. When Leroy died, right around the time the boys were finishing up their schooling, some in town thought maybe they ought to send Social Services out to the Yancy trailer to see to the boys. But Jesse wouldn't hear of it—said he and his brother could get by just fine on their own.

And so they had, it seemed. Jesse fixed up his dad's old Dodge and started hiring out for odd jobs, and pretty soon he and his brother were keeping busy enough. They took just about any job that required more brawn than brains, and truth to tell, folks sometimes hired them out of pure kindness—finding a reason to call on the boys for a weekend's worth of clearing brush, or house-painting. Now the Yancys were a fixture of the town, and their truck was a familiar sight to all of Hammerstone's residents.

Jennifer watched the pickup move on up the hill a moment longer, then turned her attention back to the garden. It was getting late, and she still hadn't begun planting the pansies that she bought that day. She looked at them. "OK, OK, hold your horses," she said as she bent back over and began again to clear the vines. No more time for daydreaming. The sun was getting low, and she hadn't begun cooking yet.

Inside the pickup, Luke was riding shotgun as usual—Jesse always kept driving duty for himself—and he was bored. Seemed like they'd been driving for hours, though it was probably more like 20 minutes. It was just that Luke didn't have a lot of personal resources to fall back on when there was nothing much to do. Not a thinker by any stretch of the imagination, on long drives he was stuck hanging his face out the passenger window and sucking up the breeze. Now that they were nearing the outskirts of Hammerstone, however, there was finally something worth looking at. He reached across the front seat and punched his brother on the arm.

"Hey, Jesse. There's ol' Jennifer. ' Member her? She's lookin' this way! Hit the horn, 'kay?

Jesse pushed his brother's offending arm away. "No time for that kind of foolishness, Luke," he said irritably. "We're on a job, remember? We got a schedule to keep." He listened to the laboring sound of the engine, already having trouble with the incline as they headed up into the foothills of Arrowhead Mountain. "Gotta concentrate on the road from here on up," he muttered, more to himself than to his brother. He spit out the window of the truck.

As the truck rolled past Jennifer in her garden, Luke managed a shy wave, but she was already looking down at her garden again, so he figured she might've missed it. Soon the truck started the steep climb that marked the start of North Indian Heights Trail.

When Luke and Jesse were just little kids, this stretch was simply known as Old Indian Trail, and it had run for several miles through the valley on its way out of town. Back in the late 80s, though, a developer bought up the mountain and put up a bunch of houses. To attract high-end buyers, this end of the old trail was rechristened North Indian Heights Trail, and the newly paved streets that ran through the subdivision were given cutesy names like "Wigwam Way" and "Running Brave Road." The developer got a lot of press when his contractors sank the first foundation holes, turning up artifacts by the shovel-full. After that, they were forced to work around several ancient novaculite mines, full of the arrowheads that gave the mountain its name.

But all that was old news now. Where once there were well-tended properties, now there was devastation. The community that graced the lower slopes of Arrowhead Mountain was all but gone, blown away by the violence of the tornado that ripped through the region six years ago.

As they began their climb, the truck gave a jarring bounce as the last of the maintained road fell away behind them and they hit the first of the ruts. The pavement from here on up was damaged by the tornado and debris and after years of neglect, much of it had eroded away. "Kinda scary, ain't it, Jesse?" Luke was gazing raptly out the window at the twisted landscape and crumbling houses. "All them big old houses, and the winds just tore 'em up."

Jesse heard the first small hint of fear in his big brother's voice—it didn't take much to spook him. "Nah," Jesse said gently. "Nothing to be scared about. The winds came, and now they're gone. You're safe with me." Then Jesse tuned his brother's chattering out as he set himself to concentrating. The road from here on in would only get worse.

Jesse cursed the town supervisors for the state of the roads. Even after all these years, the township never saw fit to at least clear the brush and fill the potholes left by the tornado's rage. Guess nobody saw the point. Ain't nobody stayed except Ol' Jack Burns. Maybe everybody felt he just wasn't worth the trouble, Jesse thought.

Jesse clasped the steering wheel tightly as he encountered a particularly difficult turn, but after that they rode a mile or so in relative peace. This job meant good money, but Jesse wasn't all that sure about the guy they were on their way to see. It seemed like he was some kind of hermit or something. At first, Jesse had figured that Burns was cooking up hootch or meth in his basement or something, what with all this secrecy. But if he was, Jesse couldn't figure out how the heck he was getting the stuff to market. Eventually Jesse had just stopped wondering.

Instead, he concentrated on doing his job. And his job was to make deliveries. Or at least, that's what it always had been. This time was different. This time he was supposed to pick something up. And suddenly, all Jesse's wondering was back in full force. He just hoped that there wasn't any trouble in the package that waited for him at the Burns house.

The sound of the roadway under their wheels suddenly changed, and the punctuating pings of small stones as they hit the truck's undercarriage lightened his mood like nothing else could have done. When he fixed up his house after the storm, Burns had extended his gravel driveway a few hundred feet down the road. Jesse knew from experience that this meant they were close. "Hallelujah!" Jesse's shout jolted Luke to attention. "We're almost there!"

Soon the road split and Jesse swung the wheel hard around, to follow the gravel road to the right. Within minutes they were pulling up in front of the house. Luke jumped down nearly before the truck made it to a full stop, bending and stretching to work the kinks out of his back. "Hang on, big brother," said Jesse as he switched off the engine and waited for the truck to quit rumbling. "We gotta look professional. This could mean more work later, you know."

Luke had already bounded to the front door and pounded one of his meaty fists on the wood. Now he looked back to his brother a little shamefaced, and Jesse felt a pang. Luke could be a pain in the neck sometimes, but he really couldn't help that he was a little dim. Jesse didn't like making Luke feel any dumber than he had to. He walked up to his brother and gave him a quick, playful jab in the arm, just to show he didn't mean nothing by what he'd said. As usual, Luke's hurt look washed clear away, and was replaced with a grin. "Sorry, Jesse. Didn't mean to get ahead of you."

Behind the door the two heard approaching footsteps. Luke stepped back, letting Jesse do the talking. They'd made many runs up Arrowhead Mountain over the last couple of years, but this was the first time they had actually talked to Burns. Heck, they'd never even been face-to-face with him. All their earlier runs had required was that they drop their load off around back. This time was different, though, and even Luke knew that Jesse was better at smooth-talking folks. The brothers waited on the stoop when suddenly, the door swung open.

"Gentlemen?" A tall, slender man stood in the doorway. He seemed unnaturally pale, like he never got out into the sun. His untidy hair stood up in tufts; clearly it hadn't seen the working end of a comb in a while, and although the clothes he wore were of decent quality—no Wal-Mart specials for him—they still looked like he'd been sleeping in them. He peered out at them through smeared glasses. "Welcome." The mild voice seemed unthreatening enough, but there was a chill behind the words.

Jesse found his voice. "You Mr. Burns?" The doctor nodded. "Got a package for pick up?" He tried to sound offhand, as if this was something he did every day but, truth be told, he was feeling a little weirded out by this guy. Thoughts of vampires and ghosts flitted through his mind, but he shook them away. He tried to collect himself. "I mean... we're supposed to take possession of a parcel." There, that sounded a little more professional.

"Ah, yes," Burns stepped back, gesturing the Yancys into the hallway. "You're a little ahead of time, but it's nearly ready. Please wait here." He turned and walked down the shadowy hallway toward a door at the back of the house. When he had slipped through, closing it behind him, Luke nudged his brother sharply in the back.

"Whatcha think? He some kinda Dracula or somethin'?" Luke's hoarse whisper made it plain that he was only half kidding around on this subject. Even though the same thought had just run through his own head just moments ago, Jesse put on a brave front.

"Naw. That's just in the movies, Luke. Now hush up." Abashed, Luke stuck his hands in his pockets, ostentatiously demonstrating that he wanted nothing to do with this house, or anything in it.

Within minutes they heard the door at the end of the hall open, and Burns re-emerged, carrying a red and white icechest. Jesse stepped forward. "This it, then?" He looked at the container doubtfully. "Don't look like much to me," he offered.

9

"Still, you'd be well-advised to treat it gently." Burns's soft voice held an undertone of, if not threat, then at least warning. "The contents are fragile. You don't want to break the flasks." Jesse stepped back, as much at the warning as to make room for Burns to move more fully into the hallway. Luke took this as his cue, and stepped up to relieve Burns of his burden.

"I'll just take this out to the truck, then. Right, Jesse?" he muttered, and headed off with the chest. "See you outside." He was out the door with a haste that betrayed how much he didn't like this house, or its owner.

Jesse was left facing Burns, not sure what to do next. He cleared his throat a few times, then spoke up. "Supposed to be some paperwork that goes with this, ain't there?" Maybe it was nervousness, but the words came out a little more belligerently than he meant them to. Burns eyed him mildly, his eyes looking huge behind the smudged lenses of his glasses.

"That's right. I have that right here." He reached into the inside breast pocket of his rumpled jacket and pulled out an envelope. "This is what your masters want," he said with a sly grin as he held the envelope out in front of him.

When Jesse reached for the envelope, Burns held onto it a moment longer than necessary, like you do before you drop an important letter in the mailbox. Finally he let it go, reluctantly, and Jesse slipped the envelope into his back pocket. Almost immediately, Jesse found himself moving toward the door as if Burns had given him a little push, but of course he had done no such thing. He just seemed so intent on returning to his solitary state that the desire itself seemed to impel Jesse out of the house.

Jesse paused at the exit. "Yeah. Well. Been right nice doin' business with you" he said as he let himself out the door. Once outside, he turned back towards Burns again, only to see the pale gentleman already swinging the door closed in his face. With a shrug, Jesse turned his back to the door and stepped down the front steps to join his brother in the front yard.

"Got it all stashed away, Jesse," said Luke, obviously wanting to please his brother. "I put it behind the seats.

"Kin we get outta here now?" The discomfort in Luke's voice was clear. He was really feeling scared. Jesse never could get over how such a big man could be so easily intimidated, but that was Luke all over. Jesse hit Luke in the shoulder playfully. "Yeah, yeah, you big dope. We're getting out of here." The boys got into the truck and Jesse backed away from the house.

At first, Jesse thought the drive down the mountain would go much smoother than the trip up had been, but he was reminded of the ruts when Burns' gravel road came to an end. Still, they were heading downhill, which was always easier. They continued to bounce along until suddenly a loud thud and clang resounded from beneath the truck's floorboards. The vehicle continued around a bend another couple hundred feet down the road before Jesse could bring it to a sliding stop amidst the clear sound of an engine without a muffler.

"Dang. Hit something, feels like," Jesse said to Luke as he frantically fought the wheel until it came to rest in a deep rut. "Sounds like we lost the muffler. We better get out and check the damage."

Jesse got out of the truck, taking care not to get too close to the edge of the road, which fell off precipitously above the southwestern corner of Hammerstone below. He could see right away that this was a mother of a rut they were stuck in. He got on his knees and peered under the truck. No muffler. He looked back up the road. He couldn't see it so he figured that it had dropped off before they rounded the bend.

"Aw, man," he shouted to Luke. "I gotta go up the road and hunt for the muffler. You stay here and hold the fort. Here, give me that rag so I don't burn myself. It's gonna be hot."

It took Jesse a while to hunt up the lost muffler. Finding the clamps that had held it to the truck frame was an even longer job. In the end, Jesse had to get down on his hands and knees and crawl through the brush. His mood was growing fouler by the minute, and it wasn't helped much by the sudden wind that gusted up and blew dirt into his face. By the time he got back to the truck he was coughing to beat the band.

Seeing that Luke wasn't in the truck did nothing to lighten Jesse's mood. The passenger door was open, but no Luke. He was just about ready to holler for his brother when he saw Luke hunkered down on the far side of the truck by the cliff, fooling with something on the floorboards of the passenger side. Approaching the rear of the truck, he put the parts in the truck bed with a clang and yelled over to Luke, "What you got yourself up to," he said, exasperation roughening his voice. Luke straightened up fast, looking scared. His posture told it all: Luke had done something he felt guilty about, and was afraid that Jesse would get mad. Jesse took a deep breath, wondering what could go wrong next.

"What'cha doing there, Luke," he said mildly. It didn't do to start out shouting with Luke. Like a big kid, if he got shouted at, he just clammed up. But when Luke looked up at his little brother, Jesse was startled to see that he looked like he was going to cry.

"I didn't mean it, Jesse. Really. I just thought... I mean... I couldn't help myself. I wanted to see what was in the cooler. I swear I was careful. Really."

Jesse looked at his brother helplessly. "What happened, Luke? Show me. I promise I won't get mad." But when he came around to the passenger side of the truck he changed his tune. The ground beside the truck was covered with white powder, although most of it had already blown down the mountainside on the wind. Offering mute evidence to the catastrophe was the empty glass flask that had once held the powder.

"You dang fool!" Jesse couldn't stop the words, but he reined in the tone of voice that he was tempted to use. "What've you gone and done?!"

"I'm real sorry, Jesse," Luke was sniveling, now. "I just wanted to see what was inside. And then the powdery stuff—it looks just like that cocaine or meth stuff you see in the movies." He turned his earnest eyes on his brother, clearly ashamed. "I thought I'd do like those guys on TV do and try a little taste. You know? And then my hand slipped and I dropped it...." The last came out in a rush, then petered out as Luke dropped his head, truly ashamed of himself.

Jesse thought fast. He looked into the cooler. There were five sealed canisters packed tightly among frozen ice packs. A sixth lay open and empty, its metal lid nearby. "Maybe we can scoop it back up," Luke said hopefully, but Jesse knew that wouldn't work. The fine white powder that came out of the sixth flask had already mixed with the dirt of the roadway and an awful lot of it was already blowing away down the mountain. Still, there had to be some way out of this jam. Jesse stared at the white powder. Maybe they could come up with something to replace what was lost, and hope the guys at the other end of the delivery won't know the difference.

"Don't worry, Luke," said Jesse. "Let's jack up the car and get the muffler back on. I'll think of something. We still have two hours before they expect us in Hot Springs." He stooped down and retrieved the empty flask, replacing its glass stopper and slipping it carefully into its container in the ice chest.

"You mad at me, Jesse?" Luke asked.

One look at his brother's hangdog face stole all the mad out of Jesse. "Naw, big fella," Jesse said. "But let's get this show back on the road, huh."

He looked over at his brother once more. "Hey, don't worry," he said. "Tell you what—when we get to Hot Springs, we'll stop off and get a package of those powdered donuts you like so much."

Luke's grin finally returned, and Jesse smiled back—he could always count on Luke's sweet tooth to get him through life's tough spots, even though the truck would look as white as snow when he was done.

While the Yancy boys labored at getting their truck out of the rut, Jennifer rocked back on her heels once again, this time to take a worried look at her watch. She'd stayed in the garden a little longer than she thought.

As she stretched her weary frame, she caught a momentary glint of sunlight reflecting off of metal. If she had looked closely enough, she might have just made out the silhouettes of two men laboring to get their car jacked up and back onto the road. But she was in a hurry, so she never noticed the Yancy boys hard at work, and she surely didn't see the fine, powdery white crystals borne on the breeze and heading swiftly toward her.

*New Year's Eve, 2002 — 10:00 pm*
*Indian Heights, Hammerstone, Arkansas*

Jack Burns was feeling restless tonight. He walked through the rooms of his big house, trying to put to rest the vague sense of unease that had troubled him since dusk. He entered his study and walked straight to the bar at the back of the room, reaching for the Waterford decanter on the shelf and pouring an inch of single malt whiskey into a stubby crystal tumbler. He held it up to the light and stared at it admiringly as his mind wandered.

It was New Year's Eve, a night for nostalgia, for taking stock of one's self. This had been a fruitful year, his purpose in Hammerstone finally accomplished, but somehow, he really didn't feel like celebrating. Of course, Jack Burns was never comfortable thinking about the past. Too much bitterness, too many disappointments.

He paused and took a deep breath as he placed the tumbler back on the marble counter and poured himself another inch of the amber nectar. Reaching once again to a neighboring decanter, he added a splash of local spring water. He replaced the decanter and took a sip. "There," he murmured to himself, once again admiring the drink, "A perfect blend of the Old World and the New."

He carried his glass out of the room and down the hallway. At the door at the end of the hall, he nervously looked around as if expecting to find himself being watched, but that was sheer foolishness. He was alone here. He was always alone. And it would be at least another month or two before his business associates discovered his little deception.

For now, it was New Year's Eve, and no one was likely to come all the way up Arrowhead Mountain to bother him. Still carrying his drink, he headed toward the staircase at the back of the house. As he had done every night since beginning his strange work in this house, Burns intended to end his evening with a visit to the basement.

At the head of the stairs he flipped the wall switch, and the room below was flooded with light. Below, where in another house one might expect to find a laundry room, perhaps a handyman's workbench, or maybe just storage boxes, Burns had an impressive laboratory set up.

Burns descended the stairs and moved around the room, admiring the state-of-the-art equipment that had thus far enabled him to make his unorthodox living. He had done some extraordinary work down here, to be sure. True, no peer-reviewed journal was ever likely to publish the results of his work—but that could not change the fact that he had accomplished some ground-breaking feats of science here in his splendid isolation.

He hadn't planned on his life turning out this way. Once, long ago, he had nurtured all the conventional aspirations of a man of science. A career in academia, tenure on the faculty of a prestigious university, a life devoted to the lab and to publishing, with every year bringing greater acclaim as he brought his genius to bear on the cutting-edge issues of biotechnology. He thought back to his days in graduate school, when he and a small group of colleagues had shared their hopes for the future.

Before he could finish those thoughts, he made his way to a corner of the basement, where he had created what he thought of as a gentleman's smoking room, all brown leather and cherrywood, surrounded on three sides by floor-to-ceiling bookshelves. He put down his drink and lifted the lid of an antique humidor that stood on the center of one of those shelves. He dipped into the humidor and pulled out what he referred to as a "Cuban" cigar, defined by his fellow students at Columbia as a cigar made by Cubans, even if the cubbyhole of a store in Union Square used South American tobacco. The cigar brought out a rare smile and he promptly busied himself with the business of cutting the tip and lighting up, and then settled into the deep cushions of the overstuffed chair that was the centerpiece of this self-indulgent nook. He drew a long pull on the cigar and reclaimed his whisky, letting his restless mind drift back once again to the days of his youth.

As the smoke wafted from his cigar, his mind began to wander again. Burns found that he could barely remember the faces, let alone the names, of most of his fellow grinds back at Columbia. Only a few now stood out in his memory: Angela, James, Bill Weston, and... who was that other guy?

He'd fallen in with them almost by accident, and they'd formed the first real social group to which he'd ever felt he belonged.

By the third pull on his cigar, all other images had faded into the smoke except that of Angela. He'd certainly taken a shine to Angela back then, but the fates were against him. With her work and her mother to take care of, she didn't have much time for socializing. She really only took time out for one thing, her computer games.

The gaming world was in its infancy in the '80s, and nearly everybody who played seriously eventually turned to writing their own games. Angela had founded a club of sorts, and posted a sign-up sheet in the university computer lab inviting fellow gamers to get together once a week to talk about their efforts at writing code. They called themselves the Coneheads, and one day Burns, in an uncharacteristically sociable mood, had turned up for a meeting.

He probably would never have returned after that first get-together, but something about Angela had drawn him in. Not that Angela ever knew that he was smitten. She just saw him as one of the gang—a neophyte gamer with an interest in learning to write code. He thought of her as the Puzzle Princess, because she favored brain-teasers over the more popular Pong or Asteroid style games. Since those halcyon school years, he'd fallen out of touch with most of the old Coneheads, but he still played at writing game code, and every so often he dropped Angela an e-mail with his latest effort.

He gazed blankly through the smoke of his cigar. "What would they think if they could see me now?" he found himself wondering. "What would *she* think?" He'd followed her career over the years and knew that she'd made good on the promise she'd shown in graduate school and in medical school as well. He even knew where she was likely to be right at this moment—not twenty miles away, living in the town of Hot Springs. He found that fact amusing—even a bit portentous. As if fate itself conspired to bring them back together again. But that couldn't happen. Not after all he'd done, all he'd been through. How could he go to Angela, when she'd done so well for herself and he had fallen so far?

Jack felt the whiskey working in him, and knew he could easily end the evening in a rage or in a maudlin funk. It was hard to hold back his bitterness. His career had begun so splendidly, and crashed to ruin so swiftly. But, it never should have happened. His fall from grace was grossly unfair. Sure, he'd fudged the data on that research project, but he was under pressure to produce, and *anybody* would take shortcuts if they saw a greater goal ahead—he was sure of it. But *no*, those righteous fools on the tenure committee wouldn't listen. He was out on his ear—virtually unemployable at anything but third-rate institutions after his academic honesty was called into question.

He'd been forced to take a more unconventional route if he wanted to stay with his science. Unconventional, hah! In his rare moments of self-honesty he could laugh at that euphemism. Downright illegal would be more to the point. But by now he had convinced all but the deepest corner of his heart that he had had no choice—that he'd been forced to take the path he'd taken.

Jack sighed and placed his now empty tumbler carefully on the table by his chair. He stood, a little unsteadily, and took one last look around the basement at the computer station, the hood, the lab benches, all the paraphernalia of a serious scientific installation. Suddenly he heard a sound from the floor above. He looked up, as if he could somehow hope to see up through the ceiling to find the source of the noise. When there was no repetition of the sound, he dismissed it with a shrug. Wooden houses like this one always made settling noises, he thought.

He returned to his reverie, but now his thoughts were on the present, not the past. He thought of the job he'd recently done, and the likely use to which it would be put. He'd truly fallen far this time—even he could no longer deny that fact. His current bosses were North Korean, and he was under no illusions that his work was aimed at easing the plight of the poor, the sick, or the hungry. He'd become a dealer in death.

At least the money was good. But he was no fool—he knew that his current masters were hardly to be trusted. Once they had what they wanted, they'd be quick to decide that they were safer if he wasn't around to expose their plans. He'd dealt with this kind of ruthless boss before, and nearly lost his life in consequence. This time, though, he was playing it smart. He had a little "insurance policy" all set.

Jack shook his head to clear it. Time to head back upstairs and go to bed. He moved toward the stairs, but a new sound stopped him in his tracks. He heard the soft tread of a sneaker-clad foot placed just a touch too heavily on an aging floorboard. He forced himself to move, but he made it only halfway back across the lab, when he heard the door at the top of the stairs swing slowly open.

"Who's there?" he called, but the shadowy figure in the doorway made no answer. He sensed something come hurtling down the stairs. Before he could react, there was the flash of an explosion, and suddenly, he simply knew nothing at all.

*New Years Eve — 11:50 pm*
*Hammerstone, Arkansas*

New Year's Eve in Hammerstone was a numbingly predictable night for those stalwarts who worked law enforcement. A couple of brawls down at one of the local bars, and a handful of disturbing-the-peace calls that required little more than the appearance on the scene of somebody in uniform. Police Chief Hank McLain had drawn duty tonight, and by quarter to midnight he was already bored with the banality of the evening. Still, the job had to be done. Or at least that's what he told himself as he slid out of his squad car in front of the small dwelling in a neighborhood on the northeastern border of Hammerstone. As he unfurled himself from the car to stand at his full 6'2" height, he looked towards the house, all lit up by the house party going full swing within. He sighed and started making his way down to the front door. As he reached the door, Hank knocked loudly, hoping he'd be heard over the raucous noise of the partiers inside. He waited a moment, then raised his fist to knock again, when the door was pulled abruptly open by a laughing girl about twenty years old.

"Happy New... Oh! Hi, Chief," the good-time laugh that had accompanied the opening of the door took on a deliberately sober note when his greeter registered his uniform. She was a dark-haired, vivacious girl, normally all smiles, but tonight she looked back over her shoulder at the obliviously uproarious crowd jamming her living room. She turned back to Chief McLain, looking a little nervous.

"Happy New Year to you, too, Judy," Hank drawled, smiling. "I guess y'all know why I'm here, now don't you?"

"Oh come on! Are the people next door complaining? But it's New Year's!" Judy wailed at the unfairness of a world that could crash her party on what seemed to her a whim.

"Yep. They did." Hank smiled at the girl. He knew her parents well, and he knew that she was a basically good kid. She just tended to let her social events get a little out of hand, especially on nights like this. As if to underscore his thoughts, he heard a crash as two over-enthusiastic dancers lost their balance and landed in an ungainly heap half across the coffee table. "All I ask is that you keep the yelling down to a dull roar. And maybe crank that stereo down a notch or two. Okay?"

Judy nodded, her dark eyes serious. Hank gave her a reassuring smile so she'd know she wasn't in deep trouble and turned to go, but just as the door swung shut behind him he heard his beeper go off. He grumbled as he tried to dig it out from under his jacket.

He looked at the number on the read-out and uttered a mild oath. Beepers were a relatively new addition to his armamentarium, but it required that he call back on his cell phone. Unfortunately, much of Hammerstone was a dead-zone for cell service—the high mountains that flanked the town on two sides rendered his cell close to useless. With a sigh of resignation he turned back and knocked on Judy's door again.

The door opened. "Chief, I didn't even have a chance to..." she stopped when she saw the look on his face.

"Sorry, Judy. The police radio doesn't work sometimes in these mountains, so I'll have to use your phone to call the dispatcher." Judy looked worried as he motioned towards the living room. "Official call. I really need to check in right away."

"Sure thing." The pout on Judy's face had been replaced by much more natural dimples, now that she knew he wasn't trying to give her trouble. "Down that way, in the hall." She grinned ruefully as she surveyed her guests. "Hope you can get through all the bodies." She laughed.

Hank nodded his thanks, then made his way through the party's crush to the phone. He dialed the dispatcher and curtly identified himself. "Chief," came the voice through the line. "We got a report of an explosion up on Arrowhead Mountain. Big fire up there in the woods." Hank processed the dispatcher's words, thinking quickly.

"The Burns' house? That's all that's still standing up there, right?" The dispatcher agreed. "I'm on my way," Hank said, hanging up the phone abruptly. He plowed his way through the partygoers and hurried to his car. Explosions? Fires? This could be bad. He slammed the squad car into gear and headed south to the outskirts of town. Arrowhead Mountain was just inside the southwest corner of Hammerstone township, clear on the other side of town.

It took him ten minutes to get across town and as soon as the mountain came into view, he could see that this was going to be a bad one. The horizon to the north glowed a dull red, the flames reflecting off the cloud bank that floated above the mountain. Hank switched on his flashers and siren and stepped on the gas, taking the roads much faster than safety would dictate. Ahead he heard the sirens of the firetrucks, heading up the mountain. He knew that his brother, a Hammerstone firefighter, rode on one of them.

The wild ride up the mountain seemed endless, but eventually he felt the roadway change to gravel and he knew he was nearly there. He pulled his squad car in behind the firetrucks and got out, then looked around to see what needed doing. The scene was apparent chaos. Hammerstone had responded with two engine companies, one ladder company and the command vehicle, carrying Mike Miller, Hammerstone's fire chief. There were eight men in all, including Hank's brother Mark, who rode with Engine Company Number Two, the second company to arrive on the scene.

Hank made his way over to the command vehicle: a group of firefighters surrounded the fire chief, who was shouting to make himself heard over the roar of the inferno that was once the Jack Burns's residence. Engine Company Number One had already established a water supply in the nearby creek, but was still relying on the thousand-gallon tanker, because the creek was running low. They had entered the east wing of the residence, and were trying to keep the flames down so that Mark's team could enter and look for Burns.

Miller acknowledged his presence and yelled over to
Hank, trying to fill him in. "Best we can tell is that the explosion
happened over there, in the west wing. If he was in
there, he's gone."

He turned his attention to the men of the second company.
"You boys," he called over to the group, "Y'all enter through
the east wing, and watch yourselves in there." One of the men
raised a hand in acknowledgement of the warning, and Hank
realized with a start that it was his brother, Mark. He tried to
get closer, to add his own words of caution, but by the time
he'd made it over to the firetruck where the group had gathered,
they had begun to disappear into the house.

Hank made his way back to the Chief. "Hope like hell the
tanker's got enough water for this, because the creek up
here's prit' near dry." Miller's laconic delivery belied the tension
that every firefighter feels when faced with a catastrophe
like tonight's blaze promised to be.

"Think Burns is still in there?" Hank scanned the blazing
mansion for a glimpse of the firefighters' progress inside.

"Probably. He never leaves that house no more." Miller
spoke so softly that Hank nearly didn't catch his words. "We
gotta try to get him out this time, though."

By now the fire had consumed the whole west wing of the
building, and sparks shot up as portions of the roof and walls
collapsed inward. The building's eastern wing was still standing,
but the situation in that wing was clearly worsening.
Hank couldn't take his eyes off that part of the house, his
inability to help making his stomach churn. Miller looked
over to him, a kindly look in his eyes.

"He'll be alright, you know. That brother of yours has some
kind of instinct for these things. He'll get the job done, and he'll
get out." But Hank could see the worry in the older man's eyes.

They watched, overwhelmed by the awe that overtakes
mere humans in the presence of such a vast inferno. Chief

Miller had a decision to make. The fire was rapidly spreading to the east wing and the roof was ablaze despite the best efforts of his men. Soon, it wouldn't be safe for anybody to be rummaging around in there. He decided to abandon the search for Burns and call his men back. But before he could shout out the order, the night was suddenly shattered by a deep boom and the windows along the ground floor of the east wing blew out in a shriek of shattering glass.

Miller charged the building with his bullhorn and bellowed his orders. "Get outta there! Outta there NOW!" His words were answered within moments by the sight of dark figures stumbling from the now blazing east wing, and Hank rushed forward to grasp the arm of the first of these to approach his position. "Mark?" But the soot-streaked face was that of a stranger, and Hank looked frantically past him, trying to spy his brother in the mob. It was a second or two before he registered that the man he held was trying to tell him something.

"Mark's still in there. Or was. Floor gave out. We're gonna need a harness." The man was drawing painful, labored breaths. Hank let him go and stumbled forward, calling his brother's name each time he passed another of the soot-begrimed group that emerged from the building. At last, as he neared the entrance to the east wing, he saw two men, one clearly injured, stumble into the yard. Behind them, the fire bellowed once more and the east wing's roof collapsed inward.

Hank raced to help them. When he helped the injured man strip off his respirator, he found himself staring into Mark's pain-filled eyes. Hank helped ease his brother to the ground, then moved out of the way so that the EMTs could get to work. Even from a distance though, he could see that Mark had taken the brunt of one of the earlier explosions. Even from a distance, he could smell the sickly odor of burned flesh. He leaned in, murmuring words of encouragement, and Mark turned toward the sound of his brother's voice. Hank took Mark's hand into his own, and was shocked at the strength in his brother's return grip. His brother raised his head slightly to speak.

"It was set." Hank nearly missed his brother's gasped words, but Mark repeated them. "It was set." Then Hank felt the strength drain from his brother's grip. He watched the light die in his brother's eyes. And he wept.

*Friday, February 7, 2003 — 5:30 am*
*Donatelli residence, Hot Springs, Arkansas*

It started as a vibration in the eardrum, tickling the bones of the inner ear. The impulse spiraled through the labyrinth of semicircular canals, then finally arrived at the dendrites of the auditory nerve, which waited to accept its coded message, ready to rush it onward to the brain. Within milliseconds, the owner of that brain was wide awake. After years of conditioning herself, Angela Donatelli responded to the sound of her beeper like a trooper. She sat up in bed and reached swiftly for the little appliance that was clamoring for her attention from the bedside table.

Wide-awake or not, it took a moment or two for Angela to make out the beeper's text message in the dim, pre-dawn light. "Call patient Linda Tackett at 555-0274." Angela was surprised and alarmed. Linda was one of her long-standing patients, and a friend of the Donatelli family, as well. She was not a complainer, so an early morning beep from her must mean trouble. Angela snatched up the bedside phone and punched Linda's phone number into the keypad. The first ring at the other end had barely ended before she heard the receiver pick up and Linda's familiar voice, clearly pained: "Hello?"

"Hey, Linda. It's Dr. Donatelli." Angela kept her voice level and cool. "What's up?"

"Sorry to call so early, Doctor," Linda's voice was whispery with exhaustion. "I had a horrible night. I tried to hold out until our appointment this afternoon, but I just couldn't stand it anymore." At her end of the line, Angela heard Linda's reluctant pause, and then came the difficult admission, "I just... the pain just got to be too much."

"Okay. It's okay." Angela sat up in bed. "Talk to me about the pain. What kind? Where does it hurt?"

Perhaps it was the professionalism in Angela's voice, but Linda's next words came out a little stronger, "Doctor, it's in my legs. I can hardly bend my knees! I took the medications last night, like I always do, but for some reason they didn't seem to work. I've had spasms before, but never like this." Her next words were a frightened plea. "I just don't know what to do."

Angela understood too well the fear that such symptoms could cause. She was a neurologist, and a specialist in the research and treatment of multiple sclerosis. More to the point, she had a lifetime's personal experience with this disease, for her mother, Marie, was also afflicted. You could say that MS was an intimate member of her family.

Linda continued, her voice now soft, almost confessional— she had reached the root of her deepest fears. "Your mother told me that before she ended up in a wheelchair, she started getting painful spasms." Linda gulped, and finally asked the question. "Is that going to happen to me?"

Linda's anguish came through loud and clear—so clearly that Angela realized her first job would be to help her patient move to a more positive state of mind. Linda's fear was understandable. Up to now, she'd managed to maintain an independent lifestyle, her only physical concession to MS being her use of a walking cane. To lose mobility was a threat to that independence. But Linda was giving her fears too much free rein. Sure, Marie had developed severe spasms a few years ago, and soon after that, she had made the transition from cane to wheelchair. But Angela knew that the course of MS was often very different from one patient to the next. She had to make Linda see the truth of this.

"What happened with Mom won't necessarily happen with you, Linda. It's at least as likely that you're just going through a rough patch and you'll be back to your old self soon. Right now, though, let's deal with the pain. Can you reach your medications? I'll wait."

"Yes, doctor," she said, the necessity of completing a task making it a little easier to get a hold on herself. "It may take a few minutes."

Angela heard the clunk as Linda put down the phone and went off to get her pill bottles. As she waited, she thought of her mother's own battles with MS over the years. Marie had been coping with the disease for as long as Angela could remember. For years before the diagnosis was made, she'd dealt with bouts of numbness and pain, suffered mild weakness and overwhelming fatigue; all so-called silent symptoms, which she hid from the entire family and most of all from her daughter. And she'd succeeded for a time.

But right about the time of Angela's eleventh birthday, Marie's symptoms became more pronounced, and conceal-ment was no longer possible. She was diagnosed with MS, and after that, she would have bouts of numbness and weak-ness that would make even the simplest tasks too difficult. And then, suddenly, after a month or two, the problems would pass, and she'd be almost as good as new until the cycle repeated itself. No one knew when these attacks would occur, what function would be affected when they did, or how long they would last. It was the uncertainty that took the greatest toll.

The sound of the phone being taken up at the other end broke through Angela's thoughts. Linda's voice, when it came through the line, sounded a little stronger now. "I've got the pills" she said, and then read off the labels while Angela scribbled them down on the pad by her telephone.

"Okay, Linda, now take a breath and listen to me." Angela didn't like practicing long-distance medicine—she'd much rather be face-to-face with her patients—but a quick, maybe temporary readjustment of Linda's dosages would give some immediate relief for the pain. She proceeded to adjust some of Linda's medications and after making a little reassuring small talk, Angela hung up the phone.

With a sigh she looked at the clock—just past six. Still too early to start her day, especially since her first scheduled patient wasn't due in the clinic until noon. But she was too fully awake to reclaim her interrupted sleep. She slid her feet into fuzzy pink slippers and shuffled to the bathroom to brush her teeth. A tall, slender woman gazed back at her from the vanity mirror. Her face was strong, with the kind of well-cut bone structure that was the envy of women much younger than her nearly 50 years. Her skin was still taut, still smooth, and she decided that the hint of crows feet around her eyes just added a touch of character to her still strongly attractive features.

She could thank her mother for the fact that her shoulder length dark hair still showed only a trace of gray. Marie had kept the glossy black hair of her youth well into her sixties. The rest, though—the lithe, fit body—Angela maintained in spite of, rather than thanks to, her mom. Marie was, after all, a great cook. Angela grinned ruefully. If she let her mother have her way, she knew she'd have ballooned out years ago on all the pasta and pastries that Marie produced like magic from the kitchen.

Her morning's ablutions taken care of, Angela slipped on

her robe and returned to her room just in time to see a black, shadowy form leap lightly from the tangle of sheets and blankets to the floor. The cat paused momentarily, casting a peremptory backward glance toward Angela, clearly demanding breakfast.

"Be right with you, Snowball," she said, and the cat stalked off, clearly indignant at the longstanding joke that was her ironically endowed name. Angela caught herself wondering, not for the first time, just who trained who in the collaboration between people and their pets. She swiftly slipped into a gray sweat suit and headed down the stairs. Might as well take advantage of her early wake-up call by getting in a good run this morning.

Snowball awaited her in the kitchen, and began insistently twining herself around and between Angela's ankles as she opened the can of cat food and scooped heaping spoonfuls into the cat dish. She looked up from her task when she heard the soft whoosh of wheels on the carpet in the hall. Marie soon entered the room.

"Up early, aren't you, Angie?" Marie piloted her chair with the alacrity of a long-time pro, swinging it over to the counter. "Why don't I just put the coffee on?"

Angela had long ago given up on trying to get her mother to ease back on the domestic chores. All her arguments—that she was fully capable of getting her own coffee, that she could cook for herself—were met with cheerful agreement, and just as cheerfully ignored. After one disastrous interlude, when Angela had offered to hire help to come in and do the cooking and the housework, Angela had finally given up. Marie had greeted the idea of an outsider invading her kitchen with stony silence, which was bad enough. But afterwards, Angela had heard her mother weeping in the privacy of her room, and finally realized that Marie needed to play an active role in the household far more than she needed a little help now and then. She needed to be needed, plain and simple. So, ultimately, Angela bowed to the inevitable. From then on, she devoted her energies, and no little cash, to making the house more friendly to the needs of a person who just happened to need a wheelchair to get around.

As Angela waited for her coffee, she surveyed the kitchen, of which she was enormously proud. When working out the floor plan, she'd made space a priority—Marie's chair needed room to maneuver. First-time visitors to the kitchen were sometimes a little disoriented because everything—sinks, countertop, even the big appliances—were set so much lower than usual. Made sense, though, when you did your cooking and washing up while sitting down. The refrigerator and cabinets were outfitted with rollout shelves, so everything was in easy reach, and there were strategically placed grab bars with which Marie could pull herself up to stand, if need be.

"Here you go," Marie said, interrupting Angela's thoughts with the offer of a small, steaming mug of espresso. "I heard your beeper go off before," she went on. "I thought you weren't on call last night?"

"I wasn't. It was Linda—she had a rough night. Spasms in her legs—they threw a scare into her."

"Poor kid," Marie said. "She's got it tough. Not everybody has the support I had, from you... from Tony." She shook her head in sympathy for Linda, who'd been a friend for years now, and who was, with Marie, a co-founder of the local MS support group. "I don't know how I'd have done it without your father to help see me through the hard times."

Although Tony Donatelli had passed away twenty years ago, Marie's memories of her husband were still just below the surface of her everyday life. Theirs had been a true love-match. Marie D'Eramo had grown up on Arthur Avenue, in the Bronx—one of New York's old Italian neighborhoods. She'd had no end of likely suitors, but she had given her heart to

Tony Donatelli on the very first day they'd met. And Tony had been just as smitten with Marie. It wasn't just her dark-eyed beauty that caught his eye. He was entranced with her easy laugh, her resolute character, her gentle strength. It came as a surprise to no one that the two were married as soon as the law, and their parents, would allow.

The young couple sailed through their early years together in love and joy, and when baby Angela came along, they thought they were rich beyond measure, though money was tight and sometimes it was a struggle getting by. The true test of Tony's love came eleven years later, when Marie woke up one morning to find that she simply could not get out of bed. Tony was at her side in an instant, and he helped her get moving again. And when the mysterious disability dragged on for days, then months, he did more. He made it clear that for all the mornings to come, he would always be by Marie's side, no matter what the future held in store.

Now, though, Tony was gone, struck by a car as he was walking home on icy New York streets one night, twenty years ago. Angela had still been in school when the call came and she hurried home to share her mother's grief. The next few weeks had been terrible. Angela almost didn't recognize the woman who seemed to have taken over her mother's familiar face and form. It seemed for a while that Marie would never emerge from the depression that had taken possession of her spirit. But Marie was a fighter, and with Angela's help she had slowly made her way back.

Angela, seeing that her mother had fallen into private reminiscence, finished her coffee in silence, and quietly put down her mug. She went outside, pausing to do some quick, limbering stretches before setting out on her run. She looked east towards her mountain, half obscured by the complicated roofline of her 1896 Victorian-style house on their seventy-acre estate, aptly named Stonemeadow Rise. The sun had already risen behind the mountain, but, it wouldn't clear the peak for another three hours. Angela stepped down from the porch, setting off at a brisk pace up the gently sloping trail that wound its way invitingly into the woods and upward onto the mountain.

Angela was no jogging fanatic, but she knew that she needed to keep herself fit, as counterpoint not only to her mother's cooking but also to her own workaholic ways. If she didn't make herself go out for her daily run, she could easily find herself spending all her time in the clinic or the research office, making excuses never to leave. Her commitment to her work was nothing new. As a kid in school, she was always quiet and studious. It wasn't that she was antisocial, but she found that she was just more *interested* in her studies than in the rough and tumble world of childhood and adolescent socializing.

Of course, she had her share of romances in her life. By college, her strong good looks had come into their own, and this, combined with her work ethic, made her somewhat mysterious and attractive to many men. She had given her heart more freely in those years, but she never met anyone who could arouse in her the sustained passion that her lifetime love of learning was able to do. Ironically, it was this willingness to be led down the path of knowledge, to try to understand the complex catacombs of thought and emotion that define the human condition, that ultimately was her most attractive feature.

Angela ran on, making it halfway up the mountain before judging that she had run far enough. She turned smoothly and retraced her steps, the distance melting away more quickly now as she headed downhill.

As the gabled roofline of her house appeared through the trees, she found her thoughts returning to her morning caller, and to her mother's struggle with the same disease. It was to

Marie that Angela owed her commitment to her work and to her patients. When the time came to decide on a specialty, her classmates had spent endless hours debating the relative merits of each, but her course had been set ever since she first understood what was happening to her mother. From that time on, she knew she would specialize in neurology and work with MS—who could better understand not just the disease itself, but the challenges it presented to the friends and families of its victims.

Angela emerged from the trees into the yard, worked through a few cool-down exercises, and was soon in the kitchen pouring herself a second cup of espresso. Marie smiled at her daughter fondly. "Have a nice run, dear?"

"Just great, Ma," Angela grinned back. "Now I've just got to figure out what to do with myself until clinic at noon. And I'm seeing Linda at one o'clock—maybe I'll be able to see what caused her so much distress last night."

"I gave Linda a call while you were out on the mountain," she said. "Thought that maybe she could use a little moral support."

"I'm sure she could." Angela looked questioningly toward her mother. "But can you tell me why she waited so long to call? I just wish she hadn't put herself through a whole night of pain unnecessarily."

"It's pride, Angie, but not the bad kind, even though it's sometimes foolish." Marie's voice was soft with sympathy for their mutual friend. "You don't want to be a bother, so you tell yourself you can cope. Then it gets late and you figure you'll just try to stick it out until morning because you hate to ruin somebody else's sleep. And sometimes it works. But sometimes it doesn't." Marie's shrug was not dismissive, just a sign of her acceptance of the way of the world. "When you live with something chronic, like MS, you need your little victories—and if she could have held off calling until it was time for her appointment, Linda would have counted it a victory. We spend far too much of our lives with no choice but to accept help, so sometimes we try to prove we don't need it."

Marie's words rang true, and from a patient's point of view they made a certain amount of sense. But a doctor's perspective was different. Symptoms ignored—even for pride's sake—meant symptoms untreated. And sometimes, that could make all the difference in the world. "Anyway," Angela said. "I'll be seeing her this afternoon. We'll see what's up then." Taking her cup, she left Marie to her coffee and newspaper and headed down the hall to her study.

In the study, Snowball's inky form was pooled on top of her desk, her silky tail swishing softly across the top of the laptop that lay to one side. Angela scooped the cat up unceremoniously and dumped her on the floor. The cat stalked off irritably, and Angela settled in front of her desk and flipped open her laptop. If nothing else, she might as well clear out her e-mail in-box.

As she waited for her laptop to boot, she sighed impatiently at the delay. How quickly we forget, she thought—it wasn't so long ago when it took whole minutes to get on-line. Now we chafe at having to wait a few seconds.

At last, though, the familiar online homepage filled the screen, and she clicked her way into her e-mail. As the new messages scrolled onto the screen, she saw that she'd received one from her former mentor, and now dear friend—Murdoch "Mud" Riordan. Mud never had much to say in his e-mails, and this time was no exception. Sometime late last night, according to the date stamp, he'd taken a minute to type "give me a call when you can." She looked at the clock—plenty of time to call him back, she thought with a smile. She shot a quick glance at the remaining messages and saw nothing that leaped out at her as urgent, so she shut the laptop down and closed the lid before reaching for the phone.

Angela's relationship with Murdoch Riordan went way back. During her internship at Hudson Hospital, Dr. Riordan was made Director of the Hudson Hospital Multiple Sclerosis Center, where Marie was a patient. It was there, at the MS Center, that Dr. Riordan first met Angela Donatelli. Actually, he met Angela's mother first, but Angela might as well have been there. Like in all Italian families, meeting the mother meant getting to know the entire family at the same time. At Marie's urging, Angela got up the courage to meet the "great man" himself and told him of her interest in neurology and multiple sclerosis. Murdoch graciously agreed to be her faculty advisor. Little did he know that this would become a lifetime appointment.

Their relationship had evolved over the years, from the lopsidedness of mentor and student to the mature satisfaction of collegial equality and true friendship. Now, as she waited for her call to go through the hospital switchboard, she felt a rare pang of regret at the decisions that brought her here to Arkansas, so far from New York. Mostly, she was well-pleased with life in Hot Springs, but every so often she missed the long talks in the lab, when she and Murdoch would talk about everything and nothing, solving all the problems of the world. These days they stayed in touch with regular phone calls and more infrequent visits. It helped that Murdoch had ties with the State Crime Lab in Little Rock. In fact, it was just those ties that helped bring Angela to Hot Springs. Still, long-distance friendships just weren't as satisfying.

Eventually the switchboard operator came back on the line. "Doctor isn't answering his page," she said apologetically. "Alright," Angela said. "I can try again later."

*Friday, February 7, 2003 — 12:00 noon*
*Hot Springs Medical Building, Hot Springs, Arkansas*

Back when she was still a schoolgirl, Angela's report cards always included the note "uses time wisely." It had become something of a mantra for her through all the years of her professional training, and as she pulled into the parking lot outside of her office building in the heart of Hot Springs, she found herself chanting it, a little ironically. After all, she'd had the whole morning to pull herself together, and here she was, running late. She hated running late.

Angela kept two offices in the Hot Springs Medical Building, a large one story building covering an entire city block in Hot Springs and housing twelve independent physician offices. At one end of the front hall was Central Arkansas Research, or CARE, with a full staff and all the necessary equipment for her to conduct clinical trials on new treatments for chronic diseases. In a separate office at the other end of the hall was her medical practice, the Donatelli Center for Clinical Neurology and Rehabilitation. Her work today was mostly in the clinic, but she pulled the car around the back of the building, where she could slip through a back door leading right into her private office at CARE. She wanted a few minutes to herself before she braved the crowd at the clinic.

Angela's private office was part of a suite she shared with her secretary Dolly Winston, and her director of clinical research, Fran DeMarco. The three of them made up what Angela liked to think of as the ruling triumvirate, presiding over what was known in the clinical research field as an investigative site. Her company, CARE, conducted independent safety and effectiveness testing on new medications under development by pharmaceutical companies. Without CARE's work, and the work of hundreds of other such independent sites, new medications could not receive FDA approval for sale to the public.

Angela was fiercely proud of the research studies she conducted here. She understood the seriousness of her responsibility, protecting the public on two fronts—by facilitating the smooth flow of new, better medications for the treatment of disease, but also by keeping unsafe or ineffective drugs off the market. Her professional independence, and that of countless other investigative sites, was an important part of the checks and balances that kept drug testing honest. Right now she was between projects, her last few studies having been completed only a week earlier, and the facility that lay beyond her office door was relatively quiet. The next round of studies would not begin for a month and her staff was busy preparing for it.

Casting one last look around at the office, Angela dropped her laptop on the desk and took a deep breath. No more putting off the inevitable—time to announce her presence and get to work. As soon as she touched the intercom button, Dolly's voice came over the speaker. "Glad you're here, Doctor. Several patients are already in rooms at the clinic but they're not ready for you yet."

Dolly, her long-time secretary, had been working with Angela from the beginning, and had carved out an unusual but indispensable role for herself, handling Angela's personal schedule and often acting as liaison between Angela and the world. She coordinated the "master schedule" that regulated patient appointments, speaking engagements, lab time, and all the other professional obligations that Angela had to keep straight. Last, but by no means least of her duties was management of the financial end of the business. For her part, Dolly gave all the credit for her organizational skills to the invention of the yellow sticky note. Her office was papered with them.

Angela began to prepare for a day seeing patients. Janie

North, Angela's nurse, would be moving among her clinic patients now, collecting a list of their complaints and updating their charts. She would call as soon as the first patient was ready. While she was waiting, Angela slipped into her white coat and looked up at the master schedule that hung on the wall above her desk. She only had fourteen days to go before her long-awaited two-week vacation. She'd already made arrangements for a colleague to cover her practice. As she lingered for a moment, a call came from Susan, the clinic receptionist, telling her that her first patient was waiting in Examination Room 3.

With a sigh, Angela made the trek down the hall of the building to her other office, the clinic facility. Janie had placed the chart in the rack on the examining room door, and Angela flipped it open, glancing quickly at the patient's name; "Good afternoon, Mrs. Williams," she said with a reassuring smile, and plunged into her day.

Mrs. Williams complaints were pretty straightforward: stiffness in the neck and arm following a bad auto accident. Angela moved smoothly through the history and physical, spoke to the patient and then walked her patient out to the front desk to schedule an MRI and a follow up visit. As Mrs. Williams walked away, Dolly caught Angela's eye. "Fran's on line 2," she said, and Angela dutifully picked up the phone. "What's up, Fran," she said into the receiver.

"Can you take a call from Dr. Lemlie at Horizon Medical? He's got a few questions about one of the patients in the MS study." It was rare that Angela allowed the research side of her work to intrude on her medical practice, but sometimes it was unavoidable. This looked to be one of those times. From Fran's tone of voice, it was clear that life would be a great deal easier if Angela could talk to Dr. Lemlie today.

Angela sighed. "All right," she said, resignedly. "I'll be right down." Hurrying to the door, she tossed a quick "Hold the fort, Janie!" over her shoulder. "I won't be more than a few minutes."

Angela was true to her word. After dealing with Dr. Lemlie's concerns, Angela hurried back to the clinic and pushed straight through the patient's entrance. Her rush carried her three full strides past the door before the unexpected scene that greeted her caused her to stop in her tracks. A small mob was crowded around the front desk, all talking excitedly, and even the unflappable Dolly stood to one side, apparently at a loss.

At first no one seemed to notice Angela's arrival, but at last one and then another face turned her way. Before she could say a word, the crowd parted to reveal Linda Tackett, grinning a little shamefacedly. "Hi, Doc," she said. "Brought some friends with me."

Mystified, Angela looked around at the crowd, then back at her patient. "Feeling the need for a little more moral support than usual?" she asked with a smile.

"Oh. No, Doc. This is something else." Suddenly Linda's grin slipped from her face, a look of dead earnestness replacing it. "It's just.... Well, I thought maybe you wouldn't mind when you found out. I mean, I didn't really know what else to do." She gave a small, helpless shrug.

Angela looked around again at the crowd. "You want to talk about it in my office?" Angela asked. Linda nodded and with that she picked up her cane and marched, after a fashion, towards Angela's office, clearly expecting everyone to follow her and, bemusedly, they did. Resigned to her fate, Angela fell in step behind the rest of the newcomers. Inside the office, confusion reigned once more while everyone found a place to settle. Angela took her seat behind her desk, cleared her voice, and said in as stern tones as she could muster "Okay, Linda. What's going on here?"

"Right. Well. After talking to you on the phone, I took the

medications like you suggested. And then your mom called and we chatted for a while." Linda's seriousness slipped away as she warmed to her role as spokesperson. "Your mother's a great believer in using work to take your mind off your troubles, you know." At Angela's impatient nod, Linda hurried her tale a bit. "Anyway, your mom suggested that I get to work on the MS Support Group fundraiser.

Again, Angela nodded. It seemed clear that Linda would get to the point in her own time. "Anyway, I thought she had a good idea there, so I figured I'd check my answering machine to see if anybody's RSVP'd about attending the event." And then she stopped, as if with these words, everything was explained.

"And?" This time Angela's impatience was clear.

"Oh, well, a few months ago I got myself a separate line wired up just for support group stuff. Otherwise the regular phone would be ringing off the hook all day." She allowed herself a small, guilty smile. "But I'm still so bad about checking the darn thing—let it go for days, sometimes. So I knew there'd be a lot of messages to wade through. She paused. "And that's when I found out about all these folks. That's Merle and Lorraine Davies," she said, indicating a thirty-something black couple who stood toward the back of the office. "And over there, that's Mr. and Mrs. Stedman and their son, Timmy." Mrs. Stedman tried a polite smile, but the attempt failed. She looked quickly to her son, in whose features Angela saw the distinctive signs of Down's syndrome. Mr. Stedman nodded a greeting but remained silent. "And this here's Jennifer Richmond," Linda went on, pointing to an attractive woman in her late thirties, who was clearly in the greatest physical distress of the bunch. Angela looked at the expectant faces arrayed in front of her, still not quite getting what was wanted of her. "And all these people had called in to RSVP?" she asked, confused.

"Well, not exactly. They called in because they saw the description of MS on the fundraiser flyers. And now they think that they have it."

Angela tried to get a grip on what she thought she was hearing. Looking around the room and addressing the group, she asked, "So, all of you called Linda's support group line over the last few days?"

There was a rumble of assent from the group. Angela sat back in her chair, her mind working quickly. "What do your doctors think about all this?"

Linda, once again, leapt to the fore. "Well, they don't seem to know what it is. You see, since old Doc Farley retired, we don't have a local doctor in Hammerstone, so we all go to different places. Some go to Fort Smith, some to Texarkana and some to Hot Springs."

Jennifer earnestly met Angela's eyes. "I had to get a new doctor and she says she doesn't know what it is I got. Sent me home with an antidepressant." Her voice was soft, with just a trace of bitterness. "Of course, it's gotten much worse since I saw her."

Merle spoke up next. "My doctor didn't have a clue either. Said to sit tight for a while and see what happens. But when I saw the flyer for that fundraiser I started to wonder. Looked up MS on the internet. Then I talked to Linda and figured it wouldn't hurt to come here."

"Us too," added Mrs. Stedman, a little hesitantly. "I don't mean to speak poorly about our doctor—he's been good to Timmy," she dropped her sad gaze to her son. "But he can't seem to say what's wrong now, so me and my husband, we just thought...." she let her voice trail off. Mr. Stedman remained stoically silent.

Linda took charge once again, turning back to Angela. "See, here's another odd thing. They're all *new!!* They've none of them *ever* had this kind of trouble before."

Angela took this rare opportunity to get a word in edgewise and briefly questioned everyone about his or her new symptoms. After a few minutes, she felt satisfied that she had at least an overview of their various complaints. But that was the only satisfaction she felt. This is impossible, she thought. Each of these strangers had described symptoms often associated with multiple sclerosis, but there simply had to be another explanation. There were too many of them, all from the same tiny Arkansas town, all getting sick between Thanksgiving and mid-December—it was statistically unlikely that every single one of them could suddenly have contracted MS at roughly the same time.

Making it even more unlikely was the nature of the patients who sat before her. Jennifer Richmond most closely fit the usual profile of an MS patient, but the rest represented extreme rarities. For example, MS primarily strikes women, yet here was Mr. Davies. He was even more curious as a candidate for MS, because it only very rarely occurs among African-Americans. Moreover, it was very unusual to see MS in children like Timmy, and even more significantly, the disease was almost unheard of among people with Downs syndrome.

"Listen," she said to the group, "it sure sounds like MS symptoms. But there are lots of conditions with symptoms that mimic MS." She paused a moment, not wanting to alienate these people, who were clearly suffering from *something*, by sounding disbelieving or dismissive.

"See, MS produces areas of damage in the brain called plaques. These can occur anywhere in your brain. That's why every MS case is pretty much unique—if it attacks the part of your brain that controls movement of your left arm, then your left arm will be weak or paralyzed. If it attacks the part that controls sensation in your right leg, than that leg will go numb. See what I mean? Each one of these symptoms can also be seen in lots of other diseases and conditions, so diagnosis can be difficult. It's best if we don't jump the gun here, okay? We can't know for sure what we're dealing with until we've done some tests."

Everyone in the room looked from Angela to Linda and back again. Mr. Davies spoke up first. "Does that mean you'll do them? The tests I mean?"

Linda piped up. She sounded a little embarrassed, but she looked Angela straight in the eye and stood her ground. "I told them you were the best in the business. I said if anybody could figure out what was wrong, it'd be you. They're kinda counting on you, Doc."

Linda's activism on behalf of MS patients had always been a part of clinic life. She was forever organizing car pools to get patients to their appointments, and she was almost embarrassing in the fervor of the praises she sang in Angela's name. As far as she was concerned, the only doctor worth seeing— especially for MS, was Dr. Donatelli. But this was different— she'd crossed a line if she planned on starting to recruit new walk-in patients in wholesale lots! Angela was tempted to send these folks back to their regular physicians to schedule a battery of tests.

But the personal appeal had touched Angela's heart, and the sheer improbability of this motley crew had piqued her curiosity. These were powerful motivators for Angela. Her best moments have always come when both her heart and mind were equally engaged, and she felt a rush of excitement as she contemplated this little mystery. She gave Linda a mock scowl for having put her in this position, but tempered it with a bit of a reassuring smile.

"Okay. I'll arrange for some tests. But we're going to have to do a complete history and physical on each of you first, which means I'll have to sweet-talk my staff into staying a little late today to accommodate y'all. Some of you may have to wait all afternoon. We'll squeeze you in when we can."

The relief caused by her words was almost palpable. It was as if everyone in the room had been holding their breath, awaiting her judgment, and now they all dared to let it out. "I knew she'd do it," Linda crowed. "Nothing to worry about now. Doc Donatelli's on the case!"

Jennifer was the last patient of this long and difficult day, but she didn't have to wait alone. The whole Hammerstone gang waited with her, even after they had been examined and were free to leave. Angela was acutely aware of the lot of them, sitting patiently in reception, as she began her examination of the young woman.

"Let's start with when—when did you first notice you were having trouble?"

"'Round Thanksgiving—just a little after, maybe. I just got so horribly tired." She turned dark-ringed eyes to the doctor. "Sleep doesn't help much. Nothing does. Some days, it's just overwhelming. I've got to hit the ground, right then, no matter what."

It sounded so familiar—from her past patients, even from Marie's experience. It was just that kind of full-out exhaustion that had finally made Tony and Angela realize that their beloved wife and mother was seriously ill.

"Okay. Give me a list of your other problems—in order of their importance to you."

"The fatigue is the worst, but there's something else that comes a close second." Jennifer looked abashed. "It's kinda embarrassing." Angela held silent, encouraging the young woman to go on. Jennifer's voice dropped to almost a whisper. "Sometimes I... I can't hold my water. Can't get to a bathroom fast enough." Angela understood her patient's great distress. This was a well-raised young woman, taught to be clean in her life and her habits. Incontinence was very hard for some people to admit, because they so feared that people would think they were dirty.

"Sssh," Angela breathed out a comforting sigh. "That's alright, Jennifer. It happens to a lot of people. We can deal with that."

"And my legs go weak. Makes it hard to walk sometimes. Or they go numb, feel all tingly. Enough to hurt. And sometimes, lately, they twitch... hard. Like spasms, you know?" Angela nodded. Indeed she did know. "But what bothers me lots more than the stuff with my legs is that I get so depressed all the time. Like I'm stuck forever in this blue funk."

Angela moved swiftly through the rest of the exam, noting hyperactive reflexes, weakness and rigidity in the left leg, and reduced sensation in both legs. At last she felt she had enough to make a few observations out loud.

"Okay, Jennifer. The examination seems to point to MS— your history and the physical exam bear it out, at least. But we can't be sure until we've done a few more tests. I'm going to order an MRI of your brain, for starters. We'll use a magnetic field to get an image of your brain. That will show us if you've got any plaques, or areas of damage, consistent with MS." Angela thought a moment. "I'd also like to get a spinal tap. There are certain antibodies that show up in the spinal fluid that might also suggest MS. After that, we'll see."

Jennifer nodded, looking grimly determined to deal with her problems, and that determination gave Angela heart. It took strength and determination to deal with chronic diseases, and MS was no exception on that score. "Meanwhile," she went on, "let's do something about your symptoms. We can treat the spasms and sometimes even the incontinence and fatigue with medications, and we can get you started with physical and occupational therapy to work on your walking."

When the last of the group had crowded onto the elevator and both Janie and Dolly had finally gone home, Angela spent a moment savoring the silence and solitude of her office, reviewing the copious notes she'd taken from her unexpected patient boom. She'd expected something to turn up in the preliminary investigation that would put her suspicions of MS to rest, at least for the Davies man and the Stedman child. But that hadn't happened. As she had done for Jennifer, she'd ordered MRIs and held out the prospect of a spinal tap to follow.

She looked at her desk clock and decided that staying a little later wouldn't do any harm—she was already well past her normal quitting time. She felt a brief pang of guilt that she hadn't made it home in time for dinner, but late nights at the clinic were not unheard of in the Donatelli household, and she knew that Marie had more than likely fixed her something she could microwave when she got home. So she might as well give Murdoch another try—this time at his home, where she had a better chance of catching him.

She punched in the number from memory, and listened as, way up north in Murdoch's sprawling Manhattan apartment, the phone began to ring. In no time, Mud's welcome voice came on the line.

"Hello..."

"Hi, Mud, got a minute?" Without waiting for an answer, Angela let the events of the day pour out. As she spoke, she found herself focusing in on certain details, speeding past others, as if the simple act of talking through a problem with her old mentor helped her to understand the data more clearly. This... *this* is what she missed from her old days in New York. Murdoch listened until she'd talked herself dry. But when he finally spoke, he seemed less than impressed with her tale.

"Angela, your data certainly sounds unusual, but I doubt that it's unique. You don't have enough information yet to rush to any kind of judgment. You'll have to wait for your MRIs, at the very least." Angela understood Murdoch's caution, but his refusal to become swept up in her own growing interest in these cases took some wind out of her sails. "Well, what about the rarity of some of the cases—a black man? A child with Down's syndrome? Don't they whet your curiosity?"

"Not in and of themselves. But you're right that these cases are intriguing, if only because they involve so *many* exceptions to the general rule.

"So you agree with me? That this is worth investigating."

Again Murdoch's reasonable tones seemed aimed at dampening Angela's enthusiasm. He was no stranger to her investigative zeal. More than once he'd found himself drawn into her mysteries, sometimes even ending with brushes with the law. At least this time, the mystery was purely medical. He chuckled. "Before you go off the deep end, stop thinking like a mystery sleuth and remember how to think like a scientist," he said. He could almost hear Angela's dismay over the phone lines, and realized that perhaps he was being too rough on her.

"Angela. Think this through, like I know you can. You're seeing MS-like symptoms, but in an unusual group of people. So, besides running the usual tests, what else should you be doing?'

The silence on the Arkansas end of the line dragged on a moment, but then Angela rose to the challenge. "Looking for alternative diagnoses—confirming or ruling out other possible causes, one by one."

"Good girl. Now, just talking off the top of my head, I'd consider something environmental. Heavy metals in the drinking water, maybe. From heavy industry? Mining? Pesticides?" He paused, considering his next question. "What do you know about the town they're from?"

"Not much. I didn't really think to ask. I just assumed that it's just like lots of the other little towns around here. They're usually more residential than anything else. But I don't know for sure, and that environmental angle does sound like something I should check out."

"Now you're talking like a scientist, Angie." Murdoch could almost feel his former student's sudden renewal of confidence over the phone.

"Here's what I suggest," he went on. "Wait for your test results to come back, then maybe take a trip out to the town—Hammerstone, was it? Bring a field-test kit, and collect some samples."

When Angela hung up the phone, she felt miles better than she had before making the call. It always happened when she had Murdoch to bounce her problems off of. Sure, she'd been deflated a bit by his stolid insistence that she keep her feet on the ground, but that's what Murdoch was always good for—reining her in when her own curiosity threatened to run away with her. And she had to admit that she'd let her curiosity run away with her for a while, there. Murdoch was right. Wait for the test results to come back and plan her next move from there. With a sigh, she picked up her laptop and headed for the exit, shutting lights off as she went.

*Friday, February 7, 2003 — 8:30 pm*
*Donatelli Residence, Hot Springs, Arkansas*

When Angela pulled into the driveway in front of her house that night, she was surprised to see Linda's car blocking her way. After the day she'd just had, she wasn't really feeling up to company, but she pasted on a cordial smile and headed toward the kitchen. She'd make a gracious entrance, greet her mother's guest, and slip away as soon as possible. At the kitchen doorway, though, the sight that greeted her stopped her dead in her tracks.

"Didn't I just say goodbye to you two?" she asked, looking bemusedly at the crew ranged around her kitchen table. Before her sat Linda Tackett and Jennifer Richmond, wearing the guilty grins of kids caught pulling a fast one on their folks. Marie wasn't much better. She rolled on over to her daughter and pulled Angela into the room. "Don't be a spoil-sport," she said, laughing. "Did you really think Linda would leave town without cluing me in on her little mystery?"

Angela tried to look stern. "You know I don't like mixing work with home life." But Marie just laughed.

"Don't give me that. Linda's practically part of the family now, and I'm feeling like maybe I might adopt this young lady." She smiled sweetly at Jennifer. "Might be nice to have a daughter who made it home for dinner on time once in a while." With fond exasperation, Angela came the rest of the way into the room. "Okay, I give up. You win." Marie beamed at Angela's decision to be reasonable and poured her daughter a cup of tea. Angela pulled up a chair and sat down.

Linda began. "Angela, I'm sorry about today. Let me explain, okay? I know some people think I'm just a bossy, empty-headed ol' fool, but I'm not, you know. I've been deal-ing with my MS for a long time now, and I've learned a lot about it. I know there's no proof yet that these other folks have MS too—but I thought it was worth finding out, so I brought them to you. You know, Angela, not everyone knows as much about the disease as you do and I think it was even worse when your mother first got sick." She looked to Marie. "I'll bet you've got stories that would curl Jennifer's hair about trying to get a doctor to tell you what's wrong, back then." Marie nodded mutely.

Linda turned her attention back to Angela. "It was that, more than anything, that made me break your rules, you know. I couldn't stand it that these people were scared and their doctors weren't telling them anything." Her voice turned harsh. "Antidepressants!"

Angela looked from Linda to Marie and saw, in both their faces, something she could only call implacability. It was so easy, as a doctor, to think in terms of caution—let's wait for the tests to come back, let's rule a few other things out first— that it was easy to forget how agonizing it was for the patient as days and weeks passed without an answer to their most fundamental question, What's *wrong* with me?

"I understand your frustration, but even *I* can't guarantee a diagnosis. Sometimes it's just not possible," Angela said quietly. "But I *can* guarantee that I'll keep on working with these people until we figure out what is going on." She paused and looked Linda squarely in the eye. Now about your methods…"

"Yes, well…" Linda looked abashed. "Probably should have called ahead. But…" Contrition didn't come naturally to Linda, so she changed the subject fast. "The thing is, *something's* wrong with all these folks—MS or otherwise. If it's MS, we got one kind of mystery." She paused dramatically. "If it's not, well—we got another kind of mystery, don't we?"

Angela had no argument. Hadn't Murdoch said the same thing over the phone, not more than 20 minutes ago? "Okay," she said. "I agree. But we've got to be clear on a couple of points. There's no reason to think that what's going on is anything but a weird set of coincidences, right? In fact, I was just speaking to a colleague of mine up in New York— Murdoch says 'hi,' Ma—and he says that this is probably some kind of environmental contaminant, not some weird new version of MS."

"Well, then," said Marie, "We've got our work cut out for us." She turned to Linda. "Mud's an old friend. Very wise. We're going to have to stay real sharp if we want to impress *him*." Turning to Angela she said, "What do you suggest?"

"You three can start collecting 'people data.' Use the support group to do a little outreach to the Hammerstone community. See if there are more people with these symptoms—people who haven't yet come forward on their own."

Jennifer gave a guilty little start. "I don't think I'm going to be much help." She looked down at the table. "I'm just not the cloak and dagger type." Her voice grew soft. "I'm having a hard enough time just keeping my business afloat."

"That's okay." Linda was quick to move to Jennifer's side. "You look like you're getting tired and I need to get home, too. We'll pick this conversation up again tomorrow." With that the two women got up and got ready to go. As they headed for the door, Linda turned to Marie. "I'll call you. Meanwhile, you tell Angela what we've done so far," she said as she and Jennifer took their leave.

When they were gone, Angela looked at Marie. "Do I really want to know?"

Marie had the grace to look a little embarrassed, but without hesitation she reached across the table to pull over a roll of butcher paper and spread it out. "We were thinking it might be useful to see who lives where, you know, among the new patients. Mud's not the only one who could think up that environmental idea. We all saw *Erin Brockovich*. So we were trying to draw up a map of Hammerstone." She looked down at the paper's markings and shook her head ruefully." Maybe our artistic skills leave a little to be desired."

"Actually," Angela said slowly, "that's not such a bad idea. I'll pick up a county map of the town and surrounding area—you can plot the locations on that." She stood up from the table, suddenly feeling the weight of the day. "I'm tired, Ma," she said. "Let's talk about this in the morning." But just before she reached the door she turned back to Marie. "Listen, when you're looking for new cases, don't just count people who say they think they have MS. Consider the whole cluster of symptoms: weakness, numbness, fatigue and so on. And ask them when these symptoms first started turning up. We should include everyone who started having symptoms in the latter part of last year, say after July first. Write down anyone who you even think might qualify. We need to cast a wide net at this point."

Marie nodded soberly. "I get it. What counts is the combination: MS-like symptoms that started turning up after July." Marie looked thoughtful. "You *do* think there's something strange going on here, don't you?"

"I don't know what I think," Angela said with weary honesty. "But it won't hurt us to look a little harder."

As Angela turned again to leave, Marie spoke up once more. "I hope you aren't too put out with me and Linda. Maybe we're making fools of ourselves, a little bit, but you've got to remember that this disease of ours is an awfully big thing in our lives. Can you wonder that we might get a little carried away? What if this is some new kind of MS? A meaner, harder, faster kind? What does that mean for us?"

Suddenly Angela understood a little better how her normally level-headed mother could have been so easily enlisted by the much more scatter-brained Linda into this wild goose chase. Of course the two of them would immediately think of this new outbreak in terms of how it could affect their own lives. Of course they'd want to find out as much as they could about it. Getting involved in solving the mystery would be, for them, a little like whistling when walking past a graveyard. It let them keep their courage up when their first instincts were to be just plain old scared.

"No, Ma. I'm not mad. Not mad at all," Angela said gently. "And that map idea is a winner. I'll make sure I pick up a good one for you to use. Okay?"

*Saturday, February 8, 2003 — 7:00 am*
*Donatelli residence, Hot Springs, Arkansas*

It's amazing, Angela thought the next morning. A good night's sleep really *can* knit the ravelled sleeve of care, just like the bard said. She had been so tired last night that she'd gone to sleep with no thought for the day to come. Now she was pleasantly surprised to realize that she had a whole weekend ahead of her. She felt rested and refreshed, and it suddenly dawned on her that this would be a good day to follow Mud's advice. A trip out to the country sounded like a great way to spend the day.

Of course, she knew perfectly well that statement was untrue. Murdoch's advice had been to wait for the test results and *then* take a field trip. But, she was the doctor, and that gave her certain responsibilities and more then a few perks, one of which was the right to make hard, if somewhat impetuous decisions. She was going to satisfy her curiosity and trek out to Hammerstone. Surely it wouldn't hurt to get a little jump on the field-work aspect of the investigation, just in case.

It had been years since she'd gone out into the field to do environmental research. Last time had been for an ecology project in college. She had led a small army of classmates on a project designed to catalog the biological diversity of a brackish salt marsh in Pelham Bay Park, in the Bronx. It was a long time ago, but she still remembered the basic field techniques.

Downstairs, she found Marie already at work in the kitchen, toast and coffee at the ready. "I think I'll take a trip out to Hammerstone today, Ma," Angela announced. "Take a look around, see the place for myself. I'll get you a map of the area while I am out there"

Marie looked worried. "You'll be careful, won't you Angie? In case there really is something out there that's making people sick?"

"Sure I will, Ma." But to tell the truth, Angela wasn't so sure that there were any precautions she could take. She had no idea what was behind this strange pattern of sickness. Marie wheeled over to the counter and pulled down a loaf of bread. "At least let me pack up something for your lunch," Marie said firmly. "You don't need to take any chances eating the food out there."

Angela was in the car and on the road by 8 o'clock, but she had a pit-stop to make before she could head on out to the highway. She stopped off at her research office, and put together a collection of pipettes, ziplock bags, and rubber-stoppered vials. Tossing in a few gauze-tipped swabs and a box of latex gloves, she decided that this would make up a more than adequate field kit. She went out to the parking lot, tossed the kit into the back seat of the car and got in. As she pulled out onto the street, she felt the first stirrings of excitement. The bright blue sky was studded with the kind of big, white, puffy clouds that only make their appearance in the best of weather, and by the time Angela turned onto the highway to Hammerstone, she was in the highest of spirits.

She was soon out of town, driving through stands of new-growth forest that ran along both sides of the road. Fifty years of logging had stripped most of west-central Arkansas of the majestic old trees that were common in the northeast. But what this part of Arkansas lacked in grand old timber, it made up in beautiful mountain vistas. Tall peaks stood crisp and clear against the horizon on this glorious day. She switched on the radio, hoping for some bright, bouncy music to match her mood.

By the time Angela approached the first of the signs announcing the Hammerstone exit, the radio had switched from the classic rock she favored to the news. She listened with only half an ear, more intent on maneuvering her car through the light traffic than on listening to world events.

Suddenly, however, a name grabbed her attention. Bo Li Yeung. She'd known him since her college years, and had followed his career with interest since then. Once a gangling engineering student who'd attended a few meetings of her old computing club, Bo Li was now a candidate for President of South Korea. He had been scheduled to give a talk in Little Rock last December, and Angela had intended to go and hear him speak, but the event was cancelled at the last minute. Something about the heightened terror threat during the holiday season. Now, at least according to the news announcer, the talk was back on. He'd be lecturing on Korea's North-South relations at the Clinton Library on the 27th of this month. Well, well, she thought with a smile. Guess I'll get to hear ol' Bo Li after all. She made a mental note of the date just as she approached the Hammerstone exit. With a quick spin of the wheel, she drove off the highway and into town.

*Saturday, February 8, 2003 — 9:00 am*
*Police department, Hammerstone, Arkansas*

Hammerstone's chief of police, Hank McLain, looked at the files on his desk and sighed. After more than a month of working overtime, he was no closer to discovering the causes of the New Year's Eve fire on Arrowhead Mountain than he had been on day one. The files were thick with forensic data, but in the end, the evidence told him nothing more than Mark had already told him just before he died—the fire had been set.

The fire marshal's investigation had identified the cause of the fire: a bottle full of home-made napalm had been tossed down into the basement of the house. Hank knew that anyone with a library card could find the recipe for such a simple device. Upstairs, the bomber had splashed gasoline around to guarantee that the initial blaze would rip through the rest of the place like... well, like a house afire. There was nothing unique about the methods that this arsonist used, nothing to give Hank the first clue as to who might have set it.

The situation regarding Burns was similar: loads of data but no answers. The fire had started with an explosion in the west wing and it was there that Burns' body was found. As the fire marshals sifted through the wreckage, it became clear that the west wing held some pretty big equipment, much of which had been reduced to smoldering piles of twisted metal. His team had been stumped at first—aside from the computers, they'd been unable to figure out just what all Burns had been working on in his basement.

Hank had finally called on help from the medical school at the university up in Little Rock, and they'd sent a crew down to check things out. They had been impressed by the extensive laboratory that now lay in the ruins of Burns' house. When Hank heard this, his first thought was that Burns had set up a drug manufacturing operation, but they were quick to shut him down on that one. It wasn't that kind of lab, they said. Near as they could tell, Burns had to have been doing some kind of biotech or genetic research—like that Human Genome Project that used to be in the news all the time.

But that just didn't make any sense. Why on earth would some kind of scientific genius hide himself away in the Arkansas hills and build a secret lab like that in his basement?

Who *was* this guy, anyway? A quick background check turned up the facts that Burns was British born, came from a good family, and attended good schools. He'd earned an advanced degree in bioengineering from Columbia University. On these facts alone, Hank would've reckoned that Burns was nothing more than an academic who'd managed early retirement and just happened to choose Arkansas as the place to spend his golden years. But the closer Hank looked into Burns' past, the murkier things got.

For example, Hank had had no trouble unearthing Burns's biographical information for the first twenty-eight years of the man's life. Burns seemed to have started out strong—won a pretty impressive faculty position at a university out in California, fresh out of his post-doctoral studies. But he left that job under some kind of cloud—some big academic scandal. And then he just dropped out of sight. Hank could find no trace of him after that until about six years ago, when Burns had turned up in Hammerstone and bought the big house up on Arrowhead Mountain for cash on the barrelhead. Since then, he'd lived up there in relative obscurity, until the tornado hit.

He never mixed with the town—rarely left the house at all, as far as Hank could tell. Took his groceries by delivery. Ordered whatever he needed by phone. People talked about the hermit on Arrowhead Mountain, and rumors flew through the town. After the tornado, he had earned some grudging respect for standing his ground and rebuilding even after all his other neighbors had cut their losses and moved away. Not that anybody much warmed to him—he was still considered a bit too odd for most folks' tastes. But they cut him some slack and just left him to himself, which was all he seemed to be asking for anyway.

However, it was plain to see by the artifacts in the ashes that if Burns was a hermit, he was a pretty rich one. After all, a six thousand square foot house full of antiques did not come cheap. Hank ran a check on Burns' financial dealings, but the only thing that seemed really odd was what *wasn't* on the record—Hank had never found out where or when Burns had bought all that equipment, or even how he'd paid for it. This really stuck in Hanks craw. To hide something like that took more organization than one man could muster... and now that man was dead. And there was no getting around the fact that he was dead because somebody wanted him that way. But who?

Hank stood up from the desk, stretching the kinks out of his back. It was obvious that he wasn't going to get anywhere by staring at these files. He looked out the window to see that this was going to be one of those crisp, clear, late winter days that made living here in the country such a treat. Heck, he wasn't even supposed to be in the office this morning—it was his turn on the rotation for a Saturday off. Might as well take advantage of the day. He strode to the door, snaring his hat off the hook as he passed, and went out to the front office where one of his officers was shuffling some papers.

"Mornin', Thelma," he said.

"Mornin', Chief." Officer Thelma Wilkins gave her boss one of her trademark dimpled smiles. An eight-year veteran on the force, she'd time and again proved her competence, but dang if she didn't look like a school kid.

"Looks to be a good, slow day." She opened her desk drawer to show him the thick novel she'd tucked away in there. "Maybe I'll finally get a chance to finish this thing," she said with a laugh. Then the phone on her desk rang and she broke away. Hank headed out the door into the parking lot.

Yep, on a day like this, a man could do worse than head up into the hills, preferably on horseback. And like that, Hank knew what he wanted to do. He got into his car and drove off home to the ranch house, where his horses waited in his stables.

Minutes after Hank drove out of the police station parking lot, Angela pulled into the space he'd just vacated. She walked into the police station to find Officer Wilkins at her desk, engrossed in the final chapters of her mystery novel. Angela politely cleared her throat. "Excuse me," she said, tentatively.

Startled, Thelma looked up at Angela with mild annoyance,

reluctantly lowering her book. "Can I help you?"

"Sorry to interrupt." Angela flashed an apologetic smile. "Hope I didn't drag you out of a really good part."

Thelma offered a grudging smile and a shrug in return. She dog-eared the page she was reading and stashed the book back into the drawer. "No problem. It'll still be waiting for me once we're through doing business. What can I do for you?"

"Just a few little things. First off, do you have any county maps showing the town of Hammerstone? You know, the kind of plats that engineers use?" Angela hoped that this Officer Wilkins could help her out —she'd already noticed that the town hall was closed for the weekend, and she wanted to surprise her mother by returning with the map she'd promised last night.

"You know? I think I just might have a copy of one of those. Got a stack when those surveyors were working their way through town a few months back." Thelma rooted through her desk, which was a marvel of dishevelment. "Now where'd I put those things," she muttered to herself as she hunted through the disorderly piles. "Ah, gotcha!" she exclaimed, victoriously, sliding a folded wad of paper out from the middle of a precariously balanced pile of forms, manuals, and paperwork. She handed it over to Angela with a grin. "Hope your other 'little things' are as easy to handle," she said.

"Well, next I need to know where the nearest coffee shop is. I could use a cup after the drive from Hot Springs."

"Well, I know just the place," Thelma responded. "We make the best cup of coffee in the county right here," she said over her shoulder as she walked towards the corner of the room and disappeared into an adjacent room. In a minute she returned with a fresh cup of coffee and little packets of creamer and sweetener. "Here you go," Thelma said as she handed it to Angela. "So, I'm battin' two for two, right? Anything else?"

"They say the third one's the charm," Angela said with a grin. She was getting to like this Officer Wilkins. "I need directions out to Jennifer Richmond's place. I know she's out by Arrowhead Mountain, but I haven't a clue where that might be."

Thelma's smile faltered at the mention of Jennifer's name. She gave Angela a doubtful look. "You a friend of Jenn's?" Angela couldn't help but hear the note of protectiveness that crept into Thelma's voice. "'Cause she's got enough on her plate right now without having to deal with strangers."

"You could say I'm a friend—but a pretty new one," Angela said, reassuringly. "Linda Tackett brought her to meet me yesterday. I thought I'd return the visit, since I'm passing through town anyway."

Thelma's worried look cleared away in an instant. "Well, if you know Linda, I guess it'll be OK." She seemed to realize that an explanation for her earlier reaction might be in order. "You see, Jenn and me, we went through school together. Got to be pretty close. Let me tell you, that girl's something special. I guess I get a little protective, but then you'd be hard put to find somebody in town who didn't feel that way about her."

Angela smiled. "She cuts a pretty wide path through the community, does she?"

"You said it. Course, what with her running the antique store downtown, just about everybody knows her, but it's her good works that makes her popular." Thelma propped her elbows on her disheveled desktop, threatening to trigger a small avalanche of paperwork as she did so. She leaned forward and lowered her voice confidentially. "That Jenn's got the world's greenest thumb. Every year she plants a big ol' chunk of her yard in vegetables. More'n a skinny girl like her could ever hope to eat. And every harvest, there she is, dropping off baskets of her vegetables at houses where they'd be the most welcome, if you get my meaning." But now Thelma's sad and worried look returned.

"So maybe you'll understand why this is such a tough time for her right now. It's coming up on planting season, and I think that if that poor girl can't get back out into her garden, it's just about going to break her heart. As it is, she hasn't been able to work at the store very much for a good couple of weeks now. People are starting to miss her." Thelma let her voice trail off as she considered the unfairness of a world where bad things happened to good people.

Then she favored Angela with a rueful little smile. "But here I go, forgetting what you asked for." She stood up from her desk and walked Angela toward the front door. "To get over to Arrowhead, you want to get on Main Street heading southwest out of the center of town." She pointed to the road that passed in front of the station. "Then go on about a mile or two until you see the road split. Take the right fork and go about another three miles on the Old Indian Trail." She walked Angela to her car, offering a last bit of clarification. "You can't miss her house. It's the last one before the road heads up into the hills. Set back a ways from the road."

*Saturday, February 8, 2003 — 11:00 am*
*McLain ranch, Hammerstone, Arkansas*

Right about the time that Officer Thelma Wilkins was filling Angela in on the town's affection for Jennifer Richmond, Hank McLain was easing his favorite horse, Cornbread, along the trail up behind his ranch house. Both horse and rider knew the way—they'd made this ride many a time since the fire. It seemed he was drawn up the mountain, to the charred remains of the old Burns house and the place where his brother had breathed his last.

Cornbread trotted past the big brown barn and out into an open field. Hank always gave the horse free rein here, where the land was relatively flat, and she soon broke into a flat-out run. Hank felt the smooth muscles of his horse rippling and bunching with the movement, enjoying the power and the speed as much as Cornbread did. All too soon, though, he had to rein in her exuberance. They had come upon the start of the woods that marked the base of Arrowhead Mountain. From here on, the going would be treacherous.

Soon, they picked up a stream coursing through the woods. A little further on they emerged from the trees into a small clearing. Hank dismounted, ground-tied the horse, and allowed himself a few moments with his memories. When he and Mark were kids, they used to camp out here on warm summer nights. Back then, they'd been inseparable, despite the difference in their ages. Now Hank was left to carry on alone, and sometimes the loneliness seemed too much to bear. He picked up a rock and threw it into the stream. With a sigh, he got back up into the saddle and set Cornbread to moving again.

Hank made the ride up into the hills to the Burns place just about every time he had a day off. He knew that solving the case wouldn't bring his brother back, but he hoped that by closing the case, maybe he could also close the door to the past and move on with his life. He'd never forget Mark, of course—he didn't want to. But he needed to know what had gone on in that house—what had set into motion the chain of events that ended in Mark's death.

When at last Hank and Cornbread emerged from the cover of trees into the yard behind the ruins of Jack Burns's house, Hank slipped down from the saddle with a sigh. He wound Cornbread's reins around a tree branch and began his slow, watchful walk through the charred stone and wood that littered the clearing floor, looking for something, anything, that would help him understand.

*Saturday, February 8, 2003 — 11:30 am*
*Jennifer Richmond's house, Hammerstone, Arkansas*

Thelma's directions were good. Angela had no trouble finding Jennifer's small frame house at the foot of Arrowhead
Mountain. She walked up to the front door, and was greeted
with a smile.

"So," Jennifer said as she invited her in, "you're really going
through with it! Come on in and have a cup of tea. Or are
you too busy doing your detective work?"

"Tea would be fine," Angela said as she followed Jennifer
into the bright yellow kitchen. She took a seat at the table
and watched as her hostess set the kettle on the stove and laid
out a plate of cookies. Her experienced eye saw that Jennifer
was finding these simple tasks difficult, but she made no move
to take over. After all these years of living with Marie, she
knew that Jenn would rather do these everyday chores herself
than let somebody else do them for her. As her mother would
have said, "it's pride, but not the bad kind." At last Jennifer settled herself into one of the gaily patterned vinyl chairs.

"So," she said, "where are you going to start?" Jennifer
reached for a cookie. "How do you investigate something like
this?"

Angela smiled. "Right now I'm just making it up as I go along.
I figure I might as well check to see if there's something special
about Hammerstone that could explain what's happening to you
and your neighbors. So I came prepared to collect samples—soil
and water, things like that." She gestured to the makeshift field
kit she had carried in with her from the car.

"Is that how MS starts? With something in the environ-
ment?"

"No." Angela was firm. "Not that we know of. Of course,
there's a lot we still don't know about MS. And one of the big
things we don't know for sure is exactly what causes it." She

sighed. "I'm just trying to cover all bases in case this unusual outbreak is not MS, but is the result of some kind of environmental poisoning instead. That might account for why all these cases are in the same area." She took a last sip of tea and stood. "So, if it's okay with you, I'd like to check around your house—take samples of the water you drink, maybe even check out your garden."

"Sounds like a plan," Jennifer said. She struggled to get herself up, leaning heavily on her cane. She took a few unsteady steps around to the other end of the table. "Mind if I just wait here while you get your samples in the house? All the strength seems to have run out of my legs." She tried to keep her tone light, but Angela heard the anguish beneath.

"Sure thing. You just wait here and take it easy." Angela went about her work, her sympathies for Jennifer fully engaged. It was always heartbreaking to watch someone in the early stages of coming to terms with this kind of disability. But it was always inspirational, too. The strength that people—perfectly average, everyday people—found within themselves to cope with hardship like this never failed to fill Angela with a kind of awe. She moved quickly through the house, filling her little sample flasks with water drawn from each of the faucets. Down in the basement, she looked around for unusual household chemicals but found nothing worth collecting. When she came back upstairs, Jennifer was standing again, a little wobbly but game.

"Ready to see my garden?" she asked.

"Lead on," Angela laughed in reply.

Outside, Jennifer pointed to the left of the driveway. "It used to be a little patch by the side of the road. But then I got carried away, and it just grew and grew. Of course, right now there's nothing to see but the pansies I put in last fall. It's still too early to plant my vegetables, but pretty near all that side of the yard is garden by the time growing season gets underway."

Her voice dropped to a darker, sadder register. "At least, that's how it used to be." She fell silent, and Angela refrained from speaking for a moment. She knew that Jennifer had just realized that her days of kneeling between the rows of well-tended plants might well be over.

It seemed to Angela that she couldn't let this sad moment drag on for another instant. "Right," she said brightly. "Why don't I take a few scrapings from the soil over there, then?" She busied herself with her ziplock bags, taking her time about collecting her samples so that Jennifer could have a moment to pull herself together. When she judged enough time had passed, she stood up and looked out across the yard, still intent on giving Jennifer a little privacy to deal with her sorrow. However, as her eye traveled up the road to where it disappeared into a wooded area, a thought struck her. "What's up that way?" she asked.

"Used to be a fancy neighborhood. Big houses on big, private lots, looking down on us regular folks from the mountainside." She shrugged. "Now there's nothing much to see. Most of the houses up there got wrecked a few years ago when the tornado blew through, and just about everybody moved away. One guy stayed on—rebuilt his house with the insurance money, but his house is gone now, too. Blew up like a rocket last New Year's Eve."

Angela let her gaze travel up the mountain. She saw the glitter of flowing water—a small stream that ran along the side of the road. That same stream flowed right past Jennifer's house and joined a larger stream to cut through the middle of the valley.

"You get your water out of wells down here?" she asked idly.

"Yup. This country's got more natural springs than you can shake a stick at," Jenn replied. "One thing we don't have to worry about around here is a water shortage."

"How about up on the mountain? Any big industrial development up there?"

"Nope. Or at least, nothing I ever heard of, and I've lived here most of my life. Some stone mining, of course. But that's pretty small scale."

"Maybe I ought to just poke around up there a bit, anyway." Angela's voice was thoughtful. "I'd like to follow that stream, see where it leads." When Jennifer responded with a vague shrug, Angela recognized the signs of real fatigue. Their little visit had already taken most of the starch out of Jennifer and she probably would welcome a chance to rest.

"Tell you what," Angela said brightly. "Why don't you go on back into the house and I'll get out of your hair. You've been a great help, but I've kept you lots longer than I should have." Jennifer made vague, polite sounds of denial, but she was clearly glad at the suggestion. Once she'd gotten Jenn back inside and comfortably ensconced on the sofa, Angela made her exit and headed up the mountain in her car.

*Saturday, February 8, 2003 — 12:30 pm*
*Arrowhead Mountain, Arkansas*

Almost as soon as Angela started on North Indian Heights Trail, it turned downright ugly. Deep ruts threatened to scrape off her undercarriage, and deadfall littered the landscape to the right and left of her. Getting up this mountain was going to challenge every one of her driving skills. But still, the ride up gave her a little time for thought.

As she drove, Angela considered what she'd learned so far from her inspection of Jennifer's house. Obvious sources of contamination were entirely lacking. Jennifer didn't keep exotic pets, which sometimes carried equally exotic germs and parasites. She shared her house with an aged greyhound, long retired from the West Memphis dog track, but he hadn't budged from the living room hearthstones during her entire visit.

Of course, Jennifer was an avid gardener, so there was the chance that some toxic pesticide or fertilizer might have been the culprit. But Angela had checked all the bags and bottles in the garden shed, and she'd seen nothing that wasn't in use in gardens and greenhouses all across the country. For the sake of thoroughness she'd made a list of all the garden chemicals anyway. She could ask the state's poison control center to review them, but she was pretty sure that would turn out to be a dead end.

A sudden thump and a strong jolt from the front of the car brought Angela's attention back to the road, where it belonged. And not a moment too soon. Dead ahead, a large, fallen tree completely blocked her path. With a sigh Angela shut down the engine.

The sudden silence was striking. She could tell right away that she was never going to be able to move that tree out of the road, and briefly considered turning around and going home. But the day was still young, and the weather was fine. Besides, she'd missed her morning jog. A little hike up the mountain wouldn't hurt. She retrieved her field kit from the car and set off up the road.

As she strode up the mountain on this glorious day, taking in the cool mountain air, she began to get a better sense of her surroundings. She could hear the stream running parallel to the road and feel the cool breeze as it rustled through the trees. In nearly no time, she came to a fork. The road itself wound off to the left. To the right, a well-marked gravel drive led up into the trees. For sheer ease of traveling, the gravel drive looked like the better bet, and when Angela saw that the stream followed the drive to the right, her decision was made for her.

She didn't get far, however, before she was brought up short once again. Stretched across the drive was a length of tattered yellow tape, black lettering spelling out the words "Do Not Cross." She stopped and stared at it a moment, nonplussed by the incongruity of a crime-scene barrier out here in the middle of nowhere. Suddenly, she heard a voice.

"Can I help you, ma'am?"

Angela looked over to the sound and saw a man step out of the trees into the sunlight. He was tall, a little raw-boned, but attractive, in the lanky, cowboy sort of way that seemed to be common currency in these parts. He came forward, stopping just short of his side of the bright yellow tape, and Angela saw that he sported a police badge on the breast pocket of his brown leather jacket.

"Name's Hank McLain. I'm the police chief round here," he said, tipping his cowboy hat and nodding. Angela acknowledged his greeting with a guilty smile, somehow feeling as if she had been caught with her hand in the cookie jar.

"Don't get many visitors up this way these days." He smiled; a lopsided grin that Angela was sure caused many of the local ladies to swoon. "Mind telling me what you're doing here?"

"I'm Angela Donatelli. Doctor Donatelli. From Hot Springs." She stopped, not sure how to continue. Her hesitation was not lost on Hank, who gave her a closer once-over. All in all, she made a good impression. But there was no escaping the fact that she was standing on the edge of a crime scene with a backpack slung over her shoulder and a determined look in her eyes. This needed some explaining. He waited, willing to let the silence spin out until she felt compelled to talk. An old interrogator's trick, but it worked just as well in the real world as it did back at the station.

Angela saw Chief McLain give the backpack a curious glance. She stuttered slightly. "Ah... well. I guess that's what you'd call a collection kit. For taking samples, you know?"

"What kind of samples?" Hank's tone was not quite forbidding, but he was clearly not going to be satisfied without more explanation on her part.

"Uh, well, like water, soil, stuff like that." Angela took a deep breath. This was silly, letting some strange officer of the law make her nervous like this. She wasn't doing anything wrong. How was she supposed to have known that this was some kind of official crime scene?

"Look," she began again. "I'm up here trying to do some research." She paused a moment to consider how best to begin to explain her mission up here in Hammerstone but before she could find the words, Hank interrupted her, almost harshly.

"Research? Up here? Why?" The urgency of his tone startled her.

"I'm a neurologist. I have a practice up in Hot Springs, like I already told you. I was visited by an unusual bunch of patients, all from Hammerstone, and, well..." She stopped, helplessly wondering how she could explain this without going into too much detail. "Look, it just might be possible that my patients got sick from something in the water or the soil. I wanted to see what I could find by doing a little field work."

"Don't know many doctors who go tramping through the woods to treat their patients." Hank's laconic drawl carried a note of disbelief. "And if it's a public health problem, aren't there proper channels to go through for this kind of thing?"

Angela felt like a fool. Of course there were. This whole trip was an exercise in foolishness. How could she hope to explain to this total stranger that she was here partly because she wanted to indulge her mother's desire to play private eye? How could she get him to understand about her own overpowering curiosity about what might be going on out here in Hammerstone? Anyone who knew Angela knew that, more than anything else, she hated being cut out of the loop when it came to solving a puzzle. And if she turned this mystery over to the Department of Public Health, that's exactly what would probably happen. She couldn't bear that. But she could hardly expect this police chief to understand that.

Hank gave her a long, level stare, clearly wrestling with the decision of how much to trust her word. Angela held her breath and waited. At last he gave a small grunt. Then he surprised her by lifting the tape and offering her his hand.

"Watch your step here. There's a little drop where the road caved in some." Next thing Angela knew, she was on the inside of her first crime scene. She paused a minute to give the experience its due respect. When Chief McLain offered to relieve her of the backpack, she hesitated a moment, but decided that relinquishing it would show him that she wasn't here on some nefarious errand. He hoisted it up under his arm, and led the way up the drive to the devastated clearing that marked the site of the Burns house.

Angela stood at the edge of the ruins. At first, it looked like nothing more than a charred hole in the ground, but as she accommodated to the scene, she could see the melted remains of what was clearly some big equipment on the western end of the property. While Angela surveyed the scene, Chief McLain gently lowered the backpack to the ground and walked over to Cornbread, retrieving two small bottles of water that he had tied to the horn of the saddle.

"I was just thinking about taking a break up here myself when I heard your car," he said, handing one of the bottles to Angela. She looked back the way they'd come. It seemed to her that was a long way for somebody to have heard her from here. Hank caught her look.

"Sounds can play tricks on you up here in the hills. Carry a lot farther than you'd think, sometimes," he said.

"Well, I was getting a little hungry—this is as good a place as any to break for lunch." She pulled a sandwich out of her backpack and offered half to the chief. "Share?"

Hank demurred. Instead he hunkered down by a tree, leaning his long back against the bark, and pulled a cigar out of the inside pocket of his jacket. You mind?" he said, raising it for Angela to see. When she offered no objections, he lit up. Between puffs, he asked her to tell him a little more about herself and her reasons for being out here in the wilds.

Angela started slowly, explaining about her new cases but being careful not to name names. Police chief or not, there was still a little thing called patient confidentiality, and she had no intention of violating it. It turned out, though, that she needn't have bothered. Chief McLain seemed to know everything about everybody in his little town.

"Okay," he said. "I'd guess you maybe talked to Jennifer, down the hill a ways. And prob'ly Merle, too. He took sick all of a sudden. And those poor Stedmans—little Timmy's been hurting some as well. Oh, and the Bright girl, most like. And the McMasters boy. You're right. There's a lot of folks who've come down with health problems this year. I never gave a thought to them being linked."

Chuckling to himself and shaking his head. "Heck, I thought nothing would slow down ol' Jimmy McMasters once his daddy let him buy that old car. Now he's lucky if he can manage to get out into the yard to rub on a coat of wax. Breaks your heart to see the boy like that."

Angela was aghast. If the Chief was right, there were at least two more cases like the ones she'd already seen. She tried to cover up her reaction, but she resolved to speak to Linda about this, first chance she got.

"I came up here because there seems to be something fishy about the way the cases turned up." She paused, weighing her words. The last thing she needed was for the local police to think she was some kind of excitable nut. "Now, sure, it could be some kind of fluke, but I think maybe it could be something more. Something like an environmental toxin that's only recently started leaching into the town's water supply, maybe." She pointed across the clearing, where several rills of water were flowing down to join the stream that she had been following. "A stream like that would be the perfect source for any number of contaminants."

Hank sat a moment in silence, taking a few contemplative puffs on his cigar while he considered what this pretty lady doctor had just finished telling him. "Toxins in the water." He turned the words over in his mind while Angela watched him anxiously, hoping he'd at least accept her explanations enough to let her get back to work. The strong light of mid-day had already eased back somewhat. Now the sky had taken on the mellower glow of a waning afternoon. When that light was gone she wanted to be well down the mountain, heading home. Finally, Hank seemed to come to a decision. "Okay. I'll buy your story. But I've got to tell you, all this talk about poisons and such, and then you turn up here... It sure sets me to thinking."

"Why?" asked Angela. "What happened up here, anyway? Someone in town said there was an explosion, but that's all I've heard."

"Explosion's only the half of it. The guy who lived here was a pretty odd character. Turns out he was some kind of mad scientist, seems like. Had this big ol' laboratory in his cellar."

"So what happened? An experiment got out of control and he blew himself up, or what?" Angela imagined some variant on the old Dr. Frankenstein routine. It seemed a little far-fetched, though.

"No. That's the thing. You'd think with a set up like that, that's the way it would turn out, right? But this ol' boy, he wasn't that kind of scientist. No smelly, smoky chemicals just waiting to blow. Did most of his work on the computer, near as we can tell, though he had other equipment here, too." Hank paused for another draw on his cigar, then puffed out a pretty impressive ring of smoke. "See, when we first heard about the lab, we thought maybe he was into processing dope. Crystal meth labs are a big thing out here in the boonies. It doesn't cost very much and they can be set up just about anywhere in the woods. Don't even need to build shelter. With an operation like that, the explosion would make sense. Either he blew himself up, or the people he was supplying did the job for him."

"But you're saying it *wasn't* drugs, right? So what was he making up here?" Angela was completely perplexed.

"No one can say for sure. We called in a team from the university up in Little Rock, and they said this set up could only be for one thing—bioengineering of some kind. Looks like our Jack Burns was some kind of maverick biotech genius."

Angela was startled. "Did you say Burns? Jack Burns?"

Hank turned a curious eye on her. "Yep, that's the name. Been living out here for the past five, six years now. No one knows where he was before that. Guess guys with those kinds of brains can pretty much do what they want, right?"

But Angela was still hung up on the name. It couldn't be the Jack Burns she knew, could it? One of her computer-gaming gang? Still, the life-history Hank just recited sounded about right. Everybody knew that Jack had gotten caught on the wrong side of a research ethics scandal during his first year at Stanford. And while he'd stayed in touch with Angela, it was only by way of increasingly infrequent e-mails. Nobody really knew where he'd taken himself off to after that big research scandal. She pressed Hank for more details.

"He was a tall skinny guy. Real pale. With big owl-eyes glasses. He had a British accent and acted superior, if you know what I mean, like he was always smelling something bad." Hank chuckled at his description, thinking it was good that 'ol Jack wasn't listening.

"That's him! I'm pretty sure I know this guy." Suddenly she

was struck by the implications of what Hank had told her. "And now you say he's dead." She shook her head sadly. "That's a shame. I mean, Jack was a little weird, but he wasn't that bad a guy."

Hank looked at the burnt out hulk that was once Burns' home. "Yeah. He's dead. But we don't have a clue as to why. See, the explosion was no accident. The fire was set deliberately. Hank looked down and saw that his cigar was finished. He buried the tattered remnants of tobacco just beside the tree, then stood. Angela stood with him, and suddenly became acutely aware that the top of her head came just under his chin. At 5'9" she was a tall woman herself, and unaccustomed to feeling like a little slip of a girl. She decided that it wasn't a bad feeling.

Hank put on his hat, then turned to look Angela square in the eye. "Maybe we've got something in common here," he said. "I don't know how, but maybe Burns was up to something that was related to y'all's problem, too. Maybe it wouldn't hurt if we joined forces, so to speak. Work as a team?"

Angela gave the proposition a little thought. It certainly would help make things go a lot more smoothly if she had an ally in the local police department. She couldn't see how the work Burns was doing, at least as Chief McLain had described it, could have any bearing on her mystery, but it was far too early in her own investigation to rule it out. She smiled at Hank. "Sounds like a plan to me," she agreed.

"Okay, then. Maybe I've got something you should see." He brushed leaf crumbs from his jeans and strode off, not waiting to see if Angela would follow. She scrambled to catch up with him and finally made it, nearly crashing into him when he stopped suddenly. "See up there?" he asked. She followed the line of his pointing finger, and finally spotted, camouflaged by the trees, what appeared to be a small concrete enclosure with a tin-roof.

She looked at it a moment, not recognizing it for what it was. "Looks like a miniature bunker," she said.

"It does, doesn't it? But it's a collection tank, for spring water."

"He had his own personal springhouse?"

"Yep, real common up here. There are springs everywhere."

Hank led the way up to the tank. Once there, he stood back and watched while Angela set about exploring. The walls of the tank were made of poured concrete, about six feet square and about seven feet high, with a tin roof over half of it. The other half was open to the elements. On both the uphill and downhill side was a hole about six feet off the ground, each connected to a hose. A drainage plug was set close to ground level. Angela climbed up on a large rock so that she could peer into the tank. She saw that it was full of water to about a foot from the top, and a thick mat of dead leaves floated on the surface.

"There'd have been a hose-pipe carrying water straight into Burns's house," Hank explained, pointing to the now naked downhill outlet. "Once the place burned down and the hose got detached, the water began pouring out through this hole, directly into the stream."

Angela climbed back down from the rock and went straight for her field kit. "I think I'd like to sample the water here, but I'd be even more interested in getting a sample from the actual source. Where does this water come from?"

"You've got to hike up another couple hundred yards," Hank warned. "You up for it?" Angela didn't even bother to answer. She slung her pack over her shoulder and headed up, following the vague outlines of a little-used trail.

As they hiked along, Hank filled Angela in on the local springhouse lore. "These mountains are full of natural springs, you know. But they're usually too high up for people to use—nobody wants to hike this far just to fill a pail of water."

Angela, finding herself challenged by the steep terrain, grunted in agreement. "So, the early settlers had to make the water come down to them. When they found a spring, they'd set to it with shovels, widening it. Then they'd put a container in the hole to collect it. These days, most folks use a plastic garbage can with the bottom cut out." Angela found herself wondering how this man could maintain his untroubled conversational tone—the gradient was getting ever steeper and she knew she'd never be able to make this climb and talk at the same time. She let his words flow over her.

"Anyway," he went on, "once you got your water collecting in the can, you're more than half-way home. All you have to do is make sure the can sticks out a few inches above the ground. Then you cut a hole in the side, attach a hose to the hole, and it carries the water to the collection house down below."

Angela finally gave up and flopped down on the path to catch her breath. At least it allowed her to ask a question. "Why not just pipe it straight to your house? What do you need the collection tank for?"

Hank grinned and hunkered down beside her. "Oh, you wouldn't want to drink the water that comes straight from the spring. It'd be all muddy. But while it sits in the collection tank, all the solids settle to the bottom. The outlet is set high enough that only pure water comes out to the house."

"Got it," said Angela as she scrambled back to her feet. "How much farther?" she asked, eyeing the trail ahead.

"Just over that next ridge," Hank said.

Angela didn't know what she was expecting, but when she finally pulled herself up over the ridge, the sight that greeted her took her by surprise. A half-dozen containers—some ceramic, some tin, some made of wood—were scattered across the ridge. Water gushed over their tops, and their hoses were cut short. Only one, off to the side, bore any resemblance to the set-up Hank had described on the climb up. Seeing her bewilderment, Hank explained.

"These ones here are all old. Probably their hoses got plugged over time—the minerals in the water clogs 'em up. But there are so many springs up here that most folks don't bother cleaning out the hoses—not when it's just as easy to tap a new one." He pointed to the one off to the side. "That's probably the one that's feeding the collection tank right now."

Angela stepped over to the one Hank indicated. She slipped on her latex gloves, then cut away the overgrowth of honeysuckle that had spread over the edge of the tank and moved in to fill a few of her collection tubes. The scummy, leaf strewn surface looked singularly unappealing. Taking another moment to roll up her sleeves, she looked up at Hank. "If I fall in, do you promise you'll fish me out?"

Hank grinned. "Sure thing," he said, "What kind of Southern gentleman would I be if I left a lady to wallow in that muck?"

Angela pasted a brave smile on her face, took a deep breath, and plunged her hand into the cistern. She pulled up handfuls of dead leaves, clearing the surface so that she could get a clear look at the water. The water was startlingly cold—but that was only to be expected from a mountain spring. Probably never got above forty-five degrees, even in summer, Angela thought.

The actual sampling didn't take much time at all. She filled a couple of tubes with the water, handing the full ones back to Hank for labeling. "Maybe I ought to take a little of the sediment, too," she said out loud. She reached down into the makeshift cistern and pulled up a handful of the muck that lined the bottom. When she handed the sample back to Hank this time, she looked thoughtful.

"Should there be anything at the bottom of this thing other than dirt?" she said as she handed the tube to Hank. Before he could reply, she continued. "I think I felt something funny under the mud," she said. "I'm gonna pull it up."

She plunged her hand back into the icy water, and rummaged around at the bottom. "Gotcha," she finally grunted, pulling up an opaque plastic box. "What the heck is this?" She said, holding it up so they could both look at it. The box was about four inches square, with a watertight lid. Duct tape secured several fishing weights to the box's top, no doubt to ensure that it would stay on the bottom of the cistern.

"Had to have been put there intentionally," Hank observed. "Somebody hid it there. Maybe Burns." Angela was exhilarated by her discovery. "I can't wait to get this back to the lab to open it," she said.

"Whoa there," Hank said. "I know y'all got your own puzzle to work out, but you got to remember that this is a crime scene. I can't just let you take it out of here like that."

Angela turned to him, her exasperation clearly evident. "Well, what do you suggest, Chief? If it's got some bearing on the Hammerstone disease cluster, I've got to test the contents, and it's bad procedure to open it outside of lab conditions."

Hank saw her point, but there were rules for police work, too. He wasn't about to break the chain of evidence just because she wanted him to. After a moment's thought, he came up with what he thought would be an acceptable compromise.

"You can keep your water and soil samples—it's not like I can't get some of my own if I want. But that box might have belonged to Burns, and that makes it potential evidence. I've got to log it in and send it up to the crime lab in Little Rock." He saw that Angela was about to protest, but he rushed on. "Once the lab is done with it, I'll ask them to pass it along to you. Don't see why they wouldn't—but even if they refuse, I'll make sure you see any results they come up with. Deal?"

"Okay." Angela hated to let the box go, but she recognized the logic of Hank's position. "But they should send the samples to Dr. Riordan in New York when they're done. He is a friend of mine and consults with the lab. They'll know him."

"Fair enough," said Hank.

She gave Hank a quick smile. "Just promise me that you'll send it off to the lab right away. If it's got something to do with the sickness that's hit Hammerstone, even a day's delay could mean another person gets the disease."

They walked back down the mountain in companionable silence, with Hank carrying Angela's backpack like a schoolboy carrying his sweetheart's books. At the crime-scene tape he handed it over and watched as she got back into her car.

"Hey," he called out, just as she put the car into gear. "Want to take a look at the case file for the Burns fire?" Angela thought a minute—it seemed a shame that Jack had died so violently, and so alone. Perhaps she owed this to her old colleague.

"Sure thing," she called back.

"Good." Hank said. "You go on ahead, then. I rode in on my horse—I've got to get her back to the stable. I'll meet you at the station when I'm done." Angela acknowledged the plan with a wave, started the car, and backed gingerly down the gravel drive.

*Saturday, February 8, 2003 — 7:30 pm*
*Police department, Hammerstone, Arkansas*

By the time Angela's car reached the bottom of Arrowhead Mountain, it was already dark. Arriving at the station, she had an unmistakable feeling of *déjà vu.* She encountered Officer Watkins, still occupied at her desk in the center of the room. Once again she was so caught up in her novel that she didn't notice Angela's entrance.

"What, you working double shifts?" Angela asked. "Don't

tell me your boss is such a slave driver he keeps you on duty day and night."

Thelma looked up, a bit surprised and then smiled. "No way." Thelma laughed at the thought. Hank was hardly the most demanding of bosses. "I just got caught up in my story," she said as she raised her novel, her finger marking a place that had to be no more than a chapter or two from the end. "Nobody's waiting on me back home, so I just figured I'd stay here and keep on reading till I got to the end." She gestured off toward the back of the big room. "Vern Fogerty's on duty now, but he's off somewhere, probably sneaking a smoke." Thelma dog-eared her latest page, put down her book, and got up from her desk. She looked inquisitively at the pack Angela carried.

"Don't tell me you brought us dinner," she said, only half-joking.

"'Fraid not," Angela laughed. "These are soil and water samples I collected up on Arrowhead Mountain. Ran into your chief while I was up there—he was at the Burns property. He asked me to come here and wait for him while he brought his horse back to the stable." Angela couldn't help but notice that Thelma's interest sharpened considerably at the mention of Burns.

"Find anything interesting up there?" Thelma asked.

"Maybe. Your chief seemed to think so, anyway." Angela looked around. "Mind if I sit down and wait?"

Thelma gestured at the empty desks around her. "Be my guest," she said. When Angela seemed to have nothing more to say about Burns or the chief, Thelma popped open her book and was soon drawn back into the final chapters of her story.

It wasn't long before Hank strode into the office. Thelma spoke up before Angela had a chance to say anything. "Heard you mighta had a breakthrough in the Burns case today," she said, nodding toward Angela. She glanced inquisitively at the small box he carried.

"Maybe. Maybe not." He headed straight to his office without pausing, motioning for Angela to follow him. When he swung his door shut, Thelma realized that he wasn't going to satisfy her curiosity just now, and returned to her book with a sigh.

"Hope you didn't have too long a wait," he said as he settled behind his desk, placing the box squarely in the center.

"Not too long," Angela replied, but Hank was already preoccupied, pulling out a form on which he logged the description of his newly found evidence. Rather than interrupt him, she walked around the office, peering at the pictures that hung on his walls. One in particular caught her eye. It featured a younger, darker-haired version of the chief, wearing the distinctive uniform of a firefighter.

Hank finished his task and looked up. Seeing Angela's interest in the photo, he spoke. "That's my brother, Mark. He died in the Burns fire."

Angela found that she had no words with which to respond. She waited and Hank eventually continued.

"He was killed when the west wing exploded. I saw it myself. Guess that's the reason I can't let go of the case, doctor. Whoever killed Burns, killed Mark, too."

Angela wanted to reach out and offer comfort, but of course that would never do. She hardly knew the man. Instead she let the silence draw out, occupying herself with the rest of the photographs on display, giving him a moment to collect himself. At last Hank broke the silence. He held a thick file out to Angela.

"Well, doc, we might as well get this over with so you can be on your way home," he said. "This is the Burns file."

Angela took the offered file and flipped open the cover. Jack Burns' graduation portrait stared up at her. So it was true, she thought. Her old Coneheads colleague and the hermit of Arrowhead Mountain were one and the same. Angela couldn't help but feel a pang of loss. For all intents and purposes, Burns had dropped out of her life years ago, but she still remembered him from the old days, back when he and the rest of her small circle stayed up late at night, writing game code and talking about their futures.

"It really is him," she said aloud, but speaking half to herself. She looked up at Hank. "This is the guy I went to school with."

"Okay then," Hank said. "Anything you can tell me about him?" Angela shook her head. "I don't know. It's been a long, long time."

Hank didn't press her. "Why don't you give it a little time—see if anything comes to mind." He sighed. "Heck, I don't know what I'm hoping for. At this point, just about anything you could tell me might give us a new direction for the investigation."

Angela looked doubtful, but she nodded cooperatively nonetheless.

"I've got business in Hot Springs tomorrow," Hank offered. "Maybe we could get together in the afternoon and talk about this some more?"

"Sure," Angela agreed, "but I don't see what my 20-year-old grad school reminiscences could do for your case." She reached across Hank's desk for a pen and paper, then jotted down her home address and phone number. "I'll be there all afternoon, Chief McLain," she said. "Come early enough and my mom'll probably insist on feeding you lunch."

Hank grinned. "Sounds good to me," he said. "But if your momma's gonna feed me, we might as well be on a first-name basis. Call me Hank."

Angela smiled back—the first full-out smile she'd offered Hank, and he found himself looking forward to seeing it again, and often. "Sure thing... Hank."

*Sunday, February 9, 2003 — 8:00 am*
*Donatelli residence, Hot Springs, Arkansas*

If Angela had hoped for a lazy Sunday morning sleep-in to make up for yesterday's hike in the mountains, her hopes were dashed early. She was awakened by the sound of women's laughter as it drifted upstairs from the kitchen. She eased herself out of bed, just a little annoyed by the noise. What on earth was Ma up to now? She shuffled, bleary eyed, to the bathroom to splash water on her face.

She'd gotten home late last night, after stashing her samples back at the office. She'd expected to find the house dark, but when she opened the door, there was her mother, wide-awake and avid for details about the trip to Hammerstone. Marie had only let up on her questioning after Angela pulled out the county map. With this new prize, Marie had at last ceased her questioning and whisked over to the kitchen table, where she could spread the map out for closer scrutiny. Angela had left her to it and trudged upstairs to bed.

Now, however, it was morning, and from the sound of it, Marie was wide-awake again. Angela snatched her robe up from the foot of her bed, slid her feet into her slippers, and headed downstairs, still rubbing the sleep from her eyes.

In the kitchen, she found Linda and Marie hunched over the table, where the map had spent the night. The map bristled with yellow sticky notes. The two women looked up briefly when Angela entered, but quickly returned their attention to the map.

"Good morning, Angela. Coffee's ready if you want it and there are bagels in the fridge. Help yourself," Marie said absently, as she gestured towards the counter, still concentrating on the map. This was a real break from routine—Angela couldn't remember the last time her mother had voluntarily left her to get her own breakfast. Mumbling "Good morning,"

Angela was still not awake enough to register her surprise at this unconventional greeting.

As Angela poured herself some coffee, Linda looked up from her work. "Morning, Doc," she said. "We have a little problem. We're writing down the names of people that we've identified and sticking them to the map, but they just keep falling off. You don't have any of those colored push-pins, do you?" She gestured at the map. "We could sure use 'em."

Angela wandered over to the table to see what they were talking about. Yawning, she looked at the map. When her sluggish brain at last registered what lay before her, she woke up quickly. "That can't be right," she said. There were seven yellow slips stuck to the map, each with a name and address. "*Seven* cases? You sure?"

"Pretty sure," Marie replied. "In fact, we think this might just be the tip of a pretty big iceberg." Linda nodded in agreement.

"That's right. We've still got a whole slew of people we want to contact."

"But it's only been a day!" Angela exclaimed.

"I know," said Marie. "But we got busy while you were gone yesterday. And the Stedmans and Davies pitched in too. We all spent the whole day on the phone, calling our friends. Then they called *their* friends, and so on down the line. You can cover a lot of territory pretty quickly that way," she said, smiling at Linda, who grinned smugly back.

Angela nodded. These new cases got her to thinking. She began with the raw numbers. Hammerstone had about 2,500 residents. According to national statistics, there should be an average of about three people with MS in a town that size. But these new cases, on top of the ones she'd already known about—patients like Linda—brought their total to more than double the number they would normally expect! The very idea of it was enough to touch off a small shudder of incipient panic. Angela quickly shook off the feeling. After all, Marie and Linda were canvassing people about a pretty broad range of symptoms. She would need more time to think this through. Still, this was a pretty spectacular beginning.

Angela glanced back at the table where Linda and Marie were once again hard at work. She slipped quietly out of the kitchen and headed to her study, hoping that a little private reflection would help her make sense out of what was happening.

But once at her desk, Angela found that she simply couldn't slow her brain down enough to think productively. Better to push it to the back of her mind and let it stew for a while. She searched the study for some mindless activity to keep herself occupied while her brain sorted things out. Eyeing her laptop, she thought that she might as well check out her e-mail.

Like most professional people, Angela kept two e-mail accounts: one for work and one for personal communication. Angela always kept her work account current, but she'd developed a bad habit of ignoring her personal e-mail for weeks, sometimes months, on end. With nothing better to do, she decided that this was as good a time as any to brave the chaos that was likely to reign there now.

As soon as she logged onto the account, she regretted it. There were hundreds of messages waiting in her in-box. With a sigh, she moved her cursor up to the top of the list, where the oldest messages still languished. One by one, she called them up, deleting the obvious spam as she went along. Suddenly she saw a name that stopped her cold, her index finger frozen above the mouse. Dante1 was the e-mail handle that Jack Burns had always used, years ago, when he still stayed in periodic contact. But this message had been sent on November 29 of last year—just a little more than a month before the explosion that had killed him. She felt a chill. She was looking at an e-mail from a dead man. Even as she considered what to do, her hand moved the cursor to the OPEN button and clicked on it. The message appeared:

Hello Angela-
Remember me? It's been quite awhile since I've been in touch. Are you still the "puzzle princess" I used to know? I hope so, because I've got a real stumper for you to try. Let's see if you've still got what it takes to beat the game and find the secrets hidden inside.
Jack

At the bottom of the message was an icon indicating that Jack had attached a separate file to his message. This time more deliberately, Angela moved her mouse and clicked it open, letting the new file download onto her desktop.

E-mail housecleaning now forgotten, she returned to her desktop where the new file now waited. Judging from the file name, she realized it was a program, not a text file, and briefly worried that she might have just unleashed a virus onto her system. Too late now, she thought, and clicked on the icon. Immediately her screen filled with a crudely drawn cartoon cat, beneath which a banner bore the words "Welcome to Cat Tag." Tinny synthesized music played in the background. She grimaced—this was so 1980's she thought—but she double-clicked the START button and the game began.

A few seconds were all it took for Angela to see that this was just a silly rip-off of the kind of shooter games that were all the rage more than fifteen years ago. She spent a few half-hearted minutes clicking away with her mouse, shooting down the serried ranks of grinning cats' heads that drifted slowly down from the top of the screen. No challenge here, she thought—he didn't even have the wit to make successive rows move faster. In no time at all she'd cleared the screen.

"So where are the hidden secrets, Jack?" she murmured as she waited for the end-game animation to appear.

But all she got for her efforts was a black screen, in the center of which was a blue box that obviously waited for her input. She typed "Cat Tag" and hit the enter key, but nothing happened. She typed her name, then Jack's—nothing happened. "Damn!" she muttered in disgust. "What a waste of time!" She shut down the game and pushed the laptop away irritably. Jack had never been all that good at writing game code, but this was lame, even for him. She cocked an ear toward the kitchen. By the sound of it, Marie and Linda had finished working on their map—the house was silent. Angela decided that maybe she could venture back in there in search of a late breakfast.

She found her mother alone in the kitchen, sitting at the table and looking at her map, a crease of worry lining her forehead. "Hey, Ma" Angela said, as she entered the room. "How's the sleuthing business going."

"Hi, honey," Marie said, still looking thoughtfully at the map. "Sorry we ignored you when you came in earlier." She gestured toward the map. "You're right, though. There's way too many names." Angela joined her mother at the table. "What do you think it means?" Marie asked. "All these people—scared and hurting. How on earth could something like this happen?"

"I don't know, Ma. I honestly don't know." Angela was silent for a moment. When she spoke again, her voice was resolute. "But I do know that we're going to do our darndest to find out."

Marie remained troubled, and for a moment she would not speak. At last, she shook off her blue mood and glanced up at the kitchen clock. "Well, would you look at the time!" she said. "I'd better get started on lunch!"

Angela was suddenly reminded of yesterday's arrangements

with Hank. "Oh! I should have told you sooner," she said. "We may have company any minute now."

Marie gave Angela a severe once-over. "Well then, young lady—don't you think it's time you changed out of that robe and put on something decent?" Angela looked down at herself in dismay. "Sure thing, Ma," she said, and she headed back upstairs to change as Marie bustled around the kitchen.

By the time Hank turned up on the Donatelli doorstep, Angela was just coming back downstairs, more appropriately dressed for the day. At the sound of Hank's knock, she called "I'll get it" to her mother in the kitchen and opened the door.

Hank's smile of greeting was uncharacteristically shy. He felt a little out of place, dropping in on Angela like this. Last night he'd had a chance to think about their meeting earlier in the day, and while he was grateful that her trip to Hammerstone had yielded the first hard evidence he'd turned up on the Burns case in a long time, he doubted that her college memories could shed any light on what happened last New Year's Eve. He probably shouldn't have come here, he thought—but, truth be told, he'd wanted to see the pretty doctor again, and Burns provided as good an excuse as any.

"Hope I'm not intruding," he said. But Angela's smile set him at his ease. "Not at all, Hank. Come on in. Mom's just started making lunch." She led the way to the kitchen, where Marie gave him a smile as welcoming as Angela's had been. "Won't be but a minute before lunch is ready," she said. "I hope you're hungry."

"Yes ma'am," Hank drawled, belatedly sweeping his hat from his head. Still feeling as awkward as a teenager, he looked around at the bright, warm kitchen. His eyes fell on the table, where Marie's map still lay spread out. "What's all this?" he asked.

Angela hurried forward and scooped up the detritus of her

mother's morning's work. "You better watch out, Hank. I think my mother's planning to go into your line of work," she said with a laugh. "She's been playing Nancy Drew with my medical mystery."

Hank reached out a hand toward the rolled map that Angela now held. "May I?" he asked. With a shrug, Angela surrendered the papers, and Hank spread them out again on the table. "You're plotting the locations of our sick folks?" Hank asked. Marie nodded. He took another long look at the map. "I think you're maybe missing one," he said, and Angela recalled the unfamiliar names he'd mentioned out on the mountain yesterday. "But don't let me tell you how to do your business." He backed away apologetically. "Don't mean to butt in."

Once again Angela cleared away the papers, making room for the minestrone soup and salami sandwiches Marie was now carrying over to the table. "Oh, don't be shy," Marie said. "We'll take all the help we can get." She passed around bowls and spoons and set the soup tureen by Angela's place, nodding for her daughter to start serving. "After lunch, maybe you'd be willing to tell us who we've left out?" When she flashed her smile, Hank was struck by the close resemblance with her daughter—two handsome women, indeed.

"Well," said Angela. "Since you two seem so willing to talk business over lunch, I might as well join you. Wait here." She left, but was back in a flash, carrying a sheet of paper. "It's the darndest thing," she said. "I hadn't given a thought to Jack Burns in years, and now he's popped back into my life two days running." She handed Hank the paper. "That's an e-mail Jack sent me last November."

Hank quickly scanned the brief text. "This the kind of thing he usually sent you?"

"Well, there's no 'usual' to judge by. Years ago, there was a gang of us who used to write games—Jack was one of the group. And back then we used to send our latest efforts back and forth—you know, getting everybody to try them out. But it's been an awfully long time since I've heard from any of the old gamers—and Jack was one of the first to drop away from the group." She thought a moment. "On the other hand, Jack was pretty hopeless at writing game code—and from that point of view, his latest effort is pretty typical."

"So you've already played the game?" Hank asked.

"Yeah, but that's the funny thing. The game was a no-brainer. I breezed through it in no time. But at the end there was nothing—just a blank screen with a box where I guess I'm supposed to type in a password."

Hank looked back down at Jack's note. "No 'hidden secrets'?"

"Not a one."

"Well, keep at it," Hank said. "If nothing else, the timing is too coincidental for us to ignore it. And while we're on the subject of Burns, I've finished the paperwork on your sample—I'll be running it up to Little Rock myself tomorrow morning. I'll see what I can do to get it released to you when the lab boys are finished with it."

Angela nodded and thanked Hank, who promptly rose from the table. "I guess I've taken enough of your time," he said. "Best be heading on home. Thanks for the fine lunch, and the even finer company." Angela walked him to the door. As he stepped through, he turned back once more. "Make sure you let me know what you get back from the lab on those samples you took, okay?"

## Monday, February 10, 2003 — 8:00 am
### Donatelli Clinic, Hot Springs, Arkansas

When Angela reported to the clinic on Monday morning, she had already been hard at work in the hospital for the past four hours. It had been a crazy morning, and the clinic promised to offer no relief. In addition to her regularly scheduled patients, she would need to make time to prepare and ship her field samples for testing at the state lab. Not to mention that she was hoping to see some of the MRIs come back on her Hammerstone patients from Friday. Going straight to the clinic from her car, she squared her shoulders and marched in to see her first patient of the day.

It wasn't until close to lunch that she realized her staff was having as rough a time of it as she was. That's when Dolly caught Angela on the fly. "The phones have been ringing off the hook this morning. I had to come over and help the girls answer them." Dolly rarely complained, but she was clearly aggrieved this time. "We've had at least six new people call—all claiming they've got MS and all demanding to see you." Dolly knew that there was no way she could fit all these new people into Angela's already overcrowded calendar. "What can I do?

Angela was too busy to get agitated. "We'll talk later, at lunch," Angela said. "Let's just finish with the morning's appointments."

Only slightly mollified, Dolly bustled off. But as soon as the last of the pre-lunch patients had left, she tracked Angela down and began right in again. "We're up to eight calls, now—all claiming that Linda Tackett sent them." Dolly was exasperated. "You've got to do something about that woman!" She crossed her arms over her chest and glared at Angela, sure that the doctor would put a stop to all this craziness.

But Angela said nothing for a moment. "Dolly" she said, finally. "I think I'm really going to need your help on this."

Her serious tone caught Dolly by surprise, immediately dissipating her irritation at Linda's high-handed behavior. Angela saw this and was grateful—without Dolly's formidable organizational skills, she knew she'd be sunk. "I need you to get hold of all these patients. Put together a list for me, with their addresses, the names of their regular doctors, and so forth. Then ask Janie to take a brief history of symptoms over the phone and get permission to have their primary physicians fax us their records." Dolly nodded—she didn't relish the extra work, but was game to help if Angela thought it was important.

Angela went on. "I'm going to have to see these people in person eventually. Put Susan to work scheduling appointments. If anybody has a real emergency, she can schedule them for me after my regular hours. I'll make the time."

Dolly nodded and went off to put her orders into action, leaving Angela alone with her thoughts. This sudden surge in potential patients didn't really come as a surprise—Linda and Marie had been busy all weekend doing their outreach work. But if a single weekend had turned up this many new cases, she was likely to be swamped in no time. She needed a way to get this onslaught under control. She slipped into her office and called home. "Hi, Ma," she said when Marie picked up. "I need a favor."

"Sure thing, Angie," Marie replied. "What can I do?"

"We're getting swamped here with all of Linda's new referrals. She's got to stop handing out the number to everybody she meets. *You've* got to put some brakes on her, Ma." Angela paused and drew a deep breath. "From now on, you've got to help us keep this organized. When you turn up somebody who seems to fit our criteria, take down their particulars and get them to sign a medical release form—I'll bring a batch home with me tonight—and only *then* pass the information on to Susan, so Janie can call them. Do *not* tell them to call or walk in here without warning."

"Okay, Angie," Marie was quick to see the wisdom of Angela's suggestion, and equally quick to apologize. "We weren't thinking about the effect our calls would have on your schedule."

"Thanks, Ma." Angela was pleased. This new procedure would solve a number of problems. Besides imposing some organization on the process, it would give her the information she'd need to begin her assessment of each potential patient's condition. It would be a lot easier to determine the likelihood that any particular person had MS.

Angela hung up the phone and checked her watch. She had about a half hour before the afternoon's roster of patients started filling her examining room. That would be just time enough to duck out to the research lab to pack and ship her water and soil samples. She hurried off to the task.

The afternoon was no less hectic than the morning had been, and it was only during a brief lull towards the end of the day that Dolly had a chance to corner Angela again. She handed over a sheaf of papers and moved on. Angela only had time for a brief glance through them, but she could see right away that they held the information she'd requested just before lunch. Some of these people were already on the list from yesterday and some were new. If they all had MS, then Hammerstone would have about *four* times as many as she would normally expect to find in a town this small. This was really looking bad, but Angela knew she was still working blind. She still hadn't seen any test results from last Friday's patients, and these new cases still had to be worked up.

At the end of the day, Janie came to find Angela at the reception desk, where she was ordering a follow-up appointment for her last patient. "Doctor? You wanted to know about those tests." She held out a file folder containing the MRI reports. "Their films are by the view box." Angela took the folder and flipped through it, her eyes darting back and forth as she scanned the contents. When she looked up, she saw that her staff had clustered around and were waiting anxiously to hear the results. "So far, it looks like all three of our Friday walk-ins are showing the classic MRI signs of MS. She put a few of the films up on the view box. "See those white spots there? Those are most likely the plaques." She paused. "Of course, we haven't done a spinal tap yet. So let's not jump to conclusions here. Still...." Her voice trailed off, thoughtfully, "Every one of them can claim an unexplained neurological episode and a positive MRI—they meet the new McDonald criteria for a diagnosis of MS."

The McDonald criteria were the most recent diagnostic standards used in formally identifying new MS cases. In the old days, doctors wouldn't make such a diagnosis until a patient had reported two entirely separate neurological episodes—an arm that went numb, for instance, and then got better, followed some time later by a period of weakness in a leg. But sometimes that second episode did not come for months, even years. Meanwhile, the patient waited in a kind of diagnostic limbo, because doctors couldn't make an official diagnosis of MS, and therefore couldn't begin treatment. Doctors came to recognize that this delay in treatment was harmful, so they called for a change in the diagnostic criteria, requiring only a single neurologic episode as long as it was backed up by a positive MRI.

With the test results in hand, Angela decided she had enough to give Murdoch a call and bring him up to date. When she got him on the line, she poured out all the events of the weekend, and the startling early test results.

Murdoch let her talk on without interruption. When she finally ran out of words, he spoke. "When you first told me about these cases, I wanted to make sure you didn't jump to a diagnosis too soon. But now it seems to me you've got a real problem on your hands." His voice was thoughtful. "I'm at a loss to explain it."

Angela sighed. "I know, Mud—MS just doesn't work this way. At least, it's not like anything I've ever heard of before. If I didn't know better, I'd say this was some kind of contagion. But that's out of the question, isn't it?"

"Well," said Murdoch, "there's at least one possible historical precedent." He thought a moment, then dropped that subject as quickly as he had brought it up. "Let me think about that one for awhile, though. It seems a bit far afield for us, right now, and your data would support an environmental cause just as well, wouldn't it?"

"True," said Angela. "But it's going to be a few days before I see results back on my test samples." Her voice trailed off and Murdoch couldn't help but chuckle. He'd known Angela and her insatiable curiosity for a long time. He could just imagine how she was feeling right now.

"Well, then, it would be disgracefully premature to start jumping to conclusions, don't you think?" he chided gently. "Have you never outgrown that hair-trigger impatience of yours? You're just going to have to take this slowly—don't try to force the data, let it lead you instead."

"Yeah, you're right," she said. "But, there was one thing I found that seems more than a little weird." She explained about the small, plastic container she'd fished out of the spring.

"Submerged in the spring, eh?" Murdoch thought about this new information for a moment. "That's an old camper's trick. Just as good as a refrigerator."

"Oh no! It didn't occur to me that the point might be to

95

keep it at a constant temperature. I just thought Jack had found himself a good hiding place," Angela said regretfully.

"You didn't keep it refrigerated?"

"No, Mud, and I feel like a perfect fool. It spent the weekend in an evidence locker at the Hammerstone police department."

Murdoch brushed it off. "Well, there's nothing we can do about it now. Maybe it's still okay. Is it still in Hammerstone?"

"No. They were going to take it up to the state crime lab in Little Rock sometime today. But Chief McLain said that they would send some of the sample up to you after they are finished testing it."

"That's fine," Murdoch reassured her. "I'll give my friends over there a call in the morning. Maybe we'll find something useful."

*Monday, February 10, 2003 — 8:30 pm*
*Donatelli residence, Hot Springs, Arkansas*

Marie glanced impatiently at the kitchen wall clock. Today had gotten away from her. She'd spent most of it working on her map with Linda and hadn't even had time to cook dinner. Maybe she was obsessing about this whole thing. But then again, maybe obsessing about it wasn't so bad. She was sure she and Linda were onto something, and she was equally sure that the two of them could play important roles in solving it. It had been a long time since she'd felt like this—totally engaged in a problem even bigger than her own everyday battle with MS—and while the implications were scary, being part of solving it was exhilarating.

She glanced at the clock again, her impatience mounting. When *would* Angela get home? At last she heard the familiar sound of her daughter's car pulling into the driveway, and she was on the move to the front door as fast as her wheelchair could carry her. As soon as the door swung open, she started in: "You've got to see what we did today." Angela let herself be herded into the kitchen. "Okay, Ma. Show me what you've got," she said.

"Linda and I started penciling in all the possible cases of our mystery disease. Just to get a general idea of what we're up against. And look at what we came up with!"

Angela looked at the map. There must have been at least 30 entries that Marie had meticulously penciled in. Looking closely, she could see that they formed a cluster that spread broadly through the town of Hammerstone. She didn't see any particular pattern. "Looks like you've done a lot of work, Ma, but the pattern really doesn't tell us anything yet. It looks pretty random." Noting Marie's crestfallen look, she immediately backpedaled. "Of course, we can't be sure that all these names really belong on the map. Once we get these people tested, we'll probably end up erasing a bunch of them. When we're sure we've only included confirmed cases, the map may tell us a very different story."

Angela moved the map to clear a space for their dinner. Neither felt much like talking as they thought about the map and its implications—or lack of them. Finally, unable to make even a pretense of enjoying her meal, Angela got up from the table and carried her plate to the sink. Then she realized that perhaps she had something that could lift both their spirits. "I've got something for you out in the car—I'd forgotten all about it!" She hurried out, leaving Marie momentarily confused. Soon she was back, however, struggling with a large corkboard and a big bag of multicolored pushpins.

Noting Marie's quizzical look, she explained. "I got to thinking about your map today, and I thought it might be easier to keep track of your entries if you could hang it on the wall."

Marie loved the idea. "Where should we hang it?" she asked, pushing aside her own half-eaten meal.

"I thought maybe on the wall in my study—it'd be out of the way, but you could get to it easily any time you wanted."

Marie's disappointment from before dinner vanished. Together they went into the study, where Marie played fore-man while Angela hung the big map up on the wall. They moved back a foot or two to admire their handiwork, when Marie spoke again. "I was thinking, during dinner—about the map, and how it doesn't really tell us much yet. I think it might be too soon to start dropping entries yet. Even if a lot of these people turn out not to have MS, they're still reporting that they're sick, and they got that way during the last half year or so. So they might still be part of the problem—who knows? Instead, why don't we use different colors—red for confirmed cases of MS, say, and blue for the 'maybes.' That way we might get a better idea of what's going on in Hammerstone."

"You're a genius, Ma. A pure genius." Angela laughed and bent down to give her mom a big hug. "But the color-coding will have to wait until Wednesday, when Janie and Dolly are finished checking out your leads."


*Wednesday, February 12, 2003 — 10:00 pm*
*Donatelli residence, Hot Springs, Arkansas*


Angela got out of her car and headed toward the house, the events of the last forty-eight hours weighing heavily on her shoulders. What had begun less than a week ago with a trick-le of walk-ins had grown almost overnight into a veritable flood, a total of forty patients in all since Linda first brought her motley crew into the clinic.

Regular clinic work had to take a backseat to this onslaught of cases, so that Dolly and Janie could follow up. Medical care out in Hammerstone was badly fragmented, its people seeing physicians drawn from a four-county radius, and Dolly had spent hours calling doctors from miles around to request full records on each of the new names on their growing list of "possibles," while Janie took a history from each of them. By Tuesday night, a total of twenty-five people had their files completed. The remaining fifteen were ready for Angela's review as of tonight.

Both nights, Angela had stayed late at the office reading each file and breaking them down into three piles, based on the degree of likelihood that a case was indeed MS. But for all this new work, her own responsibilities as a doctor couldn't be ignored. Today, for example, her clinic appointments had run late, and it was well past the dinner hour before she saw her last scheduled patient. Then she'd had her regular turn on call at the hospital. It seemed like everybody in the county needed a neu-rology consult tonight—and that the night would never end.

Meanwhile, Marie waited impatiently. It's a funny thing about time. Unlike most people, physicians take Einstein liter-ally—for them, time really *is* relative. And for Angela's most important relative, time was dragging. At last, though, Angela stepped through her front door and shed her coat gratefully. "I'm home, Ma," she called from the foyer.

Marie came whirring down the hall to greet her. "I thought you'd never get home," she said. "I can't wait to show you what we've done!" As she reached to take Angela's hand, how-ever, she caught herself, seeing the fatigue etched in Angela's face. "But that can wait. I saved you some dinner."

Even in her exhaustion, Angela couldn't help but be amused by her mother's excitement. She knew Marie had probably spent the day updating the big map. Last night Angela had brought home twenty-five files from Tuesday's patients, all color-coded according to their probability of having MS. Of those, only fifteen were to be plotted, with red pins for definite cases and blue for probable ones. The evidence for MS was not strong enough in the other cases and they were left off the map.

Although Angela was tempted by the aroma of dinner wafting from the kitchen, she wanted to show her appreciation for her mother's efforts. "I can wait for dinner, Ma," she said. "I want to see what you've come up with so far."

"Tell you what," Marie said. "I'll make you up a plate and you can eat in the study." She wheeled her chair off toward the kitchen, but Angela continued on down the hall, switching on her study light as she entered the small room. She moved over to the map wall and took a look at the fruits of Marie's latest labors. She was still standing there, dumbfounded, when Marie entered bearing her dinner on a tray.

"Striking, isn't it," Marie spoke quietly. She understood the impact of the map—it had struck her hard, too, when she'd first stepped back and seen the emerging pattern.

"Striking's the word, alright," Angela said, still eyeing the map carefully. Where, Monday, there had been a big blob of seemingly random cases, there now seemed to be some logic in the arrangement of red and blue pins. "This is what you got when you plotted the cases I brought you yesterday?"

"Yeah," Marie's voice bore a trace of pride, and Angela couldn't begrudge her the right to it. "I worked off of the records and results you brought home. I think we can be pretty confident about the map now."

Angela wordlessly opened her briefcase and pulled out a thick sheaf of ten folders. "Show me what you do, Ma," she said, handing them over. "These are the last of the cases to date." She sank into her chair at the desk, where Marie had set her dinner tray. While her mother worked, she ate a few forkfuls, but she hardly tasted a bite.

Marie spread the files out on a low table that she'd positioned near the map and opened them one at a time. Angela's staff had already color-coded them—only red and blue cases in this batch—so Marie moved quickly from file to map and back again, placing pins for every new patient address, replicating with her pins the color coding of the file. As she worked, the vague pattern that Angela had noted originally became more pronounced. Angela watched in silence. When Marie pushed the final pin into place, the two of them simply stared at the map. At last, Angela spoke. "It's shaped like a, like a... fan"

"Yes, Angela, I saw it too. Or maybe like a funnel."

Angela looked at the emergent pattern more closely. The majority of the pins did, indeed, seem to form a definite shape. But there was still a scattering of them that spoiled the pattern. She moved closer to the map so that she could better understand how the shape related to the underlying geography. Moving from the wide end of the funnel shape back toward its narrowest point, she encountered a familiar name and gave a little gasp. "The narrow end of the funnel," Angela's voice shook. "Look. Look where it is." She placed her finger on the point.

Marie peered at the map and read the legend aloud. "Arrowhead Mountain." She turned to her daughter. "Is that significant?"

"Arrowhead Mountain," she breathed. "Ma, this is where I ran into Hank last weekend. This is where Jack Burns died. And this is where I found that strange container in the springhouse."

The two women looked at one another, and for a moment, neither one of them could think of a single thing to say. Then Angela broke the silence. "I think I'd better call Chief McLain."

*Wednesday, February 12, 2003 — 11:30 pm*
*Police department, Hammerstone, Arkansas*

It was too much to expect to catch the Police Chief at work this late at night, Angela knew, but she could at least leave a message. The phone rang a few times before she heard someone pick up on the other end.

"Hammerstone Police."

"Yes," Angela began. "I'm not sure if you can help me, but I need to speak to Chief McLain. Tonight if possible." She looked at her desk clock and grimaced; it was awfully late. No doubt the chief had gone home long ago. "I guess that's out of the question, though, huh?"

In answer, she heard the muffling noise of a hand being placed loosely over the receiver. "Hey! Hank! You still back there?" the voice bellowed. Then, in much-reduced volume, "Hang on, ma'am. I'm transferring you." A few clicks, and then the laconic drawl of Chief McLain came on the line.

"Can I help you?"

Angela suddenly felt a little flustered. "Uh," she faltered at first. "Hank, this is Angela—Dr. Donatelli? From Hot Springs. I didn't expect to get you this late."

"Well, hello, Angela. What's on your mind?" She could almost hear his lazy smile through the phone. "I don't imagine it was my conversational charms that inspired you to call me so late."

"Right. I mean, no. I mean..." Angela took a deep breath to steady her voice. "Something's come up with my investigation—those strange cases I was checking out when I was in Hammerstone, you know? It may mean nothing, but...."

Hank's tone immediately became serious. "Doctor, I think you'd better just tell me whatever it is you've got."

"Right. You remember my mom's map? We've been plotting cases on it as they come in. And when we'd finished marking all the new data points... well, everything pointed to Arrowhead Mountain, and to the valley below, along Old Indian Trail."

Hank's silence drew on for so long that Angela began to doubt the wisdom of this late night call. But then he spoke. "Right. So it could be that something started out on the mountain and then spread out down the valley." He paused, thinking it through. "You're the doctor—you tell me. Do diseases work that way?"

"Depends on how the disease is passed along. Diseases that spread person-to-person, like the flu, wouldn't leave a pattern like this one. I mean, you don't only sneeze on the guy who lives next door to you. You sneeze on the guy who sells you coffee in the morning, or who works at the desk next to yours. And that guy might live in a whole different town. But if we're talking about an environmental source, then this is exactly the kind of dispersal we'd expect."

"Okay. I'm with you so far." Hank said. "But what do I do about this? Are you saying it's the watershed off the mountain? And what if it's already leached into the town's wells? Should I be calling in the public health people?"

"Maybe you should," Angela agreed. "They already have the samples I took. When you give them the call, make sure you tell them that. But I think you might also want to get the local paper to run a warning—maybe the local radio station too—advising people to switch to bottled water for the time being." She looked over at the map on her wall. "Or you could maybe send a car along the path of the funnel. The map shows everything clusters most thickly on the upper end of Old Indian Trail for about a half mile on either side of the stream."

"We could do that," Hank said. "Don't want to start a panic, though. People are already pretty stirred up by all the questions from your mother and Linda Tackett. I'll have to come up with some kind of story to justify what we're doing."

"You're right." Angela gave the matter a moment of thought. "How about this. You could mention the possibility of natural contamination, but leave out any mention of people already being sick. The people we've already contacted know, but we don't have to panic the rest of the town."

"Okay. I'll see what I can do at this end, and I'll give the public health authorities a call in the morning. Be sure and send me a copy of your sample test results as soon as they come in." Hank paused a minute, then switched the subject. "By the way, you find out anything more about Burns' e-mail? With this latest news, he's looking more interesting every day."

"Sorry, Hank. I haven't had the time. But you're right—it's looking like Burns just might be important to my investigation too. I'll get back on it as soon as I can."

"Good enough." Hank hung up.

Angela looked at her computer, but the day had been long and exhausting, and she knew she really wasn't up to dealing with Burns' puzzle tonight. The more she thought of his strange e-mail, the more she was convinced that he expected her to come up with a password to move beyond the child-ish game at the start of his program. There had to be some-thing—in the game itself? in their shared past?—but for the life of her, she couldn't come up with a single idea. She looked at her desk clock. Past midnight—too late for this kind of thinking. Too late for anything but sleep. All these questions would still be waiting for her in the morning. She got up, turned out the lights in her study, and trudged upstairs to bed.

## Thursday, February 13, 2003 — 8:00 am
## Police department, Hammerstone, Arkansas

Hank McLain arrived at the station just after his officers and promptly gathered them in his private office. "Listen, guys," he said. "We've got ourselves a situation." He filled them in on Angela's phone call from the night before. "I think we've got a responsibility to get the word out about the water, but we don't want to cause a panic. I'm thinking that a couple of you—Thelma, Vern—can take a run down to Old Indian Trail. Split up and work the houses along the street. Tell people we're a might worried about the water coming off the mountain. Tell them that we'd like them to drink bottled water for a little while until we get things under control."

Thelma spoke up. "Can't they just boil the well water, like we do after a big storm? Folks aren't going to be too happy 'bout having to switch to bottled water, chief. It gets expensive. How long are we saying they got to do that?"

"Maybe boiling would be okay for wash water, but we'd better be more careful when it comes to cooking and drinking. I think we're just talking about a week or so, most likely. And if they object to the expense of bottled water, tell them they can fill their own jugs for free over in Hot Springs, at the National Park."

Thelma and Vern gathered up their gear and headed out for Old Indian Trail. Inside, Hank picked up his phone and called the State Health Department, giving them an abbreviated run-down of his conversation with Angela. He considered giving Angela a call also, just to let her know what happened, but she was probably real busy right now. In any case, she'd be calling in with news about her samples soon enough, he thought. Hank knew himself well enough to recognize that his desire to call was prompted more by an interest in the good-looking doctor than by any professional considerations. Chuckling at himself, he decided he'd better get down to work.

*Thursday, February 13, 2003 — 9:00 am*
*Central Arkansas Research, Hot Springs, Arkansas*

Every other Thursday, Angela scheduled a day without patient appointments in the clinic. In the normal order of things, this was her day to devote exclusively to the research side of her business, but today she had other plans. Spread before her on the desk were more than forty charts of what she had come to think of as her mystery patients, and she was hard at work reviewing their contents.

So far, she'd managed to rule out a diagnosis of MS for about fifteen of the cases, but the rest were either confirmed or likely to be once tests were complete. Sixteen cases of definite or probable MS were in the funnel, starting with Jennifer Richmond's case at the base of Arrowhead Mountain. But another nine definite or probable MS cases were scattered around the town and even further out in the county. The reason for this distribution eluded Angela—and troubled her, as well. Unless she could figure this out, she'd have nothing.

She began to address the pile of charts. Putting aside the rejects—the ones that were definitely not MS—she paged through the remaining files, one by one. Deep in thought, she lost track of time until her concentration was interrupted by the buzz of her intercom. She looked up at the clock—10 o'clock already. She had an unusual appointment to keep. She hit the intercom. "Be right there, Janie," she said, and hustled over to her clinic.

"Well!" Angela said as she entered the reception area. "Looks like the gang's all here." The waiting room chairs were filled with familiar faces. All her visitors from Friday's impromptu office mob scene were here for a quick follow-up and a lesson on injection techniques so that they could self-administer their regimen of MS medications. A glance told Angela that the conditions of all three patients were worsening. Jennifer, in particular, was having more difficulty walking, and Angela thought she might have to add five days of high-dose steroid treatments to the other drugs she had already prescribed—it could at least provide some relief for the most troubling symptoms. She'd have to set it up with the Home Health people. Maybe physical and occupational therapy would help too. Physical rehabilitation was too often over-looked by doctors who treat MS, but Angela was a firm believer in its usefulness. She knew that in addition to building up strength, it gave her patients an important psychological boost. Jennifer looked like she could use a boost.

Angela didn't make it back to her research office until well after noon, and she settled back into her review of the charts with a resigned sigh. She dove into the stack of charts, look-ing for a new way to look at the data that would give her some insight. She began with what she knew best. She split the charts into two piles, one for everybody who lived in the "Arrowhead funnel" and the other for people who lived fur-ther afield. No matter how hard she looked at them she could find no significant differences between the two. The mix of definite and probable cases in each pile was about the same, the average ages and sex distribution was comparable. Even the average date of onset of the symptoms was not significant-ly different between the two groups. After computing the last bit of data, she put down her calculator in disgust.

As she sat back and stared at the numbers, it hit her. The date of onset. Even though their was no difference between the piles, there was something to be learned here. It seems that almost all the cases began between December 1 and

January 5, with the bulk occurring between Christmas and New Year's. Only Jennifer reported feeling sick earlier, in the last week of November. But most important of all, there had not been a single new case since January 5!

"Point source transmission!" she exclaimed out loud, to no one in particular. A single, possibly temporary, source of illness that rages through a community in a solitary wave. Everybody gets sick at once, and then nobody else gets it. A one-shot deal. Like food poisoning.

It made a certain amount of sense. The funnel shape marked by Marie's pins was all downhill from the mountain, marking out a natural path for the disease to travel if it were water- or even air-borne. But point source transmission from an environmental source couldn't explain all those pins on Marie's map that marked addresses outside the Hammerstone valley. Their existence argued more for the idea of contagious spread of the disease.

No, Angela thought. It couldn't be contagious. Otherwise, all the Stedmans would be sick, not just Timmy. And Rainie would be showing at least some of the symptoms that were troubling her husband Merle. And the time factor wouldn't apply—people would still be getting sick. This was getting confusing once again.

Just then, Dolly came in. Welcoming the excuse to turn her mind to something new, Angela looked up with a tired smile. "What's up?" she asked.

"The answering service just passed along a couple of calls," Dolly said. "It seemed so strange I thought I'd come tell you personally. It looks like we're not the only ones with these strange cases now." She looked down at her notes. "You're getting requests for consults on new cases of suspected MS from some of the other doctors in the region— and their patients are *not* from Hammerstone. They're faxing charts now."

Angela was stunned at the news. "How many patients?"

"So far, ten. Doc Millstone, from up in Harper's Creek; Stein, from out Elgin way; and Doctor Johnston." Dolly paused to see Angela's reaction to this last name.

"Dave Johnston?" When Dolly nodded, Angela couldn't conceal her shock. Doctor David Johnston ran a very large general practice, right here in Hot Springs.

"Yeah. He said he's got four patients of his own."

"This is crazy!" The words seemed to burst from Angela, unwilled. These new cases were far outside any preliminary pattern she and her mother might have thought they saw when gazing at the map on her study wall. "Hammerstone's a good twenty miles from Hot Springs. And Elgin's another 15 miles to the north! These just can't *all* be related. I must be missing something." With a commiserating glance back at her boss, Dolly let herself out of the office.

Alone again, Angela looked down at her charts. The way all these cases turned up at the same time still argued for a point source type of outbreak. But with all these new cases coming to light, the distribution pattern was knocked all to hell. She had to think. She would certainly want to know when the first signs of MS were seen in these new cases, but there were a few other things she'd like to know too. Picking up the telephone message slips that Dolly had left behind, she dialed Dave Johnston's number first.

If Dr. Johnston was a little put off by the intensity of Angela's questioning about his patients, he was soon joined by Drs. Stein and Millstone in his disgruntlement. But when Angela hung up her phone, she felt certain that time would vindicate her high-handedness. Over their several protests, she'd cajoled, begged, and even bullied them into contacting their patients to secure one piece of information missing from their histories. She needed to know if they had ties to Hammerstone—and if they'd visited the town recently. She knew that her office would have to follow up on this and buzzed Dolly with yet another task to put on the list.

The afternoon brought no further insights, and one major disappointment. The health department finally came through with a preliminary report on the samples she'd sent them for testing. Nothing. Nada. Zip. They'd found no trace of the usual contamination culprits in the water or the soil—no heavy metals, no toxins of any kind. Just good, old fashioned spring water, and good, old fashioned Arkansas dirt.

Okay, Angela thought. Back to square one. If it's not the land or the water, how about insects, like in West Nile or Lyme disease? That seemed unlikely—early winter in Arkansas wasn't a big bug season. Still, it was something worth checking into. The problem was, she'd already stretched her resources too thin. Maybe it was time to call for reinforcements.

Angela reached for her phone again, this time punching in the numbers for the Centers for Disease Control in Atlanta. The CDC would surely be better equipped to handle this. Their whole reason for existence was to investigate unusual outbreaks and clusters of illness. Surely they would be able to come up with something to help.

When her call was finally patched through to the appropriate CDC official, Angela swiftly ran through her findings to date. When she finished, she waited expectantly, but instead of interest, she was met with a long silence. At last the official spoke. "Write up your data. We'll want to take a look at it ourselves," was all he said. You'd think he was talking about the weather, Angela thought. She wanted to be angry at his lack of engagement but she kept a cool head. After all, maybe they get calls like this all the time. She hung up and noticed that the building had gone quiet. It was well past quitting time.

### *Thursday, February 13, 2003 — 6:00 pm*
### *Donatelli residence, Hot Springs, Arkansas*

For the first time in days, Angela and Marie sat down to a normal dinner and banished from the table all talk about their deepening mystery. The brief respite from work and worry was pleasant, but neither woman was inclined to linger over their meal. Together they made short work of the washing up, then by silent agreement they retired to the study.

Marie wheeled herself over to what was now her customary spot by the map, while Angela settled at her desk. She explained about the new cases, including the several in Hot Springs. "We're waiting for the answers from the doctors. If we don't get them by Friday, we'll call these patients ourselves and ask them about their travels to Hammerstone."

Marie listened, growing ever more thoughtful. "Well I hope they understand how important this is." She paused. "I think it was very smart of you though, asking them about their visits to Hammerstone," she said at last. "That's something Linda and I didn't think to do." She looked thoughtfully at the map and continued. "I think I'm going to talk to Linda about calling our folks. We know where they live, but we don't know where they might have been when they were exposed to their sickness. Maybe one of the little restaurants in town had contaminated food in the refrigerator for a week or something. Who knows?"

It seemed so obvious, now that her mother had said it out loud. "Okay, Ma. That would be great. Make sure that you write down *when* they were there too, not just where they went. Maybe we can put it all together tomorrow." But Angela's voice trailed off, for she'd suddenly noticed something she should have seen before. As Marie lifted the cup of tea that she had brought into the study with her, her hand began to tremble.

"Oh, Ma. I didn't realize. When did the weakness in your

arm start?" This was something Angela was always on the watch for—any sign that her mother was approaching another relapse in her lifelong struggle with MS.

"It's not so bad, dear." Marie's voice was brave. Not for the first time, Angela felt a rush of admiration for this brave woman. "It's been creeping up on me over the past couple of days. But maybe we could move the map down a little lower, so I can reach it easier? And maybe we could find some pins with bigger heads?"

"Sure thing, Ma," Angela said. "Anything else?"

"No," Marie shook her head. "And don't go making too much of this. Frankly, I'm past due for another round of these nuisances." That's what Marie always insisted on calling her symptoms: nuisances, as if they were no more troubling than a touch of mild arthritis or a pesky head cold. Angela knew they were much more than that, but Marie believed that understatement was best. She called it "cutting the disease down to size." Even when the symptoms grew more pro-nounced, she refused to dignify them by complaining. "It's a nuisance," she'd say, "but could you make dinner tonight?" Or "It's a nuisance, but do you mind helping me get into bed? I need a little extra rest these days."

In time, these episodes would pass, and she'd start feeling like her old self again, but each time she made her come-back, she'd done so with a little less function than she'd had before. Both Angela and Marie understood that one day, there might be no coming back, no remission of the disease. But until that day came, they dealt with it on Marie's terms—unflinchingly, courageously. Now Marie shrugged off Angela's concern, returning to her contemplation of the map. "I'll call Linda tonight and by Saturday we should know who all ate in Hammerstone recently," she said with a smile. She wheeled off to the kitchen to use the phone out there.

Taking her cue from Marie, Angie decided to do a little

work of her own. She snapped open her laptop. Time to try again to crack Jack's little puzzle, she thought. When the desktop icons appeared, she quickly moused over to the grinning cat icon and double clicked. Once again, she hit the start button, and once again she found herself faced with screen after screen of targets to shoot. With a resigned sigh, she started clicking away. When Marie finished up with the map and wheeled off to bed, she put the game on pause only long enough to listen and assure herself that her mother didn't need help getting into bed. Then she dove back into the game. Ten minutes later she'd exploded the last of the grinning cat's heads and found herself once again staring at the blinking blue password box in the center of the screen.

But inspiration wouldn't come. She tried entering the name of the tavern the Coneheads used as their weekly hangout. Nothing. The names of all the other gamers in her group. Nothing. Snowball jumped up into Angela's lap, offering her the back of her head for a good behind-the-ears scratching. "Girl," Angela said to the cat, "I'm as big a fan of the feline species as the next guy, but I just don't see anything in that game worth the time it takes to launch it!"

She turned to her e-mail, where she found a note from Murdoch saying he'd gotten his hands on a bit of the mystery sample from the springhouse. His old buddies at the crime lab had come through for him. She fired off a reply with the news about the water and soil results. Then, nudging Snowball back off her lap, Angela stood up. "Don't know about you, Snow, but I've had enough. Time for bed."

*Friday, February 14, 2003 — 9:00 am*
*Donatelli Clinic, Hot Springs, Arkansas*

Angela's day started normally, with hospital rounds and a roster of scheduled patients to see in the clinic. Among her long-time regulars, Janie managed to squeeze in a couple of Hammerstone newcomers, but things stayed on a relatively even keel throughout the morning. Angela almost managed to put her investigation out of her mind until Dolly slipped a phone message to her as she passed from one examination room to another. She glanced at it briefly, noting that all it said was "Chief McLain—Please call at your convenience."

Angela let the call wait until the end of the day. By that time, Angela had forgotten about the phone message, and only remembered it when she slipped her hand into her pocket and felt it waiting there. She retreated to her office and tapped in the number. McLain picked up on the first ring.

"Hey, Chief," she began. "What's new?"

"Just reporting in. I sent a crew up and down Old Indian Trail with the warning about the water. Can't say that it was appreciated—this isn't your designer-water kind of community—but I'm pretty sure most folks will do as they're told. I only hope it doesn't drag on too long."

Angela reddened with embarrassment, grateful that her color couldn't be seen over the phone. "Oh, Hank. I should have called you yesterday. It may not have been necessary after all." Hank's cold silence spoke volumes about his displeasure. "The samples all came up clean," she finished lamely.

Hank was irritated. He'd just tied two of his officers up on a day-long wild-goose chase. But his irritation was tempered by his honest relief that it was all a false alarm. He hadn't relished the prospect of dealing with a full-fledged environmental catastrophe. In the end, his relief won out, and his next words were mild.

"Okay," he said, "I'll let folks do the bottled water thing for a couple of days, then call the all clear." He chuckled. "If I cancel it right away, they'll just think we're all a bunch of screw-ups around here. So I might as well make it look good."

"By the way," he continued, "I got a call-back from the crime lab on that box we found. No drugs, but they found something weird. It had some dried out powder in it, but they couldn't say what it was, exactly. Some kind of protein, they said. Probably nothing, but they're storing it at the lab for now. Oh, and they sent some of the sample up to your professor friend in New York. It went out yesterday."

"Well, we'll see what Murdoch can make of it. In the meantime, I've got some disappointing news for you, too," she said. "I tried everything I could think of for a password on that e-mail from Burns. Still can't get through."

Hank's heartfelt sigh came through the line loud and clear. "I guess I was pinning my hopes on something turning up there," he said. "Burns is the only handle we've got on that arson investigation. We just can't seem to find out anything about him we can use."

"I can keep trying," Angela offered. "But I just don't know what password he might have picked." Trying to brighten the mood, she moved on to report on the few successes she'd had over the last couple of days. "We've got a lot of work done on tracking the disease outbreak," she finished up. "And I gave the CDC a call—maybe with all their resources, they'll turn up something we can both use."

*Friday, February 14, 2003 — 9:00 pm*
*Downtown, Hot Springs, Arkansas*

Angela wanted nothing more than some time for herself

tonight. She needed to get away for a few hours and forget about her frustration with the whole affair. It seemed to her that she had only succeeded in establishing beyond the shadow of a doubt that there was a problem, but had not been able to shine any light on the solution. It had been another stressful day, but now, standing at the second floor nurses station at Hot Springs Medical Center she had reason to smile. She had just seen her last patient and now she was free. On top of that, tonight was special in Hot Springs—the Gallery Walk was still in full swing.

Angela had always been a fan of the Gallery Walk. Hot Springs had a long history as a home for the arts. Its film-industry connections were probably the best known, because of all the attention the Documentary Film Festival brought to the city each year. Less known, but equally vibrant, was the city's thriving community of poets and writers, painters and sculptors. And one night each month the city drew in crowds of art lovers who came to walk the downtown circuit of galleries and view the latest works on display.

She turned her car toward downtown past Bathhouse Row, with its landmark bathhouse buildings, all dating from the late nineteenth and early twentieth centuries. They'd been built to take advantage of the natural hot springs that bubbled up out of the local mountains, harnessing their highly mineralized 147-degree water for the restorative baths that had for centuries attracted visitors to the area.

Angela hunted up a parking space in front of another of Hot Springs' famous tourist sites, the Arlington Hotel, and worked her way south on the main drag, going from gallery to gallery until she ended up at the Belle Arti restaurant for an Italian feast to cap off the night. For three whole hours, she managed to put all thoughts of Hammerstone and its mysteries out of her mind.

*Saturday, February 15, 2003 — 8:00 am*
*Donatelli residence, Hot Springs, Arkansas*

On Saturday morning, it all came crashing back in at her.
The day had started off normally enough. Linda and Marie
were hard at work on the kitchen phone, calling all the
patients on the map, trying to find out if they'd been anywhere near Old Indian Trail between Thanksgiving and New
Year's. Angela grabbed herself a cup of coffee and left them to
their work. Alone, she stepped into her office.

Once again she flipped open her computer, scrupulously
avoiding even a glance at the grinning cat icon on the desktop. Instead she logged on to the internet—she'd do a journal
search for information on point-source disease transmission
and environmental toxins. She wasn't sure what she hoped to
find, but it seemed the logical thing to try.

Hours later, all she had to show for her work was an incipient headache and more detail on industrial pollution than
she'd ever wanted to know. She pushed back from her desk
and cocked an ear toward the kitchen. There, silence reigned.
Perhaps her over-age Nancy Drews were finished for the day.
Angela decided to go and find out.

In the kitchen, she found Marie sitting alone at the table,
staring moodily into her coffee mug. To Angela's critical eye,
her mother seemed more drawn and tired than usual. This latest relapse was taking a heavy toll on Marie, and suddenly
Angela was stricken with doubt as to the wisdom of her mother's intense involvement in the investigation. Maybe it was
getting to be too much.

"Mom?" Angela came quietly into the room. "Are you okay?"

Marie smiled tiredly. "Just... just resting," she said. "I sent
Linda home early—I just don't have the energy she's got. She
could probably have kept going for hours more." She laughed
a little ruefully. "I'm just feeling a little fatigued."

Angela knelt by her mother's chair. "Mom? Do you think maybe you ought to give this whole thing a rest?" She gestured to the papers that littered the table. "You've done an awful lot already—why not let the rest of us carry the ball now?"

"No!" Marie's temper flared immediately. "I got into this at the start, and I want to see it through!"

Angela was a little taken aback by her mother's vehemence. "Don't you think that it might be a little... unhealthy to let yourself get so involved?"

"Unhealthy?" Marie rejected the word contemptuously. "You listen to me, young lady. There's nothing unhealthy about my interest in all of this. If anything, it's perfectly natural. Even before I had the diagnosis, when I was just having unexplained episodes, I felt like an outsider. My disease marked me as different. When you were little, I didn't feel like I fit in with the other mothers at PTA night. Whenever I went out in public, I was always sure that everybody knew, and that everybody was staring at me. Sometimes it was hard to keep from feeling sorry for myself." She looked fiercely at her daughter, the intensity of her feelings clear.

"Now, all of a sudden, that's just not a problem anymore." She gestured at the map. "All these poor folks, they've got it much worse than me. At least I know what I've got. I've got a general idea what to expect. These folks, they haven't a clue what to expect. You said yourself that even though their symptoms are *like* MS, there are lots of elements that make what they've got *different.*"

Softening a bit, she said, "Honey, I know sometimes Linda and I come across like a couple of foolish kids, playing at mystery solving. But that's just on the outside. We've talked about this long and deep, Linda and I, and we've come to the same conclusion. We're doing this because we feel like it's our duty. We're the closest thing those poor people have to a community. We understand at least a little of what they're going through. So we feel obliged to help them in any way we can."

"I understand, Ma, really...."

"No, I don't think you do. Do you know that in addition to looking for new cases, Linda's got extra support group meetings organized over the next few weeks, or that she goes around and personally invites our new 'cases' to come to them? Or that while you're away at work, Linda and I share the many calls that come into her support group phone line. We've rigged it up so that the calls from her line can be transferred here. And I get calls, Angie. Calls that would break your heart. And every one of them boils down to the same questions: 'What's happening to me? *Why* is it happening to me.'" She stopped, breathing hard, and Angela was startled to realize that her mother was close to tears.

"I didn't know. I'm sorry," was all Angela could say, as both women sank into a brief silence. Marie calmed down and collected herself.

"Well, let's get back to the mystery then, okay?" Angela said, breaking the silence. Together they gathered up the papers from the table and went into Angela's study.

Marie moved directly to the map. "This morning, Linda and I were able to reach all twenty-five people with probable or definite MS. We put each person's name on an index card, and under their name, we wrote down the names of all the places in Hammerstone where they had eaten in late November or early December. I hope you don't mind that we mentioned our food poisoning theory. Now, to cross reference the information, we took another group of index cards and wrote the name of each eating place they visited on a card. On each one of those cards, we listed all the people who had been to the same place at about the same time.

She proudly handed Angela two packs of index cards. As Angela began riffling through them, Marie continued. "Lots of people ate out in Hammerstone township during that time, but very few of them went to the same places, and most of the places that they did go were downtown, not in the Old Indian Trail area. One place did stand out though. More than half said they went to the Hammerstone Regional High School bake sale.

Angela looked up from the cards, startled. She went over to the map, scanning it rapidly. And there it was! Right at the foot of Arrowhead Mountain: Hammerstone Regional High School. Checking the file cards against the names on the map, she confirmed what she suspected. Every one of her anomalous cases—the ones who seemed to fall outside the funnel pattern on the map—had attended the bake sale. Only a few who lived in the funnel went to the sale.

She turned to her mother, who had been somewhat startled by her daughter's change of demeanor. "Don't you see what this means!" She said excitedly, "This is the answer! They were all exposed at the base of Arrowhead Mountain during the bake sale, but when they turned up on our case list, we naturally placed their residences on the map, and that's what made it look scattered! Maybe this is what is going on with the other cases, the ones from out of town! If I remember correctly, Hammerstone Regional is an agricultural Magnet school. Their students come from all over the region. Maybe these out-of-town patients attended the bake sale to support the school."

As luck would have it, the list of visits to Hammerstone by these patients had not been ready when she left the clinic for the hospital on Friday night. The doctor's offices that she had called were only able to reach half of them, but Janie and Dolly stayed late last night to try to get them on the phone when they got home from work. A quick call to Dolly clinched it. Yes, all of the out-of-town cases had been at the Hammerstone bake sale, but none of them could remember exactly when it was.

Once again, both women turned their eyes to the map. "Does this mean that all those people got food poisoning from the bake sale?"

"Not necessarily," Angela explained, "but I think this clearly supports a point source epidemic. Everyone who has gotten sick was in that funnel in late November or early December, but not everyone in the funnel went to the bake sale. No, Ma, there is something about the air or water in that funnel around Thanksgiving that caused this," Angela said, lost in thought.

*Monday, February 17, 2003 — 9:00 am*
*Police department, Hammerstone, Arkansas*

Hank was feeling a little lost this morning. He had always felt confident in his ability to do the job, but the last few months had brought bigger challenges than he was used to. First, there was the Burns fire and Mark's death and now there was this. Twenty five people in his town—neighbors who relied on him to keep them safe—had come down with a terrible mystery disease, and Hank didn't have a clue as to what to do about it. On top of that, the whole mess had something to do with Arrowhead Mountain, and for Hank, Arrowhead Mountain meant the Burns case.

He knew that the two situations had to be related, but for the life of him, he couldn't figure out how. As he rifled through the Burns file for the umpteenth time, he stopped to stare at Jack's picture, as if bringing enough intensity to bear on the image would cause his head to somehow leap from the page and begin to speak. Suddenly, he was interrupted by a knock on his office door.

He looked up to see Thelma standing hesitantly at the

121

threshold. "Chief," she said, "there is a man outside who wants to speak with you. He says he is the special agent in charge of the FBI field office in Little Rock."

"The Little Rock field office?" He put the Burns file aside. "I wonder what they want." He motioned for Thelma to send him in. It was unusual for someone from another law enforcement agency to show up in his office out of the blue, without even a phone call. And the SAC, no less. He'd had occasional dealings with the Bureau's Hot Springs office, but that usually involved local moonshine or methamphetamine labs in the woods. This ought to be interesting, he thought.

Before Thelma could exit the office, the SAC from Little Rock shoved his way past her and planted himself before Hank's desk. Hank was a little jolted by the man's intensity, but quickly recovered. "And what can I do for you, Agent...?" He let the end of the sentence hang.

"John Holmes," he barked. "I'm just here as a professional courtesy," he said, as he advanced on Hank's desk brandishing his ID. He put it away almost as fast as he produced it and sat down. "I'm in your county conducting an investigation with the highest national security implications," he said. "I expect your full support and cooperation."

It wasn't every day that the special agent in charge personally oversaw an investigation in a place like Garland County. Hank couldn't see why this odd little man had to be so pushy, but he saw no reason to balk at offering his help. Of course, that would require having some idea of what Holmes was up to, and so far Agent Holmes seemed unwilling to surrender any information of the kind. After listening to Holmes bluster for awhile, Hank decided to cut the unproductive harangue short. He rose from his chair.

"Well," he said. "We're always pleased to cooperate with our federal brethren," he said, with what he hoped was a genial grin. He walked around the desk, slapped Holmes on the back a shade too heartily, and tried to steer his visitor to the door. From this angle, Holmes, almost six inches shorter than Hank, was not so imposing. He was a banty-rooster of a man, about 5'8, mid-forties, whose rumpled suit looked like it had been slept in once or twice. His most striking feature was his scowl, which looked to be a permanent feature.

He wouldn't budge. "I want some of that cooperation right now, Chief, if you don't mind." Hank looked down at Holmes determined face, shrugged, and went back to his seat at the desk.

Holmes pulled out a worn leather-bound notebook and flipped it open, taking his time as he paged through to the proper place. "Right," he said finally, without looking up from his notes. "I need to know if you've ever heard of a Doctor Donatelli."

Whatever Hank had been expecting, this certainly wasn't it. Regrouping silently from this unusual twist, he managed a weak response. "Well, sure. I met her just the other day."

Holmes seemed like he already knew the answer and just continued. "Where'd she go? Who'd she talk to?"

"She went up the mountain—that's where I ran into her. As to who she talked to, I can't say for sure. Officer Wilkins—she brought you in here today—had a couple of words with her. For the rest, you'd be better off asking the good doctor herself."

"Don't you worry. I will. Right now though, I'm talking to you. What do you know about this Donatelli?"

"Not much," he said truthfully—but what little he did know was enough to make him resent this man's nasty, insinuating tone. "She's a doctor from Hot Springs and she came up here to collect some water and soil samples. She had a few more patients than usual turning up with some unexpected symptoms and she wanted to see if maybe there was something environmental that was causing the trouble."

"Doesn't that strike you as just a little odd?" Holmes said, sarcasm dripping from his words. "Does *your* family doc head for the hills to look for germs in the dirt whenever *you* get sick?"

"Well, no. He doesn't." Hank chuckled. "But Donatelli's different—she does research, too. On top of a regular medical practice. So, no—I wouldn't say her coming out here was all that strange."

Holmes merely grunted. "You said she was collecting samples," Holmes was speaking slowly now, looking at his notes. "Did she collect any from up at the Burns place?"

And all of a sudden, Hank felt cold. Why would the feds know about the Burns place? It was just a local unsolved arson case. Oblivious to Hank's sudden silence, Holmes kept pushing. He leaned forward and looked Hank in the eye. "Did she tell you that she knew Jack Burns?" Hank merely nodded.

The volume of Holmes voice went up a notch as he continued to make eye contact with Hank. "What's their connection, McLain? Do you really believe that this is all a coincidence, that a woman who went to school with Jack Burns is found prowling around the scene of his death, taking evidence… er… samples and then claiming to be just looking out for her patients?"

Holmes suddenly switched gears again, lowering his voice to more normal levels. "So you ran into her up near Burns' house. And she was taking environmental samples. What'd she find?"

"Turns out, nothing much," said Hank. "The dirt and water she sampled turned up clean. And that weird box…."

"Box?" Holmes was on the word like a terrier. "What box?"

"We found a plastic box in one of the springs above the Burns place. Thought it might be important, so I sent it up to the Little Rock crime lab for analysis. Turned out to be nothing important. Just some kind of powder."

Holmes demeanor changed suddenly. Minutes before, Hank had been convinced he'd have to wrestle the man to get him out of the building, but now Holmes seemed in an almighty hurry to leave. He snapped his notebook shut and headed for the door, but then he paused and turned back to level another glare at Hank. "I expect to be able to interview your deputy, and any other personnel who may have had dealings with this Dr. Donatelli at a later time." And then he was gone.

When Holmes was securely on the other side of the precinct door, Thelma came over to Hank's office and peeked in. "What the heck was that all about?" she asked. But Hank had no answer. He was still a little shaken by Holmes' questions—and even more by the man's attitude. He suddenly thought it might be a good idea to give Angela a call.

*Monday, February 17, 2003 — 10:30 am*
*Donatelli Clinic, Hot Springs, Arkansas*

Angela was in between patient visits, waiting for Janie to come out of the next examining room, when the phone rang. She picked it up reflexively. On the other end was Hank, clearly disturbed about something. As he told her about the visit from the FBI, she felt her alarm grow.

"What?! What on earth would they want with me?" Angela didn't wait for an answer. "Okay," she said thoughtfully, "maybe these days it does make some kind of sense to call in the FBI on a case like this. After that anthrax scare, maybe this is just a normal precautionary measure with any new clustering of disease. But what put them onto me to begin with?"

"I wondered about that, too," Hank said. "But I'd guess it

was your call to the CDC last week. Since 9/11, federal agencies are supposed to share information and I guess that's what happened here." He paused for emphasis. "Angela, this guy was really scary. And I hope you believe that I don't scare easy. He didn't seem to be interested in the disease. He was only interested in you—and your relationship with Burns. I suspect Burns was up to something that had already caught their eye, and when you and the illnesses popped up so soon after his death, a few pieces fell into place for the boys at the Bureau." There was silence on the line for a moment and then Hank continued in a slightly more thoughtful tone. "But for the life of me, I don't have any idea what those pieces might be."

When Angela spoke again, she was surprisingly calm. "It'll be okay, Hank. I sent the CDC a full report four days ago. Maybe they've turned up something—maybe this is not an isolated outbreak. Maybe they found something scary enough to call in the FBI."

Put in those terms, Hank had to acknowledge that federal involvement might be reasonable. But the memory of Holmes' aggressive behavior still didn't sit well. "You might be right," he said. "But you didn't talk to this Holmes fellow. I'd be more inclined to worry about him, if I were you." Hank's voice trailed off a moment. "I don't think he cares about your patients. I don't think he cares about you. He's the kind of guy who sees *everybody* as the enemy, and I wouldn't want him coming after me."

But Angela wouldn't let Hank's mood affect her own. "Listen, Hank. Maybe this guy Holmes is a nasty piece of work, but I haven't done anything wrong. I'm sure that once he comes and talks to me, I can make him see reason. After all, I've got nothing to hide."

Hank would have given anything to believe that Angela was right, but he didn't. She hadn't been here to see Holmes in all his bullying glory. And she hadn't heard the insinuation that lurked beneath his every word. "I hope you're right," was all he could say. "But Angela—I still think you'd better watch your back."

Angela hung up her phone, troubled by the intensity of Hank's closing words. The more she thought about the situation, the less sense it made. Why would the CDC call in the FBI before they even followed up with her? Wouldn't the welfare of her patients be the top priority? Wouldn't it make more sense to send someone from the CDC down here, a clinician maybe, to help solve the medical mystery? If they also want to call the FBI, fine, but how could an FBI agent help her or her patients?

But right now wasn't the time for such ruminations. Angela had a full schedule of patients waiting for her and their timing couldn't have been better. When she was uncertain about things to come, Angela could always take refuge in the company of her patients. These were people who needed and trusted her. Even with all the changes in medicine, with HMO's, unpredictable government regulations, frivolous lawsuits, even with all of this, one thing stayed constant. No one could intrude on that moment in the privacy of the examining room, when a sick person, more vulnerable than they have ever been in their life, looks towards a doctor and says "help me." It was a tremendous responsibility and a privilege, and it kept Angela grounded.

Problem was, it didn't work this time. As she worked her way from patient to patient, she felt unequal to her task for the first time since her days as an intern. Back then, her self-doubts came from a profound awareness of all that she didn't know, and now—surrounded by all these new patients—she once again felt as if her store of knowledge was inadequate. Angela knew that she could treat them for their symptoms, and that many of the protocols for MS were likely to work here. But there was something else lurking just beneath the surface of these new cases. Something sinister, something evil. The disease in these new patients was beyond normal medical experience, and she felt personally responsible for discovering its cause.

As she bid goodbye to her final patient of the day, she listened absently to the sounds of the clinic staff closing up shop. As usual, Dolly was the last to leave. She offered to lock up, but Angela told her to go on home. She wanted some time alone, here in the clinic, to work things through.

After seeing Dolly out the door, Angela went into her office to call Murdoch. If anybody could talk her out of her current funk, he could. She reached for the phone, and when she heard his clipped greeting, she couldn't hold back.

"Oh, Mud, it's me. I have to confess that I'm more confused than ever about this whole mess, and I need some advice." But when Murdoch didn't reply right away, Angela only felt worse. "What's wrong, Mud?" she asked.

"Actually, Angela, I'm glad you called. I've got some rather strange news."

"Talk to me," Angela said, anxious to hear what Murdoch had to say.

"It's that sample I got from the Little Rock crime lab," he began.

"Oh," Angela's heart sank. "I'm sorry about that, Mud. I got the results from Little Rock only this morning. I shouldn't have wasted your time."

"Waste my time!" Murdoch fairly roared. "I was just about to call you—to thank you for one of the most interesting extracurricular challenges I've had in years."

"But it's just a bunch of protein powder, isn't it? That's what the state lab reported to the police," said Angela.

"No doubt," Murdock said. "But they were probably only asked to test for a limited list of scheduled drugs."

"That sounds about right," Angela replied.

"Well, then. Of course they'd have missed the interesting stuff. I took a different tack. I started by taking a look to see if the powder had any particular structure." He paused dramatically. "And the scanning electron microscope turned up something remarkable. I think what you have here is a denatured virus!"

Angela's jaw dropped so suddenly that she was sure Murdoch could hear it on his end of the line. "A virus?"

"A *denatured* virus. Couldn't infect a flea—no doubt because you exposed it to higher temperatures than it was designed to tolerate. And that's the other thing. It's not a natural virus—at least, I don't think it is. Still got a lot of tests I want to run on it. But if you were to make me hazard a guess, I'd say this little critter got its start in a test tube, not in nature."

She was silent as she processed this new information. For many years, it had been postulated that a virus has something to do with MS, but it had never been proven. But she knew she shouldn't jump to conclusions. It's still not clear if a virus *could* cause MS and even if it could, how could it affect such a wide area all at once? Moreover, to understand if this virus is capable of causing the disease, Murdoch would still have to do many more tests to identify the virus and sequence its DNA. And then Angela would have to test those patients in the funnel to see whether they have actually been exposed. She still had a long way to go.

She continued in a more subdued tone. "But who knows if it has anything to do with our cluster of cases. Besides, why didn't it show up in the soil and water samples I took?"

"Probably because they weren't looking for it. Lab tests follow strict protocols. They can only find what they look for. So your lab probably tested for known pesticides and industrial toxins. I know for sure that they wouldn't have looked for this particular virus. The only reason *I* found it was because I wasn't limited to normal testing procedures. And, frankly, because I had a little bit of luck. Otherwise, I could easily have missed it myself."

She barely heard Murdoch's last words, as the reality of the FBI investigation and its implications entered her mind again. She felt a mild twinge of panic. "Oh my God, Murdoch! What kind of jeopardy have I put *you* in?" she exclaimed.

Murdoch laughed gently. "Oh, don't worry. I've grown excessively cautious in my old age, you know. When the package arrived, the seal on the container had been replaced by my buddy at the Crime lab, and I wouldn't have dreamt of opening it without taking all the proper precautions. But it turns out they weren't needed. The little critters were already dead. They may be stable at room temperature for a little while, and in fact, if this is the cause of your mystery disease outbreak, they'd have to be, but if you leave 'em at room temperature long enough, they'll eventually die."

"Mud," Angela tried again. "Stop. I didn't mean that kind of jeopardy." Something in her tone caught his attention. He listened intently.

"Murdoch, I think maybe we ought to stop talking about this. The Hammerstone police chief just had a visit from the feds, and apparently they're awfully interested in me. Which means they just might get interested in you." She paused. "Last week I contacted the CDC in Atlanta—I thought maybe they could help out, once I realized just how many people were affected. Next thing I knew, Hank was calling me to say the FBI was involved. Hank thinks they're starting from the assumption that I had something to do with *causing* this terrible disease."

"Well, that's ridiculous! How did they get involved anyway?" He didn't wait for an answer. "They must have known something was going on around there to begin with and your report was a trigger for them to take action."

That's exactly what Hank said, Angela thought. Then she continued. "But, once the FBI gets hold of the sample from the crime lab, they'll also know it is a denatured virus, right?"

"Most probably. And then... well. Then things could get pretty scary. There'll always be at least one bright boy who'll want the military to make it themselves. And in this new era of terror attacks—I don't like to even think about what could happen next." He paused. "You know, all this just might explain a little call I got from the Little Rock crime lab an hour ago. My old friend there gave me roughly the same warning as you're giving me now—said 'certain people' were very interested in the samples he sent me. So they may know fairly soon."

"There is nothing we can do about that now," Angela interrupted. "What matters now is that whatever their reasons, they're investigating me. And that means that everybody I dragged into this mess may be next on their list. I may have set you up for some unpleasantness, Mud," she finished miserably.

"Don't you worry about me," Murdoch said with a gentle chuckle. "If my reputation can't survive a little controversy, I've been wasting my time all these years. But your tale of rampaging federal agents doesn't do much to make me feel more secure, either. Listen, Angela, you may not be hearing from me directly for awhile." His voice was more somber than Angela had ever heard it. "Discretion might just be our best course of action....As for you, I suggest we just wait and see for a bit. The FBI is bound to contact you directly, sooner rather than later. Let's see what you think then."

"Okay, Mud," Angela said soberly. And then she hung up.

*Tuesday, February 18, 2003 — 6:00 am*
*Temporary FBI field office, Hot Springs, Arkansas*

Special Agent in Charge John Holmes stood in the doorway
of his temporary Hot Springs headquarters off Central
Avenue, surveying the nearly empty streets of the city. He
was alone; his men weren't due for another half-hour. To the
uneducated eye, this run-down storeroom was an unlikely
place to put a suite of offices for such an important investigation. But it was not aesthetics that caused John Holmes to
choose this location near the Downtowner Hotel—it was history.

To his left rose the white flanks of the grand old Arlington
Hotel, to his right stood the equally venerable Majestic. He
felt a certain ironic righteousness that his own team would
be working in the shadow of these notorious neighbors,
which in their heyday had been favorite haunts of the
Chicago Mob. Holmes enjoyed the peculiar history of this
town, where underworld figures, Al Capone and Bugsy Moran
included, declared a temporary truce in their bloody battles,
the better to enjoy themselves in the fabled casinos and
whorehouses that lined this stretch of real estate back then.
It was only as recently as the late 1960s that this sleepy spa
town finally lost its outlaw reputation.

That was when Lynn Davis, retired from the Bureau, but
still in law enforcement as the head of the Arkansas State
Police, took to heart his orders from then-governor
Rockefeller and shut the local operators down. Holmes could
easily imagine himself a warrior in that fight, sitting atop one
of the bulldozers and crushing slot machines in the street, as
was done in 1968 in the ultimate show of victory and power.

The image sat well with Holmes. His view of the world
was about as black and white as it could get—lock up the
bad guys and throw away the keys. And if you have to twist

the rules a little to do it, so what? They didn't deserve any better. But he did. Not that his superiors thought so. His posting to the Little Rock office a few years back was technically a promotion, but Holmes chafed under the knowledge that it was really an attempt by higher-ups in the Bureau to sideline him. Back then, the political winds were blowing the wrong way for an unreconstructed J. Edgar Hoover fan like Holmes. The Bureau was getting altogether too civilized, and they objected to Holmes' bullying tactics.

He laughed. His bosses thought they were putting him out to pasture, but now he was heading one of the most important investigations since 9/11. He was dead certain that once those birdbrains back in D.C. saw how he handled this job, they'd be falling all over themselves to transfer him to a plum assignment. Then he'd be able to shake the red Arkansas clay off his boots and live like a real person.

But enough of that, he told himself as he stepped back into the office; he had work to do. He moved over to a flip chart that he had placed at the head of a conference table and began to write. Soon, the rest of Holmes' team began filtering in. First to arrive were three young agents—rookies—far too junior for Holmes to bother to remember their names. But bringing up the rear came Roosevelt "Rosie" Jones. Rosie was one of Holmes' best agents. Nobody could intimidate a witness like Rosie. Standing six-foot plus and weighing in at a solid 260 pounds, all Rosie had to do was stand like a glowering black wall and most bad guys would just cave in and blab anything he wanted to hear.

Holmes waited until the newcomers had shed their coats, and then called the group to attention. They settled in at their desks and faced the display board where Holmes had posted items relevant to their current investigation. Occupying pride of place in the center of the board were the words "Healthright Labs."

"This is where our mission starts. This is why we're here." Holmes rapped the chart sharply. The agents sat up in their chairs, listening attentively. "Starting in late October of last year, our boys in Washington noticed an unusual traffic in equipment and supplies moving from a distributor up in St. Louis to this outfit in Hot Springs. Problem is, the supplies were all wrong for a facility like Healthright—more suited to a bioengineering firm than a clinical lab. What with the current national security climate in the country, this immediately sent up a red flag. They backtracked and found out that the shipment had been going on since the spring of 2001.

"That's when I got called onto the case. Trouble is, when I went to check out this Healthright outfit, it didn't exist. The deliveries were being shipped to a bogus address—an abandoned warehouse in Hot Springs. Witnesses in the area said they'd noticed a little unusual traffic—big trucks dropping off crates; and a couple of hours later, a couple of guys in a pickup coming by to haul the crates away."

Holmes directed the agents' attention to the board, where he pointed to another entry: 'Caymans.' "Turns out that this Healthright was just a paper enterprise, a front for a holding company in the Cayman Islands. From there, the trail gets murky, but at least a pair of the officers on the board of that company have ties to a North Korean bank in Kaesong City." He added that name to the board with a question mark. "And then we hit a wall. We couldn't make any headway on Healthright, and we couldn't figure out where all that equipment had ended up." Now Holmes walked to his own desk and picked up a photo, which he tacked onto the board as well.

"And then, there's this joker. Jack Burns." He wrote the name below the photograph with a flourish. "Just when we thought we'd have to drop our investigation of Healthright, this guy fell into our lap."

"On New Year's Eve of last year, this guy had a *really* bad night. Somebody blew up his house—and him along with it—out on Arrowhead Mountain, in Hammerstone. Turns out, he was something of a mystery man to the locals, so they were hot to find out more about him. After the fires were put out, the local fire marshal found a mess of lab equipment in the basement and managed to salvage some of the serial numbers. He called 'em in to the field office. The numbers were eventually pumped up the line to me and damned if they didn't match some of our missing Healthright shipments."

"Needless to say, I got interested in Burns real fast. But he's a shadowy character. He was one of those bright boys who got into the biotech field back when it was just getting started, even started to make a name for himself as something of a genius in the field—then... pffft. Nothing. He just disappeared. There was some kind of scandal about his research, and we think he left the country. But his trail just goes cold from the late 1980s, until he showed up in Arkansas and bought that house on the mountain."

"So. Now we've got these links—Healthright to North Korea, Healthright to Burns. A little more digging turned up another link. Burns was getting payments out of the same Cayman Islands holding company tied to Healthright. We didn't know what he was getting paid for, but the whole thing was starting to smell a lot like a possible terrorist plot—maybe some kind of bioweapon thing, like sarin or anthrax. The question is, why? And what was the target?" He paused a moment, letting his question hang.

"Thanks to a little inter-agency cooperation, we think we know, and it ain't pretty. The CIA routinely monitors North Korean communications traffic. They started noticing a big increase in coded chatter starting sometime last summer—right about the time that we started hearing about a new unification initiative from South Korea. The unification movement is being led by a long-time South Korean peace activist named Bo Li Yeung." Another name was added to the board.

"Now Bo Li's been around for years, but lately he's risen to new prominence—he's got his eye on the South Korean presidency. Been making lots of waves on the international stage, giving speeches and such. And he was due to come here—to the Clinton Library in Little Rock—in December. When we told the State Department about possible North Korean terrorist activity in the area, the speech was cancelled. Right after that, Burns goes out with a bang."

"We were ready to let things drop—we figured that averting disaster was a win for our side, right? But a couple of things have happened that brought the whole mess right back to the front burner. First, Bo Li rescheduled his visit to Little Rock. Second, we finally got a line on what Dr. Burns might have been making in that lab of his."

Holmes turned back to his board and scrawled another name: Angela Donatelli. "Just last week we got a call from the CDC. It seems this Dr. Donatelli was nosing around Hammerstone recently, checking out a strange disease outbreak. We'd already told the CDC to be on the alert for any odd activity in this region, given our suspicions about Healthright, so they passed Donatelli's report on to us. Well, we did a little checking and guess what? Turns out Donatelli went to school with this Burns guy!"

He took a deep breath and started pacing. "So, what do we have? We have a now-defunct holding company with possible North Korean ties sending laboratory equipment capable of genetic engineering as well as wads of money to a 'mad scientist' in rural Arkansas at about the time of a visit by a hated South Korean dignitary to Arkansas. The 'mad scientist' is murdered and his old classmate from New York, who just happens to live in Arkansas, reports an outbreak of a strange illness in the vicinity of his house." The volume of his voice went up a notch. "Is that enough for you, people?" He paused once more, for emphasis.

"So, that's where we start. We don't have any idea just what kind of relationship existed between Donatelli and Burns, and that's got to change. We need to know everything that she knows. Maybe her involvement is innocent—maybe her tie to Burns is coincidental. But I'm not a big believer in coincidence." He slapped some papers on the desk in front of him. "These are federal search warrants and a subpoena for her medical files. We're going in hard, we're going in fast, and we're going to find out just what our little local doctor has to tell us."

*Tuesday, February 18, 2003 — 7:30 am*
*Donatelli Clinic, Hot Springs, Arkansas*

When Angela pulled her car into the clinic parking lot, she was surprised to see that it was unusually full. Of all the clinics in the building, hers opened earliest. On most days, the only car ahead of her in the lot would be Dolly's—but today there were a couple of unfamiliar vehicles parked off to the side as well. She shrugged and dismissed them from her mind—today was going to be a long day, and she was in a hurry to get started.

Holmes watched as the doctor let herself into the building, then checked his watch. "Let's give her a couple more minutes to get settled in," he said to Rosie, who was riding shotgun for this raid. When he judged the time was right, he raised his hand to signal the rest of his team. The five men piled out of their cars simultaneously and moved briskly to the clinic entrance.

Holmes paused only briefly in the building lobby to check

the directory for Donatelli's office number, then led the way to her office. When they got there, he motioned for the team to stand back. Alone, he marched to the door that bore the legend "Donatelli Center for Clinical Neurology and Rehabilitation," raised his fist, and pounded.

"FBI! Open up!" he shouted.

The door swung open almost immediately. The sheer shock of his intensity was enough to drive a white-faced Dolly a step backward, allowing him to push his way into the office reception area. Dolly recovered and began moving toward him, clearly intending to try to toss him out. Fat chance. He ignored her and turned his glare on the doctor instead, who was standing by the reception desk.

"Are you Donatelli?" He barked the name. Never use their titles. The implied disrespect helped put them off guard.

"We've got warrants," he waved the paperwork in her face. Don't ask—tell. Another way to keep them off-balance. He could see these tactics were already working. Holmes felt a moment's satisfaction when the doctor's dark eyes went wide. A little fear went a long way in this business, he thought, and surely she was showing just a little. He allowed himself a small, shark-like grin.

"We gotta talk. Here or your office. It doesn't matter to me." Some folks said never let them claim their home turf, and would have faulted him for giving her the choice of her own office. But Holmes had found that if you give them the sense of territory, then yank it away, it was even more demoralizing. He hoped she'd pick her office. It would split her away from her pal, who was looking mighty angry.

She didn't disappoint him. "Come this way," she said in a soft voice, and led him to a private room, but left the door open—she didn't like the idea of being stuck alone with this man for any longer than necessary. She settled behind her desk, perhaps hoping its bulk would give her the sense of a barrier between them. Dream on, lady, Holmes thought. He let her get comfortable, then began what could only be described as his assault.

"You called the CDC." A statement, not a question.

She nodded, mutely.

Holmes planted himself directly in front of her desk, leaned forward to balance his upper body weight on his knuckles on the desk, and thrust his face close to hers. Invade their personal space—it really freaks some people out.

"Got some questions for you," he said intensely. But he didn't follow up with any, not right away. Instead, he turned away and flipped open his walkie-talkie, getting the other agents in the hall.

"Come on in, it's a go." He flipped the phone shut and turned back to Angela.

If he'd hoped to see her still cowering behind her desk, he was disappointed. Instead, she too had initiated a call. She ignored Holmes and spoke into her own phone instead. Her voice was far too calm and steady for Holmes' liking. "Mike? I'm sorry to bother you this early, but I have an FBI agent in my office. There are more on the way and they say they have a warrant. Could you come over as soon as possible? Great." She hung up the phone and looked Agent Holmes in the eye. "That was my lawyer, Mike Rhodes. He says I've got nothing to say to you until he arrives. Would you like a cup of coffee while we wait?"

Holmes realized right away that his bullying was not likely to work as well as he'd originally hoped. Still, it was worth a try. And meanwhile he could hear that the rest of his team was having much more success in reducing the outer office to chaos. Through the open office door he could see his men rooting through desk drawers and file cabinets over Dolly's angry protests. Janie arrived just as the search got underway. She stood by wringing her hands in distress. A couple of early-bird patients came in to add to the confusion. Dolly's voice rose to previously unexplored decibel levels as she harangued the strange men about patient confidentiality. Good, thought Holmes—let's see the doctor keep her cool through *that*.

He started hammering away. How long had she known about the disease before reporting it? How many were sick? Was it only Hammerstone, or were other communities involved? Holmes was pleased to see that his questions were chipping away at Angela's original calm. Mindful of her lawyer's advice, however, she kept her silence. And then he threw her a curve.

"How long've you been in touch with Jack Burns?"

She shouldn't have been surprised. Hank had warned her about this man's interest in Hammerstone and the fire at Burns' house. But coming as it did after a string of clinic-based questions, it caught her by surprise. "Off and on, for years," she stammered. "Every so often he sent e-mails."

Answering was a mistake, she realized belatedly. It only touched off another barrage of hostile questions. Had she known Burns lived in Arkansas? Why not? And then he started in on her past—her time in school, where she'd lived, where she'd hung out, who her other friends had been. The barrage went on for what felt like hours, but it couldn't have been more than 30 minutes before Mike came through the clinic doors and quieted things down. If she'd never fully appreciated her lawyer's cool professionalism, she did now.

But Mike couldn't do anything to stop the search through her records, and after he'd read through the subpoena Holmes brandished, he couldn't stop the agents from appropriating files. All he could do was put an end to the grilling. He chased Holmes out of the office and shut the door, giving Angela a few moments of peace.

Once Angela managed to pull herself together, she waded out into the reception area to lend some support to her beleaguered staff. She found Dolly and Janie together, valiantly trying to reschedule patient appointments, but Holmes shut them down in a hurry.

"The clinic's closed until further notice. We're taking over the premises." One of his agents began to herd the small throng of confused patients to the exit. Another started loading a box with medical charts. Angela could only watch, aghast, as the sacrosanct principle of doctor-client privilege was so brutally violated.

Suddenly her text beeper went off. It read "Troopers in front of the house." Alarmed, she pulled Janie and Dolly aside. "I've got to get out of here." She showed them the message on her beeper window. "Do what you can to get our patients hooked up with the other doctors in the area, just temporarily. Stick close to Mike—don't let these guys get you alone for questioning."

Ignored by the agents, Angela left the clinic and slipped into her lab office unseen. She quickly called her mother. "You okay, Ma?"

"Oh, Angela! What's going on? There are state police cars parked out front, watching the house! I don't think they plan on leaving any time soon!"

"Thanks for warning me, Ma. I've got federal agents here— they're ripping up my office right now. It seems like calling in the CDC was a big mistake."

"But why? Isn't that what you were supposed to do?"

"You'd think so, wouldn't you? But these guys aren't interested in working *with* me. It's more like they're accusing me of something. It all goes back to Burns, somehow."

"What do you want me to do?"

"Ma, I'm not feeling particularly cooperative with these guys and their jack-boot tactics. And Mud has already said he doesn't trust government motives in this kind of situation. There's nothing I can do to protect the patient files here, but I don't want them going through the stuff we've been doing at home—and it's pretty likely that they'll be going there next. My laptop's still in my car, so they won't get that. In the house, I guess the only thing I'm worried about is the map. Pull out the pins. Take it down and stuff it in a drawer somewhere. We can recreate it after they've gone."

"Don't worry. I can do that."

"Oh, and if they see the laptop docking station in my study, they'll know that there's a computer to be had and they'll hound us until we turn it over."

"Alright then." Marie took a deep breath. "I'll start packing up the docking station and all the wires in your office and make it look like there was never a computer there. I'll let them think we share mine. That'll satisfy them for a while."

"Great. I'll be home as soon as I can—maybe twenty minutes, tops."

"Maybe that's not such a good idea." Marie thought a moment, then she chuckled softly. "How about this? I'll call Linda. She and I should be able to handle a few federal agents. You go stash that computer someplace. If nothing else, your e-mails will drag Mud into this mess. He doesn't need that kind of grief."

"You sure you're up to this, Ma? These guys aren't going to win any prizes for manners, you know."

"I'll be fine, young lady," Marie said with a touch of asperity. "You need to go find Hank—he'll know what to do, I bet. Now go, I've got some organizing of my own to do."

*Tuesday, February 18, 2003 — 10:00 am*
*Donatelli residence, Hot Springs, Arkansas*

Linda drove past the parked police cars and up the drive-way to the Donatelli house, flashing a friendly wave at the offi-cers as she passed and swinging her cane jauntily as she made her way to the front door. Marie opened it just as Linda nego-tiated that final step onto the porch. "Hamming it up for our audience?" Marie laughed. "You bet," said Linda. The two women went inside and straight to the study, where they made short work of dismantling the map.

"Got any ideas about how to handle the feds when they get here?" Linda asked. "You know, I think I do." Marie's eyes twinkled mischievously. "Come on out to the kitchen, and I'll fill you in."

*Tuesday, February 18, 2003 — 10:00 am*
*Police department, Hammerstone, Arkansas*

Angela's appearance at the Hammerstone police station caught Hank by surprise. "To what do we owe this pleasure?" He said, ushering her into his office and closing the door.

"I've just had a visit from that FBI man, Holmes," she said. "You were right—he is one scary piece of work." She hesitated. "I am so sorry I dragged you into this, Hank." Without waiting for a response, she continued. "But I do have some good news from Murdoch." Hank listened curiously. "He tested the powder that he got from the state crime lab. They were right in saying the sample was free of standard drugs and the usual run of toxins—but they missed out on identifying what that powder *really* was."

"And that would be...?" Hank said, almost falling off his seat with anticipation.

"It was a virus." Hank was startled into silence. He waited for Angela to go on. "A dead virus—but only because you and I killed it, accidentally, when we took it out of the cold water of the spring."

Hank took a deep breath and leaned back in his chair. "A virus," Hank repeated, stroking his chin. "And here we are with all these sick people." He fell silent once again. "What do we do now?" he said when he finally broke the silence.

"Well, first off, I don't want Holmes to know that *we* know about the virus." At Hank's surprised reaction, she realized she'd better explain. "Murdoch is afraid that it's something pretty dangerous—maybe a bioengineered bug." She paused. "I just don't trust Holmes with this."

"Angela, the FBI needs to know that there is a virus on the loose, whether we like Holmes or not. I have to tell them."

"But you did, in a way. Now that they know about the sample at the crime lab, they'll examine it and find out on their own anyway, so you're not withholding anything. Look, our military has a pretty ugly history of playing around with bioweapons, and I just don't want to add anything more to the arsenal. I just don't want them to know that we know yet. At least not until we all know what we are dealing with."

"That's a big stretch Angela, but I guess I'll hold my peace until we hear back from this Murdoch of yours. I don't much trust that Holmes fella either."

"One other thing, Hank, I need a place to stash my stuff—my computer, mostly. And a place where I can work—someplace that Holmes won't be likely to raid."

Hank got up from the desk. "That's easy. You can set up out at my ranch, if you want. Holmes' issues with me are professional, not personal. He's likely to be a burr under my saddle at work, but there's no way on earth he'd be able to justify harassing me at home."

"That's wonderful." Angela brightened considerably. "When can I go out there and get set up?"

"You can follow me out there right now." Hank grabbed his hat and led her out of the office. "But if you don't mind, I'd like to make a stop along the way and see how Jennifer is doing."

*Tuesday, February 19, 2003 — 11:00 am*
*Old Indian Trail, Hammerstone, Arkansas*

As Hank nosed the car off Hammerstone's Main Street, he couldn't stop thinking about this virus and the central question that came along with it. Was there a continuing threat? Of course, he didn't know for sure if the virus found in the spring had actually caused the cases of MS, but he was willing to suppose that for a moment. If the sample he'd taken to the crime lab was the last of it, then maybe the threat went up in flames with Burns. On the other hand, if some of the virus had left the mountain alive, there may be someone out there equipped to launch this scourge on other unsuspecting communities. The thought made Hank shudder.

Before he knew it, he was pulling into Jennifer's driveway, with Angela close behind. They walked together to the front door, if not in high spirits, at least feeling good about the sense of camaraderie that was growing between them. But when the door swung open, Angela was taken aback. Even Hank, who'd known what to expect, was visibly affected by Jennifer's appearance. She looked exhausted, and was leaning heavily on her cane.

"Come in, come in," she said as she backed up clumsily to make way for them to pass. She smiled apologetically. "If I knew I was having company today, I'd have made myself more presentable."

145

Jennifer wore a rumpled housecoat and slippers, and obviously hadn't made much of a stab at tidying her hair. To Angela, this was a clear sign: Jennifer wasn't merely dealing with fatigue and weakness, she was struggling with profound depression as well.

"You look fine," Angela said, a touch too brightly. "We probably should have called ahead, but this is sort of a spur-of-the-moment visit." She helped Jennifer to the living room couch and sat down beside her. "How are the medications working out for you?" she asked.

"They don't seem to be helping much," Jennifer said softly. "I just keep getting worse and worse."

"Sometimes these things take time before you can feel the benefit." Angela spoke equally softly, trying hard to sound reassuring. "As long as your body's tolerating the drugs, they'll eventually start to make a difference. Right now, though, you're in the middle of what we call an exacerbation, and no medication can do much to stop it." She stroked Jennifer's bangs from her forehead. "It may last a few weeks, I'm sorry to say—but it *will* pass. And then you'll start feeling stronger again. That's how MS works sometimes—periodic flare-ups, followed by periods of remission."

"So I won't be like this forever?" Jennifer's relief was palpable. "I thought... I was afraid that I was going to feel like this for the rest of my life." She was close to tears.

"No—it won't be forever." Angela slipped an arm around Jennifer's slender shoulders. "So what do you say we try to perk you up a bit." She pulled a tissue from her pocket and dabbed away the moisture that had welled up in Jennifer's eyes.

The tender gesture seemed to break down a little of the wall of depression behind which Jennifer had felt trapped for days. "Right," she said, her voice already sounding a little stronger "Can you excuse me a minute?" She left the room without waiting for an answer. When she returned, she looked worlds better. She had obviously run a comb through her hair and splashed some cold water on her face. A little hope for tomorrow sometimes does wonders to break the cycle of depression that MS can bring, Angela thought.

"Now *there's* our Jenn," Hank said with a smile. "And I guess now it's my turn to explain why we've come." He guided Jenn back to the couch. "Are you up for a little test of your powers of observation?"

"Sure," Jennifer said, glancing questioningly at Angela. But Angela was equally mystified. "What do you want to know?"

"I want to know about Arrowhead Mountain, Jenn—about traffic up and down that road. And seeing as how you live right here at the base of it, you'd be the first one to know."

"But I already told you about that—I don't remember anybody going up or down that road on New Year's." She sounded a little defensive.

"Sure, sure," Hank said. "I know you did, and that's fine. But what about before New Year's? Ever see cars or trucks heading up that way, to the Burns house?"

"Well... yeah. But nobody important. The Yancy boys used to drive up that way every once in a while. Don't know exactly what they were doing on the mountain, but you know them—they're more likely to have been scavenging from the wrecked houses up there than visiting Mr. Burns." She looked thoughtful. "Haven't seen them head out that way in a while, though. In fact, I think I can tell you the last time I saw them. It was the Saturday just before Thanksgiving. I remember because that's the day I planted my pansies, like I always do."

"Huh." Hank took in Jennifer's information with a small grunt of surprise. "You know, come to think of it, I haven't seen those boys around in a long time either." He turned to Angela. "The Yancys are something of a fixture of life in this town. You usually see that old truck of theirs everywhere."

147

He turned back to Jennifer. "And you say they used to drive up into the mountain a lot?"

"Yeah. Often enough that it got me to thinkin' maybe they'd built themselves a still up there."

"Ever see them hauling crates, boxes, anything like that?"

Jennifer laughed. "You know that old truck of theirs, Hank. It's always crammed to bursting with junk in the back. They could have been hauling Fort Knox up there for all I could tell."

Hank nodded. "You're right." He stood and looked to Angela to follow suit. "Well, Jenn," he said, "we've taken up way too much of your time. Guess we ought to be going."

Jennifer walked with them to the door. She stopped and looked Hank in the eye, lowering her voice. "You don't think the Yancys had anything to do with the explosion at the Burns place, do you? They may not be the sharpest knives in the drawer, but there's no harm in 'em, Hank. They wouldn't be involved in anything like that," she said with certainty.

"I know," Hank said. "But maybe they saw something up on the mountain. Maybe I ought to call on them, just to ask what they were up to… and to make sure they're all right."

*Tuesday, February 18, 2003 — 1:00 pm*
*Old Forge Road, Hammerstone outskirts, Arkansas*

Angela followed Hank's squad car northeast onto Old Forge Road, a long and winding two-lane road that headed out of town. Typical of the central Arkansas countryside, the scenery on Old Forge contained a little bit of just about everything. The roadside was dotted with clusters of small wood-frame shotgun homes, beat-up trailers, and big, prosperous-looking ranch houses, all lying cheek-by-jowl to one another. These settlements were broken up by mile-long stretches of tree farms with their serried stands of pine, planted in different years and all seemingly grouped by height, like schoolchildren lining up to come in from recess. Along with pastures and stretches of natural deciduous forest, it was reminiscent of the chaotic willfulness that characterizes life at a frontier.

About ten miles down the road, Hank pulled onto a dirt drive leading through a small wood. Suddenly the road opened onto a clearing where an ancient house trailer stood. The land around it was littered by what looked to be at least a half-dozen dead cars and a motley collection of obsolete household appliances. Angela was sure she spotted an old wringer-washer piled upside-down against the rusting hulk of a vintage Ford. She pulled her car up behind Hank's and got out.

"You'll probably want to watch your step," Hank said to Angela, extending his hand as Angela stepped over an old transmission housing. "The Yancy boys ain't likely to make the cover of *House and Garden* any time soon." He laughed and led the way to the front door of the trailer. Angela followed carefully. "The Yancy family's been here for a long time. Back in the '20s they were pretty well known around these parts for runnin' moonshine. Folks pretty much leave them to themselves. Now the line is running down, I guess—Luke and Jesse are the last of 'em." As they neared the trailer, the door popped open. A wiry young man stood at the top of the steps holding a shotgun. Angela shrank back in alarm, but Hank just tipped his hat to the man. "Easy there, Jesse. Just dropped by for a chat. Ain't seen you boys in town for a while."

Jesse looked past Hank to get a better look at Angela. "Who's she?" he asked, suspiciously.

"This is Dr. Donatelli. She's a friend of mine, Jess," Hank said. He turned to Angela. "Dr. Donatelli, this here's Jesse Yancy." Angela gave a quick nod of greeting.

"Doctor, huh?" Jesse gave Angela another searching look as he put down the gun. Then he turned his attention back to Hank. "Ain't seen us in town cause we ain't been there," he said agreeably. "Luke's sick." Angela looked up in alarm at Jesse's last words.

"Sick? What kind of sick?" she asked.

"Don't know. Just sick. We could sure use a doctor."

"Can I take a look?" Angela asked. Jesse didn't answer, just grunted and moved out of the doorway. Taking this for assent, Hank stepped into the trailer with Angela following closely behind. Inside, the gloom was thick. The shades were all drawn, and no lights were lit. Jesse stepped around them and moved toward the back of the trailer. Hank and Angela followed.

The whole back of the trailer was taken up by a bedroom. As they stepped through the door they heard weak moans coming from a pile of covers on the bed. "That's Luke," said Jesse.

Hank reached for the light switch beside the door and flipped it. The sudden bright glare dazzled everyone's eyes, but it brought the wreck of the room into sharp relief. The floor was strewn with dirty clothes, the bed a tangle of blankets. Luke was sitting up in bed, and it seemed clear that he hadn't been out of it in some time. Angela went straight to the bedside, a move that caused Luke obvious distress. He rolled his eyes toward his brother, obviously dismayed at this intrusion of a stranger.

"This here's a doctor, Luke," Jesse said. "You got no call to get all scared." He turned to Angela. "Luke gets scared easy around strangers," he said by way of explanation. The gentleness of his tone surprised Angela. Jesse turned to his brother, letting a reassuring sing-song note creep into his voice. "Don't you worry none, Luke. I'm watching over you. This lady just wants to help." The sick man on the bed continued to eye Angela dubiously.

With Jesse's constant murmured reassurance, Luke eventually quieted enough to let Angela approach, passively allowing her to do a cursory examination. Even with the little he would allow her to do, it was painfully obvious that this man's legs were stiff with spasm and that he could hardly move them.

"How long's he been like this?" She turned to Jesse for answers, since he seemed to be the spokesman for the pair of them.

"Since around Christmas," he said. "Started with his legs— got a little wobbly, but then he got some better and we thought he was shaking it off." He looked mournfully at his ailing brother. "Then he got sick again, even worse'n before, and his legs got all stove up. Can't hardly walk at all now. Then yesterday, he just clammed up. I think he wants to talk, but he just can't." Jesse seemed oblivious to the tears that were now coursing down his cheeks. "Can you help him, doc?"

"Why didn't you call a doctor sooner? Or go to the emergency room?"

"Don't have no phone, but even if we did, we can't afford no doctor," Jesse said, feeling guilty that he could not provide for his brother in his time of need. "And besides, Luke's really scared about doctors. Wouldn't let me get one, even after he stopped walking. Said he'd rather wait it out till he got better again, like he did the first time."

"We're going to have to take him to the hospital now, if that's okay." Jesse nodded. She turned to Hank. "Call an ambulance. Now."

*Tuesday, February 18, 2003 —2:00 pm*
*Mountain General Hospital, Hammerstone, Arkansas*

Luke fought as hard as he could against the EMTs who came to take him to the hospital, but eventually, and with a great deal of brotherly reassurance, he calmed down enough to let the crew put him on a gurney and into the ambulance. Jesse rode with him in the back. With Hank in his squad car and Angela following behind, the three vehicles made a small procession on the drive to the nearest hospital—Mountain General Hospital. Once there, Angela collared the emergency room doctor and filled him in on what she'd learned during her brief exam. Hank sat with an anguished Jesse, asking questions and offering whatever comfort he could. When Luke was wheeled off for tests, Angela came out to the waiting room and joined them.

Luke was in the emergency department for at least two hours before he was transferred to the floor. As he was being wheeled out of the department, a somewhat sedated Luke was clearly relieved to see Jesse again as the two made their way to Luke's room, accompanied by two nurses. Angela spent a few minutes speaking with the emergency room doctor, then rejoined Hank in the waiting room. The two of them headed for the squad car.

"I made arrangements at the station to have Thelma take Jesse back home when he's ready," said Hank, as he walked through the parking lot. When he got to Angela's car, he paused and took a deep breath. "Well," he said. "Can't say I was expecting anything like this to happen." He turned to Angela. "He another one of your cases, you think?"

"Looks like it," she said thoughtfully. "The paraplegia and spasms definitely count as a 'neurologic event' and they're common enough in MS. But his inability to speak is much more troubling. It's a very unusual symptom for MS." Angela was worried for Luke. It appeared Luke's inability to talk was not due to any weakness of his mouth or his tongue but was due to damage to the part of his brain that forms words.

"Will he be able to speak again?" asked a worried Hank.

"Most likely, but he'll probably have a lot of trouble finding the right words for things or completing his sentences. That's bad enough for anyone, but for Luke, it's going to be particularly difficult." Hank could find nothing to say. He quietly saw Angela into her car, and then got into his own, leading the now shorter procession to the McLain ranch.

*Tuesday, February 18, 2003 — 4:00 pm*
*Donatelli household, Hot Springs, Arkansas*

Marie and Linda were sitting around the kitchen table enjoying lunch, when the pounding on the front door began. As Linda got up to answer the summoning knock, she cast a conspiratorial glance back at Marie. Almost immediately, the front hall was filled with commotion. Dominating everything was the abrasive voice of Holmes, which echoed all the way to the back of the house. Linda, sporting an exaggerated limp and leaning heavily on her cane, stumped back to the kitchen, leading a small parade of sober-suited men. From the back of the pack, Holmes fussed and fumed the whole way.

Once in the kitchen, Holmes flashed his badge peremptorily at Marie, and then slapped his warrant on the table. Marie looked up at the intruder. "Can I help you?" she asked with her best hostess' smile.

"I can help myself, ma'am," he said rudely. Pointing to the papers on the table, he continued. "This authorizes me and my men to search the premises."

Marie smiled sweetly. "Well then, of course you must." Holmes was a little taken aback by the mildness of her reply. He turned to stomp out of the kitchen, only to find Linda blocking the threshold, an equally sweet smile on her face. "Outta my way, woman," he bellowed. Linda just smiled even more sweetly and moved heavily out of the doorway.

Holmes and his men congregated in the living room. Calling after him, Marie raised her voice slightly. "Young man, what is it you're looking for? Maybe I can help." A moment later, Marie pushed herself back from the table and rolled jauntily into the crowd of agents. She got the desired response. Holmes was momentarily silenced—even he found it hard to play the bully with a wheelchair-bound little old lady. She took advantage of the momentary quiet and continued. "I suppose you want Angela's office?" Her voice was charming, even gracious. "Let me show you where it is," she said as she turned her wheelchair around and began to head across the room.

Passing the entrance to the kitchen again, she stopped, causing a small chain-reaction of collisions as the men who followed behind her were brought up short. "Maybe you boys would like a bite to eat, first?" Linda watched, grinning, as Marie blithely treated the intrusion like an unexpected visit from old friends.

"I... I... No, we don't need nothin' to eat." Holmes tried to bark again, but his bluster was deserting him rapidly. Two of his agents, though, looked longingly at the neat plate of sandwiches on the table.

"Maybe later, then," Marie said, as she continued along the hallway. With the dignity of the grandest society matron, she wheeled her chair towards Angela's office. "Come along, and mind not to scuff the floors." The hapless covey of feds followed her slowly down the hall as she chirped blithely away. "You know, I've always thought a career in government would be absolutely fascinating."

Linda stayed behind in the kitchen, and when she was sure the agents were out of earshot she collapsed helplessly into laughter. Three hours later, Marie escorted the bemused and empty-handed contingent of FBI agents out the door. Two of them were munching on sandwiches, much to Holmes' contempt. As they made their way back to their cars, Marie's voice rang out: "Now don't y'all be strangers."

*Tuesday, February 18, 2003 — 5:00 pm*
*McLain ranch, Hammerstone, Arkansas*

Unlike Luke, Jesse had done a little talking in the waiting room, but Hank thought it best to let Angela get settled in before they got into all of that. Angela reluctantly agreed. She set up her computer in the spare room and afterwards joined Hank in the kitchen, where he was beginning to put together a couple of baloney and cheese sandwiches. "We skipped lunch," he said by way of explanation. "Do you mind putting on a pot of coffee while I finish these up?"

Angela nodded, "Not at all." She and Hank spent the next few minutes working companionably together in the kitchen and indulging in some light conversation until Angela could stand the suspense no longer. "Let's talk about the Yancys," she said abruptly. Hank smiled and brought the plate of sandwiches to the table. After the two of them sat down, he began.

"Okay," Hank took a bite of his sandwich. "Jesse had a strange story to tell. It seems they started going up to the Burns place as early as April of 2001. But they weren't working for Burns, they were hired by some folks out in Hot Springs." Angela looked up, startled. Hank continued. "Initially, all the jobs were deliveries. It was always the same routine. They'd pick up stuff from a dead-drop in Hot Springs—crates and boxes, mostly—and haul it up the mountain. Never met the guy that hired 'em—just got phone calls telling 'em where to go. All Jesse could tell me about the caller is that he sounded foreign—maybe Chinese. Of course, with them, that could mean any kind of Asian, frankly.

"Anyway, they'd find an envelope full of money in the mailbox after every job—no stamps, no return address, so somebody must've just stuffed it in the box personally. Jesse says they must have made at least a dozen runs. Then, sometime around mid-summer of last year, the jobs dried up. But not for long." He paused and took a sip of coffee. Angela nodded for him to go on.

"In late November they got another call. This time for a pick-up, not a delivery. So they went up the mountain and got the package. They were supposed to drop it off back in Hot Springs when they were done."

"That's when things get interesting. On the way down the mountain, Luke got into the package—one of those red-and-white ice chests you keep beers in on a picnic—only this one was full of metal canisters packed in ice. Inside the canisters were little bottles filled with some kind of powder. That Luke's got the curiosity of a cat—and half the sense, and that's what caused all the trouble. Jesse told me that Luke dropped one of the bottles in the chest. The powder spilled everywhere, he said, and blew away in the wind—but not before Luke tasted it to see what it was." Angela was aghast. "Couple-three weeks later, Luke starts getting sick." Hank went quiet and let the implications sink in.

Figuring Angela needed a few moments to digest this latest news, he got up and cleaned away the remains of their late lunch. The day so far had certainly given him a lot to think about. According to Jenn—and now confirmed by Jesse—the virus *had* apparently left the mountain on the Saturday before Thanksgiving last year. Worse, it had existed in reasonable quantities and was presumably alive, because it had been safely packed in ice. Who had it now was anybody's guess, but Hank had to conclude that it was still a threat. So, now maybe he had a few answers. But he still had lots of other questions, too. Foremost on his mind were those other cases Angela had told him about. If it was the virus that caused the disease, how could a bunch of powder spilled on Arrowhead Mountain have anything to do with sick people as far away as Hot Springs and Elgin? While he was thinking about it, he turned to Angela and asked her for an update on the map. What he heard nearly rendered him speechless.

"The Hammerstone Regional High School bake sale is always held on the Saturday before Thanksgiving," he said. They stared at one another in shock and sudden understanding. Everybody—absolutely everybody showing symptoms—had been in Arrowhead Valley when Luke Yancy had spilled that strange white powder.

Hank would have liked to stay and talk about the implications with Angela, but he had been absent from the office almost all day. He thought that he should pop by again to "make sure that it was still standing." He told Angela to make herself at home while he was gone and disappeared in the squad car.

Alone, Angela wandered around Hank's ranch house, a little confounded by the speed with which these new facts about her mystery disease were popping up. Even in the face of these important developments, however, she was able to view her current predicament with something like amusement. Here she was, a nice Italian girl from the Bronx, hiding out from the feds in Hammerstone, Arkansas, of all places. Still, she told herself with a rueful little laugh, if you've got to go on the lam, it doesn't hurt to have a handsome lawman on your side. With a quiet chuckle, she picked up the phone in the kitchen and dialed Murdoch's home number from memory. The phone barely finished its first ring before it was picked up on the other end.

"Riordan here."

"Hello, Mud," she said. "It's me."

Murdoch exhaled a huge sigh of relief. "I am *so* glad to hear your voice. Even gladder you didn't call the lab. Things are getting hot up here—we had some visitors from the federal government earlier today."

"Oh, Mud—I'm sorry I ever dragged you into this."

"Don't you worry," he said. "A little excitement's good for the heart. Keeps me young. But you and I have to talk, soon. I'm flying down on Thursday. I'll be arriving on the one o'clock flight. Meet my plane, would you?"

"Sure thing, Mud. But I've got to tell you..."

"Not on the phone, Angela. I doubt they've gotten around to tapping my home line, but I wouldn't want to bet on it. I'd rather continue this conversation in person."

"Good enough." And Murdoch abruptly hung up. Angela stared at the receiver a minute before replacing it thoughtfully in its cradle. So Murdoch's lab had been searched, too. Sure didn't take the feds long to link him up with this mess, did it? Then she thought of the powder he'd been analyzing—had the FBI gotten hold of it? Maybe not. Mud would have said something about it. She'd have to wait until Thursday to hear what had happened up there. She only hoped the suspense didn't kill her first.

When Hank returned from the station, he found her at her laptop, mindlessly shooting cartoon cats that filled the screen. "Can't think of anything better to do?" he asked.

She paused the game and looked up. "I'm making another try at cracking Burns' puzzle," she said. "It's irritating, but I can't get to the password screen without running through this silly thing first." Hank pulled up a chair and watched as she methodically exploded the cartoon cats. At last the last one disappeared in a burst of pixels and the black screen and password box came into view. Angela typed "virus," "powder," "Yancy,"

"Chinese," and half a dozen other guesses before giving up in disgust. She pushed back from the machine and turned her back on the blinking cursor. "Nothing works—and I'm out of ideas," she said with a yawn. "And anyway, it's getting late."

Hank looked out the window into the dark night. "It's a long drive back to Hot Springs," he said, without looking Angela in the eye. "You can stay here, if you want." Angela smothered a grin—darned if the big tough policeman wasn't blushing! The idea had its temptations, but she knew she couldn't stay. "I left my mom alone to deal with a house full of FBI agents," she said instead. "I really ought to check and see if she's okay." She closed up her laptop and left it there, a promise of sorts that she'd be back soon. Hank walked her out to her car, and when Angela looked up at him to say good-bye, she thought for a moment he just might lean down for a kiss. She wasn't at all sure how she felt about that. To cover her confusion, she twisted the key in the ignition and put the car into gear. "'Night, Hank," she said, and drove off, flustered.

Hank stood for a long minute, watching the taillights of her car move off down the road. With a little sigh, he turned and let himself into the house, closing the door softly behind him.

*Wednesday, February 19, 2003 — 10:00 am*
*Donatelli residence, Hot Springs, Arkansas*

When Angela had arrived home Tuesday night, the house had been dark and her mother was sleeping soundly. She had tiptoed into her own bedroom and fallen gratefully into bed, asleep almost as soon as her head had hit the pillow. When she finally awoke, Wednesday morning was half gone, and the sounds of another Linda visitation came unmistakably from the kitchen. She slipped on her robe and shuffled down to the kitchen, intent on getting a good dose of caffeine into her system before doing anything else.

Marie and Linda barely looked up when Angela entered the kitchen, leaving her to fend for herself at the coffeepot. She watched the two of them in silence as she sipped from her cup. Linda was at the cutting board, where she was doing something fancy to raw vegetables. Marie was at the stove, judiciously taste-testing what looked to be chicken cacciatore simmering in a saucepan. This was the last thing Angela expected to find in the aftermath of a raid by Special Agent in Charge John Holmes.

"Welcome back, Angie," Marie said, gaily. "We're having a nice brunch this morning. You're welcome to join us." Linda looked over to Marie with a grin. "Think any of the boys from yesterday will drop in?" The two of them collapsed with laughter.

"What's gotten into the two of you?" Angela found herself grinning along with them.

"Oh, wait'll you hear," said Linda. "Your mom was amazing, yesterday. Those federal agents didn't know what hit 'em."

"Aw, shucks," Marie said in her best approximation of a self-deprecating Southern drawl. "T'warn't nuthin'." They both dissolved into giggles again, but they wouldn't say anything more about yesterday's adventures until they had the meal on the table and everyone sat down to eat.

"So come on—tell me what happened," Angela coaxed. Taking it in turns, Linda and Marie regaled her with their exploits. After yet another bout of giggles, Linda tried for the last word. "So she just 'bout wore them all down with hospitality," said Linda. "I never knew you northern gals understood how to use politeness as a weapon. Thought it was a Southern lady's special technique"

"We've been living down here long enough," Marie said. "Couldn't help but pick up some of the local customs after a while." That just set them off into giggles again.

Angela couldn't help but laugh along with them, but as she helped clear away the dishes, she felt it was time to bring everybody back to reality. She told them about her visit to Hammerstone, and what she and Hank had learned from the Yancys. Linda shook her head, half in sympathy, half in distaste. "Those Yancys," she said. "If there's trouble to be found, they've always been the ones to find it."

"I wouldn't be too quick to judge," Angela said. "I don't think they had the slightest idea of what they were getting into. And that poor kid, Luke, is paying a terrible price for it." She shook her head. "He's in a really bad way—I don't know if there's anything that can be done for him." But then she brightened as a thought hit her. "Maybe Murdoch will have some ideas when he gets here."

"Oh? He's coming?" Marie was thrilled at the news, and spent the next half-hour filling Linda in about her former doctor and great friend. Angela left them to it, slipping off for a belated morning run.

*Wednesday, February 19, 2003 — 12:00 noon*
*Temporary FBI field office, Hot Springs, Arkansas*

The boss had been in conference with Rosie behind closed doors for hours now. The other guys were not sure exactly what was going on, but they were sure it wasn't good. Even the dimmest among them could see that this case was of the highest priority to the Bureau. Holmes was on the phone to Washington at least three times a day, sometimes for hours. He had pushed hard for the search of Donatelli's office and home, and he'd come up empty. This fact had not escaped the notice of his superiors, and he alone was being held accountable.

Focused as they were on their boss' temper tantrums, it didn't take anything more than a ringing phone to jolt everyone slightly out of their seats. A rookie agent, Donny Harrison, was first to grab up the receiver. He listened a moment, put the caller on hold, and hotfooted it to Holmes' office, sure that the boss would welcome the call. After all, it might be a break in the case. He knocked confidently on the door, popped it open and announced: "Chief McLain on line 3."

"What does *he* want?" barked an obviously annoyed Holmes.

"He said he was calling as a professional courtesy."

Holmes grunted and fixed Donny with a singularly unpleasant glare. "Alright, I got it." He picked up the phone and punched line 3. "Yeah," he said into the receiver.

"I thought I'd find you hard at work, Agent Holmes." Hank said cheerily, his voice crackling on the line. "Thought I ought to tell you we've made a little headway on our arson investigation. I'm off to question a possible witness right now. Maybe you and your boys would like to sit in."

"Yeh? Who are you going to interrogate?"

"Oh, no one important, just the guy who made the equipment deliveries to Burns." There was silence on the line. Hank had been in law enforcement long enough to know that this information had to be on the top of Holmes' need-to-know list. He let the silence spin out, then gave the federal agent directions out to the Yancy trailer and hung up.

As much as Hank did not like Holmes, he'd felt obligated to share this information about the Yancys. It was one thing to mistrust a federal agent, another thing entirely to withhold material evidence in a federal investigation. The best he could hope for—and what he'd tried to insure by making the call when he was only minutes away from the Yancy trailer—was to get a few minutes alone with Jesse before Holmes took over the show.

At his end of the now-broken connection, Holmes slammed

the phone down, his bad mood now a worse one. He didn't like being one-upped by local law enforcement at the best of times, and this was hardly the best of times. Out in the main office he told Rosie to hold the fort, then collared Harrison with a brusque "Come with me" as he marched out the door. In minutes he was burning up the highway toward Hammerstone, fuming under his breath the whole way.

*Wednesday, February 19, 2003 — 12:00 noon
Yancy Trailer, just outside Hammerstone, Arkansas*

Jesse Yancy was beside himself with frustration. He wanted to go see his brother in the hospital, and the darn pickup wouldn't start. Of course, he only had himself to blame, and that always makes bad news harder to take. He'd known for months that the points needed replacing, but he'd let it slip his mind, what with Luke being so sick and all. Now, he was stuck.

It had taken him most of the morning, but he'd finally got ol' Spike McCollum on the CB. Jesse wasn't one to ask for a favor, but this was an emergency as near as he could tell, and Spike had bummed enough beers off him and Luke over the years that he shouldn't mind helping out now. When Jesse asked him to take a run out to the junkyard and pick up some parts, Spike had agreed amiably enough. But that had been a couple hours ago, and here Jesse was, still waiting.

Jesse was getting antsy. He turned on the police scanner, hoping the chatter of EMT, fire, and police dispatchers would help him get his mind off his worries. He enjoyed listening to the world on his scanner. It allowed him to dip into the hustle and bustle when he wanted to and on his own terms. Today the talk on the scanner seemed pretty busy.

He'd just settled down in his favorite chair to listen to the dispatchers calling out their radio codes when he thought he heard a truck turning onto the dirt road that led to the trailer. He turned the radio down a notch to listen, and when he heard it again, he hurried outside. Hoping to get a jump on the repair job, he popped the hood so he'd be ready as soon as ol' Spike handed over the parts. He was busying himself with the engine when he heard the truck pull up beside him. He straightened up and began to turn. "Bout time you got here, Spike. I've been…."

He never finished the sentence. Three shots rang out and just after the third one was off, the sound of tires eating gravel reverberated through the valley. Jesse fell to the ground, his clothes saturated in blood from a bullet in the chest and one in the belly. The third entered the side fender of the truck and pierced the very top of the engine, blowing off the air filter in the process.

Spike McCollum had just enough time to spin the wheel and pull off onto the shoulder of Old Forge Road when a shiny new pick-up came bursting hell-bent-for-leather out of the Yancy driveway, heading away from town. He spat a curse at the driver, glaring at the truck as it sped away. Spike wasn't the hottest tempered man in Arkansas, but there was one thing guaranteed to rile him, and that was idiots who thought they owned the road.

Much as he'd have liked to chase after the offending truck, he knew he had a promise to keep to Jesse, so he turned into the Yancy drive and bumped along the dirt road until he came to the clearing. As he pulled up beside the truck, the scene that greeted him stopped him cold—Jesse lay still in a pool of blood. "Oh my God," Spike whined under his breath.

Out on Old Forge Road, Hank and Officer Wilkins were just minutes behind Spike. Hank swung the squad car onto the Yancy driveway and when he reached the clearing he was likewise shocked by the carnage he saw. But unlike Spike, who was still sitting dumbfounded in his truck, Hank and Thelma knew what to do. Thelma grabbed the radio handset and broadcast an urgent call for an ambulance, while Hank vaulted out of the car and raced to Jesse's side. "He's still breathing," he yelled to Thelma. In a much gentler voice, he murmured "Hang on, kid" to Jesse while he tried to slow the bleeding. This looks bad, he thought, but he stayed with the boy until the ambulance arrived. It seemed like an eternity.

As the EMT crew slammed the ambulance doors shut on Jesse's stretcher, Hanks demeanor changed. Wordlessly, he turned back to the squad car. This was now a crime scene, and they had police work to do. He called the County Crime Scene Investigation Unit and set Thelma to the task of quarantining the scene. He wanted a look inside the trailer.

As he approached the trailer he drew his gun, then carefully entered the front door. The annoying background chatter of Jesse's police radio provided something like a soundtrack for his careful room-by-room search. After a few tense minutes, he decided that the trailer was clear and holstered gun. The sound of excited conversation outside caught his attention and he stepped back out into the yard, where Thelma was questioning Spike. "You'll want to hear this, chief," she called, so he walked over to join the two of them. "Spike here says he was almost run off the road by some joker in a pick-up truck. Says it came barreling out of here like the hounds of hell were on its tail. He said the driver was a foreigner—Chinese or something." Between the two of them, Hank and Thelma got enough of a description to call in an APB on a late-model, dark blue Ford truck driven by an Asian man about 40 to 45 years old.

"Well, at least that's something," Hank said. "Look, Thelma,

I'm going to take one last tour around the trailer. When Holmes gets here, I'm going to be tied up with him for who knows how long, so I'll leave you to keep an eye on things until the CSI unit arrives." He left her stringing yellow crime-scene tape around the clearing and stepped back into the musty shadows of the trailer. The scanner was still chattering away, and he reached to switch it off. Suddenly a familiar barking voice came over the speakers.

"I'm on my way out there now—McLain said he'd meet us there." Holmes' unmistakable voice came through loud and clear. Hank froze, waiting to hear what else might be coming. Suddenly the scanner squawked again and a new voice spoke.

"Alright, John. Do you think this McLain knows about the virus?" Hank grinned wryly when he heard Holmes' answer.

"Hasn't got a clue, Vince," the cock-sure fed replied. "He's just a local rube." Then the chatter cut out.

Hank stared at the scanner for a minute, trying to make sense of what he'd just heard. The scanner must have picked up Holmes' cell-phone signal, that was for sure. And Holmes had to have been reporting to his superior—this Vince fellow. Obviously, the feds now knew about the virus, but weren't intending to tell the local law about it. Angela may have been right. Maybe he shouldn't trust their intentions, he thought. In any case, Hank thought he should watch his step around Holmes a little more closely from now on. He switched off the scanner and went out into the yard again.

Holmes pulled into the yard just as Hank came out of the trailer, the county police and local CSI unit following right behind. A quick glance at Thelma reassured Hank that she had things under control, so he made his way over to Holmes. "Jesse Yancy's been taken to Mountain General—probably already in surgery."

"This Yancy—he the witness you were talking about?"

"Yeah. But it's probably going to be a while before we can

talk to him. He took a couple of bullets—lost a lot of blood. He was in a coma when he left. I'm afraid we both made wasted trips out here, Agent Holmes. We might as well head on out and leave the crime scene boys to do their jobs."

"Speak for yourself" Holmes barked. He turned away from Hank and started ordering his troops. Before long, Thelma's careful efforts at organizing the investigation were blown to smithereens as Holmes' men disrupted the work every step of the way. He waved for Thelma to join him and together they got into the cruiser and drove off.

"I just can't stand that man," Thelma fussed. "Whatever happened to all the talk about a new spirit of cooperation between the branches of law enforcement?" But Hank was too preoccupied to be drawn into her complaints, and she soon fell silent. The whole drive back to town, all Hank could think of was that he wanted to talk to Angela. Things were moving too fast now, and with Jesse getting shot, he was beginning to worry that maybe nobody connected with this case was safe.

*Thursday, February 20, 2003 — 10:00 am*
*Donatelli residence, Hot Springs, Arkansas*

Angela woke at mid-morning feeling a little disoriented. She wasn't used to the luxury of sleeping late so many days in a row, but with the office closed, there wasn't much reason to stick to normal doctor's hours. Yesterday she hadn't gotten up until nearly 11:00! After lunch, she'd made a run out to Hank's ranch with Marie's map and left it in the back room with her computer. She briefly thought of setting it up, but felt that it would be better to leave that to Marie, if the need arose. Although the map had yielded a treasure trove of valuable information, she really did not expect it to be of much help from here on in. Eventually she'd headed back home and lurked around the house, until an exasperated Marie chased her out from underfoot. She'd spent the remainder of the day poring through her old medical texts, looking for anything that might help.

When she wandered into the kitchen in search of coffee, Marie looked up at her warily. "Do you plan on hanging around the house all day today, too?" she asked reprovingly.

"No, Ma," Angela reassured her. "I got a date with a plane up in Little Rock."

Marie brightened immediately. "He's coming today?" she asked.

"Yep. Should be touching down at around 1:00," she said. Just then the phone rang and Angela picked it up. By the time she was done with her conversation, she was grinning from ear to ear.

"Good news?" Marie asked.

"The best," Angela's mood was positively giddy. "That was Dolly. The feds have finally cleared out of the clinic. We're back in business."

"I guess that means you'll be heading into work today?" Marie looked a little worried. "But who'll meet Murdoch?"

"Not to worry. I'm going into the office for a couple of hours to get Dolly and the staff started on undoing the damage Holmes' marauders did to the records. Good thing my vacation was due to start tomorrow, so the office is closed for two weeks anyway!"

"That's good," said Marie, smiling. But then her look grew more serious. "Angela. Are you bringing Murdoch back here from the airport?"

"I don't think so, Ma. I'd like to keep him off of Holmes' radar while he's here. I think it's probably better for him to stay out at Hank's place. Don't you?"

"Oh, I suppose so. It's just, with everything moving out to Hammerstone, it seems that there really isn't much for me to do anymore." Marie's hangdog expression was so forlorn that Angela couldn't help but laugh. "Now come on, Ma!" she said. "Do you really think I'd be foolish enough to cut you out of the team after everything you've done so far? We'd never even have spotted the disease pattern if you hadn't had the idea for the map! No. I have every intention of exploiting your sleuthing abilities until you drop from exhaustion!" She was gratified to see her mother's mood brighten. "Here's my plan. I'll head out to the airport and wait for Mud to turn up. Once I've taken him to Hank's house, I'll give you a call. You can get Linda to bring you over and we'll all have dinner at the ranch." She stopped. "Of course, I haven't asked Hank yet.... but I don't think he'll complain too much." She grinned, but then she caught a look at the clock. "Goodness, I'd better get a move on if I want to get to the airport in time."

*Thursday, February 20, 2003 — 10:00 am*
*Police department, Hammerstone, Arkansas*

Hank McLain was having a rough day of it. He'd been calling the hospital all morning, hoping for news on Jesse Yancy's condition, but no one had anything useful to tell him. And he wasn't making much headway on tracking down the shooter either. So it was hardly surprising that when his phone rang, he answered it with more than a trace of frustration.

"McLain here," he said brusquely into the receiver. At the sound of his caller's voice, though, his mood brightened. "Josh, you old son of a gun. Tell me you've got news I want to hear."

"Could be," the county sheriff drawled at his end of the

line. "You still looking for that blue Ford pickup? Cause we've got one for you. Found it abandoned on old Highway 43, just outside of Buckstaff. Clean as a whistle, the CSI boys tell me. But the tire tracks match the ones your boys sent out over the wire."

Hank whistled in appreciation. "Anything on the owner?"

"Nothing for you there, sorry to say. Turns out it was reported stolen in Ohio a couple of weeks ago. Don't see how we're ever gonna trace the driver."

Hank's bubble of hope burst, but he had another question. "Anything from ballistics?"

"Not yet. But I have something else I want to talk to you about. I got a call from a guy named Holmes, from the FBI. You have anything to do with him?"

"Yeah," Hank said. "The Yancy shooting may be part of a federal investigation that he's spearheading, so we're kind of stuck with him." Hank said carefully. "Hope he didn't ruffle your feathers too much." The sheriff laughed long and hard. "Don't you worry 'bout me, ol' buddy. I never much like it when the feds come in and mess up my investigations. Anything comes back from ballistics on your shooting, you'll be the first to know. That Holmes fella can wait." He was still laughing when he hung up.

*Thursday, February 20, 2003 — 1:00 pm*
*Little Rock National Airport, Little Rock, Arkansas*

Angela got to the airport a few minutes before one. When the 1:00 flight landed, she scanned the passengers as they trickled past the luggage carousels toward the exit. Her patience was finally rewarded when she spotted Murdoch on the escalator, so tall he stood head and shoulders above the

other passengers. His long mane of gray hair was unmistakable, even at this distance. As he reached the foot of the elevator she hurried over to greet him. At the sight of her, he
dropped his briefcase and carry-on and enfolded her in a
happy bear hug.

"You certainly know how to keep my life interesting," he
said as he bent to retrieve his luggage. He steered her past
the gaggle of passengers who stood around the baggage
carousels and the two stepped out into the parking lot. It
always amused Angela that Murdoch only felt comfortable
when he was in the lead, even though, in this case, he had no
idea where he was going. As they walked towards the parking
lot, Angela artfully assumed the lead, and in no time, they
were on the highway back toward Hammerstone.

Once he'd settled himself into her car, he forestalled any
thought Angela might have had about talking on the drive out
to Hammerstone. "I'm a bit tired, Angela. It was a tedious
flight, and I think I'd like a little nap during our drive." Angela
shrugged. "Okay Mud" she said, and pulled out of the lot in
silence. As near as she could tell, Murdoch was sound asleep
before they reached the Little Rock city limits.

*Thursday, February 20, 2003 — 3:30 pm*
*McLain ranch, Hammerstone, Arkansas*

Murdoch didn't reawaken until Angela was pulling into
Hank's driveway. He looked around in some confusion.
"Where've you hijacked me to, young lady?" he asked. "Or
have you and your mother changed residences since my last
visit?"

"No, Mud. I just thought it would be more discrete to settle
you in out here. Think of it as your own personal 'undisclosed

171

location.'" He laughed. "Good enough," he said. "But shouldn't I at least know where I am?"

"Sure thing. I thought I'd stash you with a friend of mine— we're in Hammerstone, and this is the home of the local chief of police." She helped her old mentor retrieve his minimal luggage and led the way into the house. "Now you just settle in the living room for a bit while I call mom and tell her you've arrived. She's chomping at the bit to get out here and visit with you, too."

By the time Linda turned up with Marie in tow, Angela and Mud had already slipped into the comfortable conversational patterns that had marked their friendship for years. Eventually, however, they got around to the business at hand. Murdoch lit up a cigar and regaled the group with his latest adventures. He had reasoned that his friend down at the Arkansas crime lab would eventually have to admit to sending a bit of the mystery powder to him, and that meant that he'd soon pop up on the FBI radar. Knowing that a raid on his lab was becoming increasingly likely, he had moved Marilyn, his best technician, and most of the sample from the crime lab across campus to a friend's laboratory. He kept a small portion of the powder in his own lab so that the feds wouldn't be completely disappointed in their search. "But," he concluded, "they were obviously hoping for more. They wouldn't give up until they had searched everywhere—I'm sure they were hoping to turn up a live sample of the virus. Eventually, and with extremely poor grace, I might add, they confiscated the dead sample and my scanning electron micrographs, and that's the last we saw of them."

Just as Mud was completing his story, Marie wheeled into the room. With her arrival, Angela knew that she wasn't going to get much more out of Murdoch any time soon. While he and Marie got caught up on each other's lives they were hardly likely to pay attention to anybody else. Linda hadn't stuck around after her chauffeuring duties were done, so Angela went into the kitchen to make herself useful by brewing a pot of coffee. That's where Hank found her when he let himself into the house.

"Hey, there," he said with a touch of surprise. "Didn't know if I'd see you out here today." His welcome, though, was genuine. Suddenly he heard the voices coming from the living room. "Who's that?" he asked.

"Well... It's my mom... and Murdoch." Angela had the grace to look both contrite and a little embarrassed. "With all the attention I've been getting from the FBI, I thought maybe..." she flashed her dazzling smile at Hank, "you wouldn't mind letting him stay here for a few days?"

Hank couldn't help laughing at her blatant attempt to wheedle him into this. But, truth be told, he was glad she'd done it. It meant she was taking the situation seriously enough to exercise caution—and after what he'd seen at the Yancy's, caution was more than called for, in his opinion. "It's fine," he said. "Come on, why don't you introduce me to this legend of yours." He led the way out to the living room.

With Hank's arrival, it was once again time to get down to business. After exchanging pleasantries, Murdoch opened the discussion. "I think, before I report on things from my end, you'd better catch me up to date on what's been happening down here."

They took it in turns at first, but soon their stories overlapped, and before they were done, they were interrupting one another to add a missed detail or embellishment to one another's presentations. But everybody fell silent when Hank spoke about yesterday's events. Suddenly, the danger of what they had gotten themselves into became clear. None of them had bargained for people running around shooting off guns.

Murdoch broke the silence. "Given what you've just told us, Hank, I think perhaps that we've been inexcusably naive up to now. We've known all along that the stakes were high, but we've been foolish to believe that we were out of the reach of danger. We must take this danger seriously." He turned to Angela and Marie. "I think you're instincts were right to bring me here to Hammerstone—but I don't think you two should be on your own out in Hot Springs, either." To Hank he said, "Do you think your hospitality could extend itself to two more guests?"

Hank nodded—he had just been about to suggest the same thing himself. "Of course. But we can't just hide out here, waiting for this trouble to pass us by. There's some kind of virus circulating out there, and we're no closer to knowing exactly what it is, where it is, or what it'll be used for."

Murdoch grunted. "I think I can help you with some of those questions." He looked around the room, standing up and facing the small crowd, clearly falling into his familiar role as teacher. This was going to be a long and complicated explanation, and he'd have to tailor the explanation to Hank, with his limited scientific background. He began.

"I think we should begin with a few basic assumptions— that the Hammerstone sickness came from Burns' lab, and that the Yancy boys were the means by which it was spread. That's as good a place as any to start." He paused to consider what he wanted to say next. "The problem with those assumptions is that it means the agent that caused the sickness—the virus, if you will—had to be airborne. That's the only way we can explain its spread so quickly down from the mountain."

"But the problem there is that we don't know of any virus-es—for MS or any other disease—that act this way. This virus would have to fly on the wind like no other and remain stable at ambient temperature for at least an hour or more. This is unheard of. So at first I couldn't imagine how your Hammerstone sickness was spreading."

He turned to Angela once again. "Do you remember our first conversation about this whole mystery?" Angela nodded. "Back then, I considered the possibility of a viral agent to be extremely unlikely. But since then, I've been thinking—and I've had a chance to study Dr. Burns' strange powder rather closely. Now, I think that maybe the key to our conundrum may be found in history—in a strange outbreak of MS that occurred just after World War II." Murdoch looked up at Hank and realized the police chief was looking a little lost.

"The Faroe Islands, off the coast of Scotland, have been important to students of MS for more than 50 years. Prior to the 1940s, there had never been a single recorded case of the disease on the islands. But then the British occupied the islands for five years and everything changed. From 1943 to 1960, 24 cases of MS turned up among the native born Faroese. All of these people had lived in neighborhoods occupied by the British or had had direct contact with them. The only way anybody could explain this phenomenon was by invoking a probable point-source epidemic, with the transmissible agent—whatever it was— brought in by the British, either on their persons or in their baggage. After this brief flurry of cases, and after the British left, the disease seems to have virtually disappeared from the islands. Only one new case has surfaced there since 1960."

Hank nodded. "Okay. But why would only 24 people on the islands get the disease—why not everybody who lived in those British-occupied neighborhoods?"

"No one knows. The best we can do is guess, and our best guess is that there's a genetic component to the disease as well. In other words, only people who've been exposed *and* have some sort of genetic predisposition to the disease will come down with it." He smiled at his audience. "If that's true, we can count it as good news—it means maybe most of the good citizens of Hammerstone won't need to fear that they'll come down with MS symptoms anytime soon. If, that is, the virus was released only that one time, when Luke spilled the powder."

"And that brings me to my next point. Marie, Angela, you both know what MS is all about. But I think Hank here probably needs a little background. Bear with us for a while, okay?" The women nodded solemnly. Hank moved in closer to make sure he didn't miss a word of what was coming next. "Hank, in normal, healthy people, we've got an immune system that vigilantly patrols the cells of our bodies, on the lookout for infection or disease. When it comes across anything that seems to threaten the body's health, that system produces antibodies and white blood cells to kill off the threatening material, restoring the body to health. But there's a small subset of ailments—MS is one of them—that we call autoimmune diseases. That's just a fancy way of saying that the disease makes your immune system go haywire. Instead of attacking outside invaders to your system, your defenses get confused and attack healthy tissue instead." Seeing that Hank seemed to be keeping up with him so far, Murdoch felt he could safely bring his discussion to the next step.

"In a way, this means that your own body's defense mechanism is functioning like an invading virus—because, just like a virus, it's attacking healthy tissue." He saw Hank nod, if a little doubtfully, and decided to forge on. "Well, autoimmune malfunctions like you see in MS can theoretically occur because of something called molecular mimicry—you could take an ordinary, garden-variety virus and splice on a piece of protein that resembles the healthy tissue you want to target. Your immune system knocks itself out trying to wipe out the virus, and eventually it succeeds. But here's where something goes terribly wrong. The immune system doesn't know its job is done. It's been conditioned to look for that protein—a protein shared by healthy tissue—so it just keeps on attacking.

Only now it's not attacking an invading virus—it's attacking your own blood, or bone—or, in the case of MS, the myelin that insulates your nerves.

"See, your nerves are like copper wires, and myelin is like the rubber insulation that surrounds those wires. If the insulation, or myelin, is removed or damaged, the wires short out and things in your brain don't work right. So, for example, if the damage occurs in the part of your brain that controls your left arm, then you will have difficulty moving that arm. It's this attack on myelin that results in the many, varied symptoms of multiple sclerosis."

Hank cleared his throat. "I think I've got it—the basic idea, anyway. And you're saying that this is something Burns created?" Murdoch nodded. "But that still doesn't explain how it spread through town. I don't see how this connects up to that Scottish island story."

Murdoch smiled encouragingly at Hank. "That's perfectly understandable, because there's one more thing I need to explain about our findings in the lab. It may be the most shocking thing of all. Burns not only created a virus that acts as a molecular mimic—it appears that he has also succeeded in creating a true dusty virus." Angela gasped—she understood the implications of Murdoch's pronouncement immediately. Marie and Hank, however, could only muster up mystified looks. "Dusty-virus technology has been the holy grail in bioweapons research for some time now," Murdoch explained. "It vastly multiplies the infectious potential of any disease agent by making it light enough to be carried far and wide on the wind, while remaining stable and virulent long enough to infect potentially huge target populations."

Murdoch continued, his voice grave. "Burns' achievement in manipulating the genetic make-up of his virus to mimic myelin was impressive, but hardly a unique work of genius— any qualified molecular biologist, given enough time, could have done the same. But no one has yet been able to make the virus 'fly' anywhere near as well as Burns did with this one. He added a protein coat to the outside of the virus that catches the wind and stabilizes it at room temperature, at least over the short term. It can float on the breeze for a few hours, infecting people along the way! There's no shortage of terrorist groups who wouldn't like to get their hands on this—not to mention certain government agencies I could name."

"The sample you've been working on, Mud—is it enough to allow you to duplicate Jack's technique?" asked Angela.

"No, not really. The dusty coat was added chemically. What I mean to say is, even though I could reproduce Burns' core virus—the molecular mimic—I couldn't begin to reproduce the dusty coat. For the virus, I've got the DNA sequence to use as a template. But the sample I have is dead—and the recipe for the dusty coat is not coded in the virus itself. The dead virus sample that we have only hints that it was there. I'd need a live sample to analyze before I could begin to try and make a functional copy."

"Then our real danger doesn't come from the disease outbreak at all—no matter how devastating it has been for the people who've fallen sick," Angela said. "The greatest danger is in the delivery system—the dusty-coat biotechnology you've been talking about."

"Exactly," said Murdoch. "While we've got to keep any more of this powder from being released if we want to avoid more outbreaks, we can't stop there. We've got to destroy the powder itself—kill it before anybody else can copy the technology for themselves. I only hope and pray that it hasn't already left the country and fallen outside of our reach."

The room fell silent. At last Marie spoke, again turning to the elderly doctor for his expertise. "But I still don't understand why they put this dusty coat on something that causes MS. Wouldn't you want a bioweapon to be fast acting, to kill people quickly. Why would you want to cause a chronic illness?"

Murdoch shook his head. "I don't know. I can't begin to guess how its makers plan on using it. But its something we'd better try to figure out—and soon."

"By the way, Angela," Murdoch added. "I haven't forgotten the plight of your local patients. I think we still need to make absolutely certain that Burns' virus truly did cause their ailments." Angela nodded. "What do you suggest?" she asked.

"I'd like to send Marilyn blood samples from your full list of infected patients. She's all set to run tests on them to verify if they show evidence of exposure to Burns' virus. If we could get them up to her by Saturday, she could probably have the results ready at the same time her sequencing is complete."

He turned again to Hank. "Speaking of the sequencing, I'd like to call my lab technician up in New York. Marilyn's working on a full DNA sequence of the powder and should have it completed by next Tuesday. She needs to know how to reach me with the results." Hank shrugged his assent, still preoccupied with the deadly import of Murdoch's long lecture.

*Friday, February 21, 2003 — 7:30 am*
*Temporary FBI field office, Hot Springs, Arkansas*

Holmes had spent the better part of last night on the phone with Vince, his National Security liaison. Vince's actual agency affiliation was still a mystery to Holmes—and most likely to all but the highest levels of power. But that didn't matter, as far as Holmes was concerned. The only thing that counted was that Vince *was* power, and as long as he remained in touch with Holmes, then Holmes himself would have access to that power. So Vince had to be kept happy.

Unfortunately, Vince was decidedly unhappy right now. Holmes had reported on the latest information he'd received from the state police, including an update about the APB on the shooter's car. For the first time, Holmes had learned that the driver seen racing out of the driveway after the hit was "Chinese." He immediately made the logical leap—not Chinese, but Korean.

This was not good news. Holmes' orders had been to run this investigation in the background, precisely because Vince wanted to avoid tipping the Koreans off. Otherwise, Holmes' own instincts would have been to simply round up every Korean in the county and treat them all to his interrogation skills. But, it was now clear that the Koreans were aware that their plot was possibly in jeopardy. Why else would they have tried to silence their former errand boy?

Vince had made no bones about it—get the live virus at all costs. Capturing the members of the terror cell was only of secondary importance. There were other, more powerful interests that wanted the dusty virus technology for their very own, private bioweapons collection. As long as the Koreans were unaware that they were being hunted, Holmes could hope for them to slip up, giving him a chance to get the job done. But with them on high alert... well, Holmes knew—and Vince most definitely knew—that the job was going to be that much tougher.

At least, with the need for deep secrecy gone, Holmes could use the kind of old-fashioned police techniques he preferred. Time was getting short and he was getting nowhere by trying to stay under everybody's radar. Since McLain now knew of the Asian connection, he was likely to start getting in Holmes' way, and might even find the shooter first. Holmes intended to beat the police chief to the punch.

He turned to Rosie. "I'm going to need you to get on the horn to Washington. Get me a list of every damn Korean in central Arkansas. Hit every department! I want citizens, green cards, work visas, tourist visas, illegals, all of them!" He looked at the rest of the team. "You're all on this detail," he barked. "As soon as the lists start coming in, you're going out! You're going to find every last name on those lists and grill 'em about their whereabouts last Wednesday."

*Friday, February 21, 2003 — 7:30 am*
*Police department, Hammerstone, Arkansas*

Hank strode into the stationhouse like a man on a mission. Like Angela, he'd been spooked by the seriousness of Murdoch's presentation last night, and this morning he needed some action so that he could shake off the feeling of helpless doom that was threatening to overwhelm him. He spotted Thelma, ever the early bird, already at her desk. He veered over to talk to her.

"Hey, I got a job for you," he said. "I'm tired of spinning our wheels on the Yancy case. I want to find that shooter, and I want to find him *now*. Spike McCollum said the guy in the pick up was Chinese, but we all know how deeply sensitive ol' Spike is to the subtleties of ethnicity." Thelma laughed. "What I need is a list of all the Asians we got in the county," he continued. "We can use phone directories, census lists— and anything else you can think of. After we find them, we're going to talk to each and every one."

"That's a tall order, Hank. We'll have to call in the county police if we want to get it done anytime this year."

"Then call 'em." Hank spun on his heel and marched over to the row of cabinets next to Vern's desk. Reaching across the desk, he opened a cabinet and he grabbed the phone books. "And just so you know," he said to Thelma as he marched through to his own office. "I'm going to be slogging through these dang things right along with you." He went inside and shut the door behind him.

*Friday, February 21, 2003 — 10:00 am*
*McLain ranch, Hammerstone, Arkansas*

Murdoch and Marie were chatting together in the living room of Hank's ranch when Angela entered the room looking troubled. When she joined them on the sofa, they traded glances of concern.

"What's wrong, Angela?" Marie asked.

Angela didn't answer right away. At last she spoke. "I'm just a little confused, Ma. I was tossing and turning all last night wrestling with the idea of what we're doing. It's not so black and white, you know? I mean, there's no question that what Jack did, making this virus, should never have been done. No gray areas there. But the fact is, he *did* make it. The monsters are already out of Pandora's box, and I honestly don't know if we're doing the right thing in trying to kill it. We can't just slam the lid shut again and pretend nobody ever opened it."

"Angela," Mud chimed in, "there are no gray areas here for us. We have responsibilities to our patients. We're healers, and it's our responsibility to destroy the agents of disease wherever we find them. The rest is just political poppycock!"

But Angela wasn't buying that. "It's not poppycock, Mud, it's reality! If our enemies have the technology, they'll find a way to use it against us. You said yourself that we need the live virus to make the dusty coat—but that also means that we need to understand the makeup of the dusty coat in order to defend ourselves."

"Defend ourselves against what, Angela?" Murdoch said.

"We have no proof that the recipe for the dusty coat or the live virus itself has gotten loose. It may never have even left Hammerstone."

"That's just the point. We don't have any proof either way." She paused, then began in a more conciliatory tone. "At least we do agree on one thing. If we could know for sure that destroying the virus would completely destroy the threat, then there's no other choice—we just destroy it." Murdoch nodded and waited for her to go on. "But that brings me right back to the beginning again!" Angela's voice rose in frustration. "How can we ever be sure that we were destroying the entire supply of virus? How can we know we've destroyed the recipe for the dusty coat?"

Murdoch shook his head sadly. "Perhaps we never *can* know. But maybe those aren't the questions we should be asking. Instead, we should simply renounce bioweapons. By renouncing them, we send the world a clear message—these things are evil. Keeping a little of it back, even if only for defensive purposes, dilutes that message. Besides we are only human, Angela. And even the best of us can be tempted."

Angela was grateful for the conversation and glad that she and her mentor had found some common ground. Nothing more could really be done now until they found the virus. Her actions then would be dictated by the circumstances. Still, it helped to think it out in advance, she thought. In the meanwhile, maybe the blood draws and the DNA sequence would shed some light on things.

*Friday, February 21, 2003 — 2:00 pm*
*Linda Tackett's residence, Hammerstone, Arkansas*

Linda's driveway and the surrounding curbside were lined

with cars and when Angela arrived there, she had to park on the side of the road about three houses down. She hadn't gotten halfway up the drive before Linda appeared at the front door, waving her in. "It's about time you got here," Linda said, leading the way through the house and into the dining room.

Angela stood in the doorway and watched the activity for a minute. "Looks to me like you've got everything under control." And it was true. Dolly was working the phones, calling people and sweet-talking them into coming in. Janie was set up at one end of the big mahogany dining room table, drawing the samples one-by-one with machine-like efficiency. Marie was at the other end with Susan, operating the centrifuge that Dolly had brought in from the CARE lab, while Linda, playing gracious hostess, was circling the crowd, offering cookies and orange juice to the patients after they'd finished having their blood drawn.

Just then Dolly hung up the phone and called out to the group. "That's the last one! We've gotten everybody on the list!" She spotted Angela in the doorway and made her way through the crush of patients to her side. "Not bad for short notice, huh?" she said proudly.

"Not bad at all," Angela agreed. "How many have agreed to come in?"

"Everybody!" Dolly grinned. "All of our definite and probable MS cases, from inside *and* outside the funnel area. Even better, Jenn talked some of her healthy neighbors into giving samples, too—so we can check to see if they were exposed, even if they don't have any symptoms." She rolled up her sleeve to show Angela the band-aid that covered a small puncture wound. "And Janie, Susan, and I made our own contributions to the cause. We figure you might want a few samples from people who were outside the exposure zone, too—as a kind of baseline for comparison."

It was clear that the team didn't need her direct participation, so instead she moved around the room, offering help when she could, and talking to each of the confirmed MS patients about getting them started on treatment. By early evening, the last blood had been drawn, and the last sample had been spun in the centrifuge. In the dining room, the team lolled around the table, exhausted but exhilarated by a job well done.

*Saturday, February 22, 2003 — 9:00 am*
*McLain ranch, Hammerstone, Arkansas*

Angela woke up on Saturday morning feeling better than she had for a long time. Yesterday, at Linda's house, she and her team had actually accomplished something important, and helping to pack the blood samples off in the afternoon had given her a sense that maybe they were finally making some progress. That and the crisp clear morning weather helped lift some of the gloom she had felt after Murdoch's revelations about the virus, two days ago.

As she sipped her cup of coffee, she decided to head out to Hot Springs. For one thing, the decision to stay at the ranch— for her and her mom, at least—had been so spur of the moment that they'd had to spend yesterday without even a change of clothes. On top of that, she wanted to visit Jesse. He'd been transferred to the Hot Springs General Hospital after the doctors at Mountain General had managed to stabilize his condition, and she felt bad that she hadn't even visited with him once since then. At breakfast, she announced her plans to the assembled household. While Hank and Murdoch were unsure of the wisdom of Angela making the trip, Marie was overjoyed by the news—she too would welcome a change of clothes and her own toothbrush.

185

## Saturday, February 22, 2003 — 10:00 am
## Hot Springs General Hospital Hot Springs, Arkansas

The trip home was quickly done. Angela grabbed up the few necessities of life that would make her stay at Hank's ranch a little more comfortable, and then was quickly on her way once more. At the hospital she went straight to the intensive care unit, where she knew Jesse could be found. Although the surgeons at Hammerstone's Mountain General Hospital had judged him safe to transfer here, he would still be in need of close, attentive care for awhile yet.

Angela snagged his chart as she entered the ICU. The notes there told a chilling story. Jesse had taken two bullets—one in the belly, one in the chest. The chest wound had missed the young man's heart, thank goodness, but it had nicked his aorta and punctured his left lung, finally coming to rest next to the spine. The stomach wound was equally serious—the bullet had pierced his small intestine before exiting out his back, causing a severe peritonitis.

When she stepped into Jesse's room, she could see that he was still in pretty bad shape. The respirator was doing all his breathing for him, and he didn't seem to register anything going on in the room. She took one of his hands in her own and gave it a gentle squeeze, but Jesse did not reciprocate. She leaned over and whispered a few reassuring words into Jesse's ear, but he was oblivious to her presence. At last she slipped out of the room, realizing that for now, at least, there was nothing she could do for him. It would be a while before he regained consciousness.

POINT SOURCE

*Saturday, February 22, 2003 — 11:00 am*
*Mountain General Hospital Hammerstone, Arkansas*

Back in her car, Angela headed back to Hammerstone. She
still felt sad at the condition she'd found Jesse in, but the visit
reminded her that there was another young man who
deserved a little attention right now. She flipped open her
cell phone and called ahead to Mountain General Hospital—
she was going to drop in on Luke, and she needed permission
to look at his chart when she got there. In no time, she was
pulling her car into the doctors' lot at the small rural hospital.

When she got to the floor, she was pleased to see that
Luke's chart recorded real progress. She could see that three
days worth of high-dose intravenous steroids were helping—
Luke was already regaining some movement in his legs, and he
was starting to try to speak again. He couldn't yet manage
much more than a word or two, but he was improving fast.
Luke's MRI results were in too, showing several plaques consistent with multiple sclerosis. Soon, Luke's doctors could
begin to prescribe one of the new MS medications that would
lessen the likelihood of further attacks.

Armed with this heartening data, Angela found it easy to
muster up a sincere smile when she entered Luke's room.
Though he was still very sick, the prospects of at least a par-
tial recovery were much better than she might have hoped
when she saw him lying there on his bed in the trailer just
four days ago. "So," she said, "how's my favorite
Hammerstone handyman?" Luke responded to her high spirits
with an attempt at a grin of his own.

"You're making a great hit with the nurses, young man," she
went on. At Luke's quizzical look, Angela explained.
"Everybody's talking about how well you're doing. It won't be
long before you'll be ready to ship out of here!" Luke beamed

187

at the news. "Porch?" he managed to say. Angela stopped for a second but then realized that he still had some trouble with dysnomia—he would be mixing up his words for awhile longer. She thought a moment and finally figured out his meaning: When he said "porch," he meant "home." She just continued as if he hadn't made the mistake.

"No, not for awhile yet. But in a week or so, they think you'll be ready to transfer over to Hot Springs General for rehabilitation." She gave him a mock scowl. "That's the hospital where I *work*," she said sternly, "and let me tell you, I make my patients work hard over there. No more goldbricking for you, young man." Her good humor was infectious, and Luke made another effort. "Go'brick'n," he repeated, grinning happily. Angela beamed with encouragement. "Good!" she said enthusiastically.

"Now, you'll still have to take medicine, of course—but you'll be done with that contraption in two days," she pointed to the IV hook up that loomed at the side of his bed. "But in the meanwhile, you're going to start working on getting strong, so that you'll be able to join the rehabilitation program when you get to Hot Springs. Get those muscles working again. And you're going to work with a speech therapist, too. Before long, you'll be chattering like a magpie—we won't be able to shut you up!" Luke's laugh told Angela that her light-hearted, joking approach was just what he needed to hear.

As she headed back to Hank's ranch, Angela wasn't sure who'd been cheered up the most by her visit with Luke. He was a fighter, that boy, she thought—in his own way, he was showing the kind of inner toughness that had carried her own mother through the battle with MS. She pulled into the ranch drive, glad to be back to what was feeling unexpectedly like home.

*Saturday, February 22, 2003 — 11:00 am*
*Yun Luck Restaurant, Hammerstone, Arkansas*

Flanked by Rosie, John Holmes paused on the sidewalk that fronted the Yun Luck Restaurant in Hammerstone. He flipped open his notebook, and scanned his list of the twenty Koreans his team had identified as living in the county. He grunted as he came across the names of the two men whose lives he was about to make miserable: Charlie and Fred Kim—the two of them had been recently hired on as wait staff here at the restaurant. In fact, they were the only Koreans living in Hammerstone. One of these Kims could easily be the shooter who took Jesse Yancy down, Holmes thought, as he headed through the door.

With his usual lack of grace, Holmes burst into the restaurant like a bull. He immediately spotted the owner, who sat at the bar going over yesterday afternoon's receipts, and strode directly over to him, leaving Rosie to follow along in his wake. He peremptorily flashed his ID and demanded to speak to the Kims. Cowed by Holmes' surly tones, the owner called the waiters over, then made himself scarce.

Rosie took up his usual position, arms crossed over his chest, his dark glower directed at the pair of nervous waiters, letting his chief take control of this show. Holmes began deceptively mildly. He asked about their backgrounds, and listened expressionlessly as they told him that they were born in South Korea but emigrated to the U.S. with their parents when they were children. Rosie kept quiet, counting on his bulk and his sullen attitude to work its intimidating magic on the two interrogation subjects. Finally, when he judged that he had let the two waiters chatter on long enough, Holmes snapped his notebook shut.

"This is all crap," he barked, and was gratified to see the

two Koreans flinch in unison at his tone. "What I want to know is, when's the last time you were back in the old country, huh?" He ostentatiously re-opened his notebook to a new page, shielding its contents from the Kim boys' view. "And I want a straight answer—I don't take kindly to liars."

Charlie cast a nervous glance at his brother; but Fred had quickly regained his composure after his involuntary reaction to Holmes' bark. He now stared impassively at his questioners. Seeing no help was coming from his brother, Charlie began to stammer. "We... we went to Seoul last year. To see family." His nervousness was obvious, but nervousness during an FBI interview told Holmes nothing. He glared at Fred, hoping to scare the young man into more details. Fred took the bait, but only to a point—he added "Got homesick. Came home."

Holmes moved on to a new line of inquiry. Questioning the boys in the rapid-fire, staccato style that he used to practice in the mirror when he was young, he grilled them separately on their whereabouts last Wednesday. At one point he thought he had caught the younger brother—Charlie—in a lie but in the end, he had to give it up. He dismissed them in disgust as he huddled with Rosie.

"They got nothing for us, right?" Rosie asked. Holmes agreed. He was already losing interest. These two boys seemed to him to have been a colossal waste of time. Try as he might, he hadn't managed to bully either one of them into saying anything useful. They claimed to have been working the lunch crowd the whole time. Holmes summoned the owner again and quickly verified their alibis with the staff that were summarily assembled before him.

Holmes marched out of the restaurant in disgust, followed closely by Rosie. Outside, he flipped open his pad again. He made a note next to the Kims. "Okay. Two down, 18 to go," he said as he and Rosie got into the car. "Head back to Hot Springs," Holmes said curtly, then leaned back in his seat and closed his eyes.

"Aren't we going to fill McLain in?" Rosie asked, but Holmes merely grunted dismissively. Rosie shifted the car into gear and hit the highway to Hot Springs.

*Saturday, February 22, 2003 — 12:00 noon*
*Police Department, Hammerstone, Arkansas*

Officer Thelma looked up from her desk and gazed out the window of the station, her eyes sore from poring over the telephone directory and recent census data. Unlike the feds, Hank lacked access to the giant federal data banks that would have made this job easier, and he knew that Holmes would not give him that access. No, they had to do it the hard way. Thelma was only grateful that they didn't live near Manhattan—now *that* would have been a heck of a directory to page through, she thought. With a deep sigh, she let her eyes fall on the scenery outside the office, steeling herself for another plunge into the closely printed pages on her desk. Just as she decided she was ready to get back to her boring task, she caught a glimpse of a dark sedan heading out of town toward Hot Springs.

"Hey boss," she shouted. "You'll never guess who's been visiting our fair town today." At his inquiring glance, she added, "Our favorite FBI agent. I wonder what business he had out here."

"All that inter-agency cooperation they've been talking about seems to have been dropped mighty fast," Hank observed. "But then again, I'm not feeling particularly cooperative with that Holmes character myself just now. So I guess I can't complain." Hank parked a hip on Thelma's desk. "How're you getting on with the list?" he asked.

"Probably another hour or so till I get through my part, how about you?" Thelma rubbed her eyes.

"Same here." Said Hank.

"Here's what I've got so far," Thelma said as she handed the list to Hank. He scanned the short list. Even when he added the names he had come up with, the final list looked like it was going to be manageably small—and that, at least, was good news. They might be able to interview everybody within a reasonable amount of time. Of course, they would have to involve the county police, and Hank had already secured their cooperation.

*Saturday, February 22, 2003 — 12:00 noon*
*Highway 37 to Hot Springs, Arkansas*

Although, Holmes seemed to be napping in the passenger seat, he was in fact wide awake and working through what he knew so far of the case. Eventually he came to the target, Bo Li Yeung. Vince had been getting increasingly demanding. Yesterday, he had made it clear that getting a sample of the live virus was paramount, but early this morning he had raised the stakes. They knew that the probable target of this engineered virus, Bo Li Yeung, was due in the area in less than a week. Vince made it clear that the need for the virus even trumped the safety of the target. Yeung was expendable if that was the only way to get their hands on the live virus. "What's one dead politician," Vince had said, "when national security is at stake?" That was fine by Holmes—it made his job that much easier.

*Saturday, February 22, 2003 — 12:45 pm*
*Temporary FBI headquarters, Hot Springs, Arkansas*

Holmes stepped into his headquarters and barked.
"Harrison!" The rookie agent appeared instantly. Holmes barely even favored the young man with a glance. "Got that itiner-
ary for Yeung yet?"

Harrison cleared his throat nervously. "Yes, sir." He looked
down at his notebook and started to read off the information.
"He's taking a commercial flight out of Seoul around 4:00 a.m.
central standard time, Thursday morning. He'll be accompanied by an aide and two South Korean secret service agents. A
third agent is already in Little Rock—arrived about a week ago
to set up advance security. The plane is scheduled to touch
down at Little Rock airport at one o'clock. A limo and a state
police escort of two cars and four motorcycles will be waiting
to take him to the Palace Hotel. Transit time from airport to
hotel should be about twenty minutes, even with traffic. He'll
be at the hotel until 5 o'clock Thursday. Then a limo—again
escorted by state police—will pick him up and take him to
the library. Guards from the state police will be posted at his
hotel room while he's there, and his own secret service will
accompany him up to the dais at the library." Harrison came
to the end of his notes and abruptly fell silent.

Holmes thought a moment. "The points of greatest vulnerability will be when he's on the move—between the plane and
the hotel, and between the hotel and the library. We'll keep
him traveling in regular traffic, so as not to draw any undue
attention to the route, and his exact route will be determined
at the last minute." He paused to let his troops digest his
words, then went on.

"The terrorists' next window of opportunity comes at the
hotel. The weapon's a powder—it would be easy enough to

slip it into his food or even blow it through the air ducts. I'm gonna bring in another twelve agents from the field office to help provide security at the hotel and at the Clinton Library." He looked at the four men who clustered around him. "Each of you'll ride heard on a three-man support team. I expect you to cover this Bo Li's butt like it was your own."

*Saturday, February 22, 2003 — 2:00 pm*
*Police department, Hammerstone, Arkansas*

When their two lists were done, Hank and Thelma had 137 names to check. They could farm out most of the work to the county sheriff's office, but the list of locals was short enough that Hank was sure he and Thelma could handle it themselves.

"Ready to get out of the office for awhile?" Hank asked. Thelma didn't even bother to answer—she was up and pulling on her uniform jacket in a flash. In the car, all she asked was "Where do you want to start?"

Hank glanced at the list, then at his watch. "Let's kill two birds with one stone and grab a late lunch at the Yun Luck."

*Monday, February 24, 2003 — 8:30 am*
*Temporary FBI field office, Hot Springs, Arkansas*

Holmes was late getting to the office this morning and it was just as well, as far as his subordinates were concerned. The last couple of days' work had not gone well. Holmes had handed off the remaining list of Korean suspects to his agents, and they'd spent the last two days interviewing every one of them. But without exception, all the suspects were able to produce alibis for the time of Jesse Yancy's shooting. Holmes himself had left town on Saturday to organize the support team from the Little Rock Field Office that was going to protect Bo Li. It was obvious to all, however, that he had returned to Hot Springs on Sunday night and picked up their reports. By now, he would be well aware that the investigation was back to square one. He would *not* be pleased.

As his car pulled into the lot, everyone in the office suddenly got busy, bracing for his inevitable outburst. But when Holmes stepped through the door, he was smiling. His unexpected good humor left them speechless for a moment, until Rosie got a grip on himself and offered to get the boss a cup of coffee. Their amazement at Holmes' mild mood only deepened when he took the offered coffee mug from Rosie with a gracious "Thanks," and went quietly into his office, closing the door on the buzz of their confused voices.

Holmes took great pleasure in moments like these. He was acutely aware of the confusion he had just caused among his agents, but it amused him to keep them off balance for awhile longer. When you're building a legend for yourself, he thought, it helps to keep the underlings out of the loop.

He settled at his desk and pulled a blank yellow pad into place before him. Out of his breast pocket he produced a scrap of paper covered with names and began to transcribe them onto the pad. Nine of them. Last night he'd called the county sheriff to demand an update on the state and local investigations of the Yancy shooting, and he'd heard about Hank McLain's parallel investigation of the region's Asian community. Sometimes working out of ignorance can score a hit, Holmes thought. Either that, or maybe it's just that Chief McLain has the luck of the devil. Whatever the case, Holmes now had a whole new list of possible suspects. And he'd never have found these guys on his own, he thought, although he would never admit that to anyone.

Holmes rationalized his near-mistake. It was just a case of letting available intelligence and technology drive the investigation—could have happened to anybody. McLain's lack of access to the federal databases and his ignorance about the Korean angle of this case had actually worked to his advantage, forcing him to check out the entire Asian community of Garland County. Instead of just the 20 specifically Korean suspects that Holmes and his team had turned up, McLain had had to wade through 137 Koreans, Vietnamese, Japanese, Chinese—you name it—he'd had to check them all. And out of that bunch, there were nine Chinese men who conspicuously lacked an alibi for the time of Jesse Yancy's shooting. Holmes had pressed the sheriff to follow up on these men today—he'd report back with the results no later than tomorrow. Holmes still believed that the terror threat originated with North Korea, but that didn't mean that the Yancy hit couldn't have been contracted out to somebody else.

Now Holmes actually benefited from all that legwork. He grinned nastily—better to tie up the locals on that kind of work anyway, he thought. He jotted the last of the new suspect names on his pad and marched back out to the common room. Holmes had another idea, but first he needed to get the attention of the team. He walked over to the conference table and announced a briefing. The agents all took their places.

He began by slamming his fist on the table, changing the mood of the room instantaneously. "Not one of you has brought me anything useful on the Yancy shooter," he said, looking intently at his men. "Maybe that job was just too hard for you. Well, we're going to change our approach, people," he said as he began to pace.

"Forget the shooter angle for now. We're going to concentrate on the terrorist cell itself. The North Koreans run a tight ship. Their sleeper cells are dispersed and isolated from each other. Individual terrorists only know the members of their own cell—

that way even if they get caught, they can't give away the plans of any other cell. But they all take their orders from the top.

"This is the classic structure used by terror organizations all over the world. Orders from the central authority are issued through some impersonal medium—a TV or radio broadcast or, most commonly these days, embedded in the graphics of a web page. To make the contact even harder to trace, terrorist foot-soldiers favor using public access computers to check those websites—and it's a good bet our local terrorists are communicating with their bosses back home in this way.

"Now, the CIA keeps lists of websites they think are used for terrorist communications. I'd bet there can't be more than a dozen or so linked to North Korea. We're going to use the list of North Korean websites to smoke our quarry out of the woodwork. Not only is the number of North Korean sites limited, but there can't be more than a handful of likely venues offering public computer access—this is Garland County, Arkansas, after all. You guys are going to find them all—internet cafes, libraries, copy centers—and check out their records—we want to know which ones, if any, are frequented by Korean customers.

"As soon as you come up with a workable list of access venues, give it to me. I'll get warrants to seize the suspect machines and ship 'em to Quantico for a search of their usage records. That'll tell us if any of the computers have been used to visit the suspected Korean sites and it'll give us the screen name of the users who made the visits. Once we know those, we can make the service providers cough up the users' *real* names." He glared balefully at his team. "Think maybe you can handle that?" Without waiting for a response, he stalked off.

Richard G. Pellegrino

*Tuesday, February 25, 2003 — 7:00 am*
*Federal courthouse, Hot Springs, Arkansas*

At the edge of Bathhouse Row, the federal building clashed only slightly with the imposing Greek Revival architecture of its neighbors. Within its walls, the walnut-clad courtrooms and judges' chambers were hushed, reflecting the serious business that was conducted there. In one such room, John Holmes stood impatiently before the federal magistrate for the Western District of Arkansas, chafing with irritation as the jurist slowly deliberated over the request for search warrants that lay on the desk before him.

Holmes silently urged the judge to get on with it. He saw no reason why this old man should be taking so long to make such a no-brainer decision. He needed the warrants to search and seize the computer hard drives at the three internet cafés frequented by Garland County residents of Korean descent. Couldn't the judge see the urgency? Didn't he know that the records of websites visited, as well as the e-mail traffic on the servers was erased from the computer hard drives by all three cafés every few days as a matter of policy? Holmes needed to recover them right away, and that meant confiscating the drives and sending them to Quantico.

The judge continued his slow perusal of the request for warrants, pausing at times as he reread particular passages. Holmes thought he could guess where the problems were going to be—he'd had to fudge his details at a couple of points to make his case against the Korean visitors—there were four in all—appear stronger than it was in fact. There was no direct evidence linking any of them to any known crime, but circumstantial evidence pointed toward the involvement of Korean agents in Garland County. The judge would want more than that, however, and Holmes had tried to oblige. He hard-pedaled the way the suspects so closely fit the profile of terrorists and hoped that this would be enough to win the day. Now it looked as though it might not be enough.

At last, the judge looked up from his reading, leaned back on his bench, and regarded Holmes silently, with obvious distaste. "I must say that I find the rationale for the warrant more than a little skimpy," he said disapprovingly. Holmes bit back an angry retort. He needed the judge's approval, and he wouldn't get it if he betrayed a hint of the lack of respect he was feeling right now.

The judge appeared not to notice Holmes' mounting anger. "I don't know, Agent Holmes, I am not altogether comfortable with the clear relaxation of judicial standards that you are requesting here." He paused, then shook his head sadly. "But, I'll allow it. For the present, we seem to have no other recourse." Indulging himself in a sigh of resignation, he picked up a pen and scrawled his signature on the bottom of the warrants.

Holmes snatched the signed warrants with almost obscene haste and turned to leave the chambers. He was anxious now to put the documents to use—he wanted to get the hard drives shipped to the Quantico computer labs no later than this afternoon. Back on the street, Holmes punched a number into his cell phone. "Got the warrants," he barked at the agent who answered. "Round up the team and meet me at the West End Internet Cafe in ten minutes."

When Holmes arrived at the cafe, his tech team was already waiting on the sidewalk in front of the entrance. They entered together, and while Holmes shoved his signed warrant into the face of the protesting owner, two network specialists were hard at work. The cafe's six internet ports were set up on a single row of tables, and the two technicians made their way methodically through each one. A quick check of the undeleted records of the last few days produced no immediately useful results, however, so the team began disconnecting the terminals one-by-one, while a couple of additional agents followed behind and packed the hard drives for shipment.

The work at the West End Internet Cafe was completed with surprising speed—within 30 minutes, the team was on its way to the second establishment covered by the warrants, and within another hour and a half, they'd finished up at all three of the cafes that had been frequented by the Koreans. By lunchtime, Holmes was settled in for a bagel at the Ambrosia Bakery and his confiscated booty was en route to the Little Rock Airport, where a courier waited to hand-deliver it to Quantico. With any luck, the lab boys in Virginia would be working on the hard-drive dump by early evening, and the results should be available within 24 hours or so.

The success of his team's raid on the computers had restored Holmes to good humor, and he was nearly smiling as he flipped open his cell and punched in the number of his shadowy colleague back in D.C. After he made his report to Vince, he pocketed his cell and tucked into the remains of his lunch with an enthusiasm he hadn't felt in days. Everything was coming together smoothly now—he was sure of it. And when this was over, he would surely have shown the pinheads in Washington how to do business.

*Tuesday, February 25, 2003 6:00 pm*
*FBI Computer Forensics Laboratory, Quantico, Virginia*

By the time Special Agent in Charge Holmes was having his first beer in the Arlington Hotel bar that evening, Special Agent Ross Turnery, head of computer forensics for the bureau, was taking delivery of Holmes' hard drives. Holmes had called him nearly every fifteen minutes since the plane carrying these drives had landed at Reagan National, so the first thing Turnery did was to call Holmes on his cell to get him off his back.

This done, he settled himself at his workstation, opened the package and extracted the first hard drive. He began the laborious process of sequentially searching its shadow data—data that, though once erased, still existed in fragmented form, hidden from view—for any traffic that linked the drive's users to the suspect North Korean websites on the CIA watch list. It was going to be a long night, he thought to himself, but if SAC Holmes would leave him alone, maybe he and his team would be able to finish.

*Wednesday, February 26, 2003 — 5:00 pm*
*McLain ranch, Hammerstone, Arkansas*

When Hank had left the house this morning to go into work, he'd had high hopes that maybe this would be the day that his luck would turn on the Yancy shooting investigation. The ballistics report was due in, and although his own interrogation of local Asian men hadn't turned up anything useful, he thought that maybe the county boys had come up with something. But when Hank got to the stationhouse, all he got was more disappointment. Everybody back at the ranch was expecting him to bring back at least some kind of news they could use, but that was just not going to happen. Rather than return completely empty-handed, he stopped off at the local bake shop.

Home again, he tried to unlock the front door of his house, but his efforts were hindered by the sack of Mueller's donuts and raft of papers he was trying to juggle. Murdoch swung the door open and grabbed the donuts, then led the way to the kitchen where Marie and Angela waited expectantly for his news. When Hank didn't say anything right away, Murdoch could no longer hold his tongue. "Well?"

"Sorry, gang, but it looks like we've hit another dead end. Ballistics could identify the type of gun used, but that's about it. And none of the nine Asians without an alibi panned out. The county boys feel that was a dead end. We're no closer to identifying the shooter than we were a week ago."

Murdoch clucked his tongue in sympathy. "I'm sorry you had so little luck," he said. "But maybe you'll feel better when you hear my news. I got a call from Marilyn, up at the lab. Very cloak and dagger-ish; she said she was calling from a pay phone at a gas station, for goodness sake." He smiled at the absurdity of the picture. "At any rate," he continued, "Marilyn said she'd be faxing us some data soon. As she put it, she was first going to 'drive around for a while to shake off any tails.'" He chuckled. "Unless she had a whole lotta shaking to do, she should be sending the first transmission over any minute now." He smiled and then looked apologetically at Hank. "I took the liberty of giving her the fax number in your study—I hope that's okay."

"Fine with me," Hank said. "What're we likely to be looking at, when she sends it?"

"The mother-lode, in a sense," Murdoch replied. "She's not only got the results on the blood work we sent her, she's also got the DNA sequencing done." As if on cue, the telltale whooping and beeping of a fax connection emanated from Hanks study. They moved in near unison down the hall.

In unspoken agreement, everybody deferred to Murdoch, who took his place by the fax's outbasket. As the pages purred through the machine, he scanned them closely, then handed them over to Angela. After all the blood test results were in, everybody moved back to the living room while the DNA sequence continued to come over the fax. Murdoch spent a moment reviewing the last sheet of paper, then looked up at his assembled friends.

"Well. Let's not waste time beating around the bush," Murdoch said, as the fax machine in the other room fell silent. "In a nutshell, every blood sample drawn last week tested positive." In a subdued voice, Angela echoed him. "Every... last... one," she said falteringly.

"Wait a minute," Hank spoke up. "Didn't you include blood from some people who weren't even sick?" Angela nodded. "What about them?" he asked.

Angela continued. "Positive. They're all positive. People who've fallen sick, people who haven't. People who live in the funnel, people who just visited there. All positive." Angela looked bleak. "The only negative results were the samples we drew from ourselves—Susan's, Janie's, and Dolly's."

Marie, too, looked shaken. "Angela," she asked gently, "are you saying that everybody—every living soul—who happened to be in the funnel on that day has been exposed to the virus?"

"Quite possibly," Angela said reluctantly. "Clearly, everyone we tested was. But, on the bright side, it looks like only some of the exposed people came down with the illness." She tried out a wan smile.

"The bright side? How do you know there's a bright side?" Hank's voice betrayed his concern. "Maybe they're just late-bloomers! Maybe we'll start seeing a whole new wave of the disease." He turned from the group, struggling to master his anger at the attack some nameless monsters had made on his town, his neighbors.

Angela went to Hank and put her hand on his shoulder. When he turned to her, she looked closely into his eyes. "It's hopeful because there just might be some people who are—well, immune to it, in a way. These people were exposed to the virus. They made antibodies to fight it, but their bodies *didn't* get fooled by the molecular mimicry that Murdoch described a few days ago. Their antibody against the myelin-mimic didn't go on to attack the real myelin in their brains. Like Jesse, for example."

Murdoch nodded. "Of course, we need to do a lot more research to understand why this happens, but suffice it to say that not everyone who is exposed will get sick—and that *is* good news. Who knows, this may teach us something about how to protect people from the real disease!"

For a moment, everyone was silent, contemplating the seriousness—and the hope—in Murdoch's words. Suddenly, Angela changed the subject. "What about the sequencing?" she cried. "Maybe that'll give us something we can use to fight this thing!"

Murdoch quickly went back to the fax machine and pulled the pages, carefully studying them as he made his way back to the living room. When he arrived there, he stood and stared at the sheets for what seemed like an eternity. When he looked up, he looked mystified. "You know, if I didn't have the highest confidence in Marilyn, I'd say she must have messed up the sequence—or that she was playing some kind of joke on us."

"Why, Mud?" Angela asked.

"Well, you know that all DNA contains what we call nonsense code." At Hank's look of confusion, Murdoch amended his statement. "Maybe that's not as widely known as I implied—but take my word for it, Hank. Everybody's DNA includes strings of genetic material that don't seem to do anything—they don't make enzymes, they aren't implicated in any bodily function. We call these DNA sequences 'nonsense DNA' because nobody understands what they mean."

"And you're seeing nonsense DNA in the sequence Marilyn sent?" Angela's voice held a note of impatience. "So what's the big deal—like you just said, nonsense DNA is a well-documented phenomenon."

"It's not the fact that the virus contains nonsense DNA

that's mystifying me," he said. "It's the sequence of the non-sense DNA." He rifled through the sequence printout, found one of the pages he sought, and handed it to Angela. "Just take a look at that—tell me what you see."

Angela was momentarily speechless. When she continued to stare at the page without comment, Murdoch looked at the rest of his companions and continued. "While it's not unusual for DNA—nonsense or otherwise—to contain repetitions of a few bases, this sample shows a pretty remarkable string—there are a great number of repetitions of a single nonsense string: C-A-T-T-A-G.

Murdoch was at first gratified that everybody seemed appropriately stunned by his revelation—but as the moments spun on and nobody spoke, he realized that perhaps he was missing something that the others already knew. "What is it?" he asked worriedly. "Was it something I said?"

It was Angela who recovered first, and when she spoke, it was Murdoch's turn to be shocked. "Mud—it's not nonsense," she said. "It makes all the sense in the world." She turned and left the room. Murdoch watched her go, confused. Marie wheeled over to him and took his hand. "Don't worry, Murdoch," she said. "Angela knows what she's talking about. We just never got around to filling you in on another of our recent mysteries, because we didn't see how it connected."

"Okay," Murdoch said. "So how about bringing me up to speed now?"

"Burns e-mailed Angela a computer game he wrote a month before he died in that explosion last New Year's. The name of the game was Cat Tag."

Any further comment he might have made was interrupted by Angela's call, summoning everyone to her makeshift computer station in Hank's spare bedroom. She had already shot through the cats a few days ago and had saved the game at the password screen.

Angela swiveled her chair around, temporarily turning her back on the computer screen so that she could face Murdoch. "Ever since this began, I naturally thought that Cat Tag referred to that silly game, but it doesn't. It refers to a DNA sequence. That changes everything. I played the cat game and got nowhere, because I could never figure out the password."

"And now you think you can?" Hank caught a touch of Angela's anticipatory excitement.

"Yup," she said. "The clue is in Marilyn's sequence data. The C-A-T-T-A-G nonsense DNA." Murdoch caught her meaning and nodded his agreement. "I'll wager you're right," he said.

"So tell *us*," Marie and Hank nearly shouted in unison.

Instead of answering, Angela put the cursor on the password box, typed G-T-A-A-T-C, and hit the enter key. All at once the screen went black. "We're in," she said. "Now we've got to wait for the *real* puzzle to load."

"Huh?" Hank and Marie expressed their mystification in unison.

Chuckling, Angela turned to her mentor. "Do you want to explain it, Mud, or shall I?"

"Let me start, at least," Murdoch grinned at Hank and Marie. "It's really very simple. Pretty much everybody today knows that DNA is made up of two strands—like the two sides of a ladder, joined together by its rungs. Only the ladder-like structure of DNA is extremely long, and it's twisted to form a double helix." Seeing that his audience was following him so far, Murdoch warmed to his theme. "Okay, then. Visualize this ladder-like structure—ignore the twists for a minute—and focus on the points where the ladders sides are joined—on the rungs, so to speak. These rung-like structures are, in fact, made up of specific nucleic acids. There are only four found in DNA: cytosine, guanine, adenosine, and thiamine. To save time, scientists refer to each of these by their initials: C, G, A, T."

"Those letters are suspiciously familiar," Hank offered.

"Right," Angela said. "They're the letters that make up the name of Jack's game."

"And you reshuffled them to come up with the password." Hank wasn't asking anymore, merely observing. But now he stopped, again mystified. "But how did you know precisely what order to type in the letters?"

Murdoch took up the tale once again. "That's where it helps to know about DNA structure. To form the "rungs" on the DNA ladder, two nucleic acids have to join—one sticking out from each side of the ladder. But there's a rigid order to the joining of these acids. Cytosine will never join with adenosine, and thiamine will never join with guanine. It's always C to G, and A to T."

And now it was Angela's turn to complete the explanation. "I just substituted the complementary letters. When you substitute the letters in C-A-T-T-A-G with their complementary DNA partners, you get...."

"G-T-A-A-T-C!" Hank and Marie roared out the answer in unison. Just then, a series of whirs emanated from Angela's laptop and everyone's eyes turned to the screen, where something finally seemed to be happening.

Slowly, an image began to emerge on the screen. Where once a plethora of crudely cartooned cats had appeared, far more sophisticated graphics were forming. The computer speakers came to life, and Angela immediately recognized the opening strains of Beethoven's fifth symphony, as fiery letters formed the words "A Journey Through Hell With Dante."

In a moment, the music faded away, and the fiery letters began to waver as a new screen image prepared to load. The screen gave way to a graphic of a deep, dark cave. Across the top of the cave's entrance, a banner carrying the classic warning from Dante's Inferno appeared: "Abandon all hope, ye who enter here." Suddenly, Angela was startled by the sound of a familiar voice from her speakers. "Congratulations, Angela. I am quite impressed. Now that you're here, I do so want to share with you the story of what I've done. But you'll have to earn the right to hear it. My life has been hell these last many years, so now it's your turn. If you want to know my secrets, you'll have to work your way through hell, and out the other side." As Burns' voice droned on, Angela's screen changed once again, shifting to a character creation panel. She saw she had the choice of playing as Dante Alighieri or Virgil.

A veteran of role-playing games, Angela quickly selected and equipped her character—she chose Virgil—and clicked the "start new game" button. Again she had to wait as the next chunk of game code loaded. Jack had clearly made huge progress in the sophistication of his graphics, but to judge by the long load times when the game had to change screens, he was still writing clumsy, overly redundant code.

While she waited, Angela spoke over her shoulder to her friends. "It seems clear to me that Jack has based this game on Dante's *Inferno*. More than likely, he's created his own graphic version of hell, and expects the player to traverse it, just like Dante does in the book, with Virgil as his guide. That means there are probably nine levels to the game—corresponding to the nine circles of hell described by Dante. That's not too bad—most role playing games involve far more levels. Still, if Jack was any good at making this game challenging, I may be at it for a few hours, at least."

Suddenly, Angela found herself facing a shadowy, claustrophobic landscape, as if she were looking through the eyes of her character. She set her character moving forward, deeper into the virtual cave, and as she felt herself being drawn into the challenge of the game, her awareness of the friends who stood behind her chair faded. When they left her, she was midway through Hell's third circle. She never even noticed that they'd gone.

Single-mindedly guiding her character through the game's maze, Angela found herself increasingly appreciative of Jack's inventiveness. The levels were growing ever more difficult to beat. By the time she finished the seventh circle of Hell—reserved for violent sinners—Virgil was definitely looking the worse for wear. She plugged on anyway, navigating her character through the maze and fending off attacking characters as she went. It was another hour—closing in on two a.m.—before she made it out the other end of the eighth level and saved her game. She leaned back in her chair and rubbed her weary eyes—she'd been afraid even to blink during the action of that last series of virtual battles.

She was startled by a noise behind her and spun round in her chair. "Oh—it's just you," she said with a nervous laugh.

"Just checking to see how you're doing," said Hank. "And I thought you might like this." He offered her the cup of tea he carried. Angela took it gratefully. "No matter what anybody thinks—beating a game like this is tough work," she said. "And there's still the final level to go." She rubbed her eyes again. "But I think I'm going to need a break before I tackle it. After staring at the screen for so long, I'm starting to see double."

Hank nodded and began to back out of the room. As he left he said, "Feel free to stretch out on the couch in here—want me to wake you in a couple of hours?"

"I don't think you'll have to," Angela said. "One of the benefits of med school training is that you learn the skill of cat-napping pretty early on. I just need to rest an hour or so and I'll get right back into the game." As Hank closed the door behind him, she settled herself on the sofa, murmuring to herself "just an hour—that's all I need." Within moments, she was asleep.

*Thursday, February 27, 2003 — 4:20 am CST*
*Seoul, South Korea*

A day ahead, and half a world away, a small motorcade made its way through the early evening, passing swiftly through the streets of Seoul on its way to the Incheon International Airport. Bo Li Yeung reclined comfortably in the back of the sleek limousine, oblivious to the group of agents who shared the car with him. His eyes half-closed, he seemed completely calm—no one would imagine him to have been the recipient of dozens of threats in the past few days alone, all warning him to cancel his plans and end his crusade for Korean unification.

When the limo pulled up on the tarmac, a team of airline representatives were there to greet him. With a minimum of fanfare, he allowed himself to be escorted onto the plane, took his seat in the first-class cabin, and gazed moodily out the window. The flight before him would be long, and he was impatient for it to be over. At 7:00 p.m. Korean time, the pilot started the planes great engines, and moments later Bo Li Yeung, and the hopes of the reunification movement, were aloft and flying northeast toward Little Rock, on the first leg of a ten-stop U.S. tour.

*Thursday, February 27, 2003 — 6:00 am*
*Yun Luck Restaurant, Hammerstone, Arkansas.*

The shabby room above the Yun Luck restaurant was still wreathed in pre-dawn shadows when Charlie Kim awoke with a start from a nightmare he could only half remember. He looked over at his still-sleeping brother, envious of Fred's stoicism. Nothing seemed to get to Fred—even the interrogation by the FBI had left him unmoved. For Charlie, though, that had been the beginning of a mounting anxiety he couldn't seem to get on top of. He couldn't bear the thought that all their work, all their planning, might go to waste. He spent a few more fitful minutes in bed, and then resigned himself to greeting the day, if not with a smile, then at least with a shower.

Fred woke to the sound of the shower water running. He jumped out of bed with the anticipatory energy of a child on Christmas morning. This was going to be a good day. As he walked barefoot to the kitchen, he yelled out to his brother, "Coffee?" No answer. Undaunted he set the pot brewing, then switched on the TV to catch CNN's morning headlines while he waited. He ignored the fatuous "happy talk" of the anchors as they blathered on about the latest celebrity scandal and instead intently watched the text crawling across the bottom of the screen. At last he saw what he was looking for—the Associated Press report that Bo Li Yeung was indeed going to make his speech today, in spite of possible threats against his life. The crawling headline had just disappeared to the left of the screen when Charlie emerged from the shower. Fred looked up at him and smiled. "Looks like we're good to go" he said.

*Thursday, February 27, 2003 — 6:15 am*
*McLain Ranch, Hammerstone, Arkansas*

In the back room at Hank's house, Angela's virtual character finally defeated the last guardians of Hell's ninth circle—the traitors' circle—and emerged into a sunlit scene of green grasses and clear skies. Somewhat surprised by the sudden ending, she let out a shriek of relief more than joy. It was over, or was it only beginning? Sitting back, she inhaled deeply and then slowly exhaled as she felt all the tension drain from her body. She paused a moment to savor the sensation.

But soon the tension returned. Fighting her way out of the nine circles of hell had been fantasy. Now came the hellish reality. As she waited with anticipation, the sunlit scene on her computer screen faded.

Before her appeared what could only be called Dr. Jack Burns' personal manifesto. As she strained to read the scrolling diatribe, her eyes widened in horror. There, in black letters on the glowing white screen, were the details of Burns' deluded work, and the rambling, bitter rationalizations of a man who had long ago lost his sense of humanity. She felt a pang of sorrow and loss that her old colleague had fallen so far, but her sympathy was more than tempered by her anger and fear. The message went on for several minutes, the author growing more delusional as the seconds ticked by.

Despite it's grandiosity, it was full of detail; written, it seems, more to impress the reader with his brilliance than to be used to save lives. Burns knew that if Angela read this while he was alive, he would end up in jail for a long time. But, in his arrogance, he was sure that would never happen. He knew that the game couldn't be opened without the password, and that the clue to the password, locked as it was in the DNA of the virus itself, would only be known if the gig was up.

Angela was agitated now. She quickly got up and peeked into the living room and the kitchen. No one was up yet. Good, there was still time to make a plan. She returned to the study, brought the manifesto up again, and sent it to the printer. As Burns' words whisked their way down the cable to the print buffer, Angela sat down on the couch and began to think about those words, and how they would affect her actions in the next few hours.

The target was Angela's old college friend Bo Li Yeung, and the virus had been right here in Hammerstone all the time. According to plan, it was to be kept by a pair of North Korean terrorist agents—Charlie and Fred Kim—in their apartment above the Yun Luck Restaurant, until it was time to be put to use. Then it was to be transported to Little Rock to be rigged to the heating duct in Bo Li's hotel room. The plan was so clear, so complete—the only thing wrong with it was that, according to Burns, it should have happened two months ago. Throughout his screed he'd mentioned December dates. "Of course!" Angela slapped her forehead as realization dawned. "That's when Bo Li was first scheduled to appear!"

But Bo Li had cancelled that trip, Angela remembered. So maybe the terrorists had had to change their plans. Again, realization hit her suddenly—the visit had just recently been rescheduled! Bo Li was making his talk sometime soon. She wracked her brain, knowing that she'd heard the announcement, but momentarily unable to recall the new lecture date. "Oh, my God," she said when her memory finally kicked in. "It's today!" She looked at her watch: 6:30 a.m. There might still be enough time to stop the terrorists. But, it wasn't that simple—they had to make sure they got the virus, too.

She took a deep breath and paused, remembering again the argument she had had with Murdoch on the ethical destruction of the virus. "If we can be sure to seize all of the virus— and the formula for making more—then we're justified in destroying it all, so *no one* would ever be able to use it," she said aloud.

She looked back at the screen where Burns' words still glowed. He claimed that he had sent the instructions for making the virus back to North Korea, but that he'd left out a few steps. He'd been afraid that if he sent the actual instructions, his masters would decide that he was expendable. That meant the science for the virus and its delivery system had not left

213

the country. As for the actual virus—he'd made only six vials of it. That would be what Jesse and Luke picked up back in November. Again according to Burns, none of that was to be used until after the attack on Bo Li, so it might just still be here in Hammerstone. Angela shuddered. The course was clear. They needed to destroy the virus and they needed to do it now.

Lost in these thoughts, she went out to the kitchen, where she found Hank making coffee. She began excitedly. "I beat the game, Hank, and things are worse than we thought.... But we might still have time."

She launched into a breathless summary of what she had read and the conclusions that she had come to. "The Yun Luck," he said. "There is not much time, Angela. I'd better go now," he said moving towards the door. But Angela put out a hand to stop him.

"Hank—we can't just arrest these guys. We need to get the virus, too. Otherwise, we'll never know what happens to it." Hank stopped and looked at her uncertainly. "If you just arrest them, the FBI will have to come in," she continued. "They'll confiscate the virus—and its delivery system. They'll be able to make more." She drew a deep breath. "But if we can find it all and destroy it first, then nobody will ever be able to use it again!"

"Then you'd better come along," Hank said. "Destroying the virus is more in your line of work than mine." Angela left a short note for her mother and Murdoch before she and Hank hurried out to the squad car.

The ride to town was short, but it gave Hank plenty of time to put a plan of sorts into motion. Hank felt that the Kims were unlikely to break with their usual routine until the last possible moment. That meant that the Koreans probably wouldn't head out for Little Rock until it was time to meet Bo Li's plane. To do anything else would be to risk getting caught. But he needed to cover himself in case he was wrong. He radioed the station and ordered Vern to stake out the highway on-ramp car while Thelma kept watch on the restaurant itself. As the squad car entered the town limits, Hank hung up his radio transmitter and turned to Angela. "Terrorists in Hammerstone! I still can't believe it!" But even as Hank spoke the words, his face grew grim. "If your friend, Mr. Yeung is the target, why don't they just shoot him?"

"I've been thinking about that all along, and I think I've finally come up with an answer. Bo Li is a powerful figure because he's so charismatic and so well-loved by his follow-ers—his following is huge. But, although his policies are truly visionary, it's the force of his personality, not his policies, that have carried him this far. If he were assassinated, he'd become a martyr to his cause—an inspirational figure that others might try to emulate. The North would want to prevent that at all costs. Better simply to render him incapable of taking office. That calls for a stealth weapon—something that can remove Bo Li from the political scene with no one the wiser. Sure, he'd get some sympathy for his tragic illness, but he'd be sidelined. And even that sympathy can work in favor of the terrorists. Bo Li's followers would likely resent anybody who tried to shove him aside and take his place."

"And you think maybe we have time to stop them?" Hank sounded doubtful. "What if there's a different target? What if these boys already shipped the stuff back to Pyongyang or wherever...?" he let his voice trail off.

"If it's gone, it's gone," Angela said. "But Burns didn't think the virus itself was intended to leave the country. He was commissioned to produce a fairly small quantity—the actual virus was to stay here." Her voice grew hard. "And now, we need to destroy it."

*Thursday, February 27, 2003 — 6:30 am*
*Downtowner Hotel, Hot Springs, Arkansas*

Awakening in his hotel room, Holmes prepared to greet a new day, and his mood was black. Thirty-six hours had past and still no results from the hard drives. On top of that, his last conversation with Vince was still painfully clear in his mind. Vince had been difficult, criticizing Holmes' handling of the case so far, and threatening to replace him if he didn't get things resolved swiftly. Now Holmes was chomping at the bit, forced to wait for the computer forensics results. He could only hope and pray that they'd point him in the right direction.

*Thursday, February 27, 2003 — 10:00 am*
*Yun Luck Restaurant, Hammerstone, Arkansas*

The morning set-up crew was hard at work getting ready for Yun Luck's lunch crowd. Fred and Charlie were in particularly good spirits, much to the surprise of their fellow workers. This was going to be their last day in Hammerstone, and they had that peculiar lightheadedness that one gets on the last day of a job that has become distasteful. Once the attack on Bo Li was successful, they hoped to slip away, back into the shadows to await a new assignment.

At precisely ten o'clock however, their mood turned sour. From his vantage point down the street, Hank radioed Thelma and gave her new orders: go in and re-interrogate the wait staff of the Yun Luck until she heard from him again. Officer Wilkins walked through the front door and spoke briefly to the owner, Mr. Woo, before moving further into the dining room.  Mr. Woo came to stand by her side, then clapped his hand loudly to call the entire staff together.

Fred and Charlie took their seats nervously as a few stragglers from the kitchen came out to join the small crowd in the dining room.  Charlie fingered his collar nervously, and thought for a brief moment of bolting for the door.  One look at Fred, however, put that thought right out of his head. They'd just have to tough this out, Charlie thought, eyeing Thelma warily.  Thelma began to question the group.

Once he was sure that Thelma had things under control in the restaurant, Hank put a quick call on the radio to Vern, ordering him back to the Yun Luck.  He checked his watch: 10:07 a.m.  He turned to Angela and gave a quick nod.

Silently they both got out of the car and made their way to the back of the restaurant building.  They stopped a moment for Hank to get his bearings.  Before them was the restaurant building itself. Behind them was the back end of an old abandoned feed store, which blocked them from the casual view of passers-by on the street.  He turned to Angela. "Maybe you'd better stay down here and keep watch," he said, but before the words were fully out of his mouth, he could see she was having none of that idea.

"You don't even know what you're looking for up there," she said. "Or what to do with it when you find it." She shook her head decisively. "No. We go in together."

Hank bowed to the inevitable and led the way to the iron fire escape. He moved swiftly up to the dark window on the second floor, with Angela following closely on his heels. At the top, he found the window had been left open an inch. He slid the window up noiselessly. As he stepped over the low sill, Angela took a last nervous glance at the alley below to make certain that their actions were unobserved by passers-by. As she let herself into the room behind Hank, she shivered—with this action, she had left legality behind.  It would matter little that her partner in crime was the chief of police—he'd no doubt be sharing the defense table, facing the same charges of breaking and entering as she was.

Angela's worries were interrupted by Hank's whispered, "Come here." Looking around, she saw that they had entered through what served as the Kim's bedroom. Two cots stood side by side, neatly made up. Otherwise, the room was largely bare. Against one wall stood a crude wooden dresser. On the same wall, a couple of hooks held the starched white shirts that the Kims wore when working downstairs at the restaurant. She moved to Hank, who had pressed himself against the door on the far wall. As she opened her mouth to speak, he raised a finger to his lips. Just in case there was someone else in the apartment, or in the hallway beyond, it would be best if they were as quiet as possible.

Slowly, gently, Hank eased the door outward, his eye to the widening crack so that he could scan the scene of the room beyond. Suddenly he grinned and pushed the door fully open. "No one!" he whispered. "But we should still be quiet as mice." He stepped through the door, and Angela followed.

They found themselves in another small room, this one obviously doing double duty as kitchen and living area. Angela scanned the bleak decor. The furniture was, almost exclusively, the kind of stuff you'd pick up at the thrift shop—a tattered sofa that had probably ended its last life in a frat house and a wobbly card table flanked by a couple of folding wooden chairs. But in the kitchen area, the refrigerator stood out in stark contrast to its fellow furnishings. It alone was brightly, shiningly new. A high-end appliance if she'd ever seen one. She moved directly to it, motioning Hank to stand back. If the viral samples were poorly corked and stored, she didn't want to expose him.

Angela took a deep breath and grasped the refrigerator handle, then pulled the door open decisively. Inside, in solitary glory, stood the red-and-white cooler that Jesse had described.

"This is it," Angela breathed as she gingerly lifted the cooler off of the shelf.

"What now?" Hank asked. But Angela was already way ahead of him. Swiftly, carefully, she carried the package across the kitchenette to the gas stove, Hank following closely behind. She opened it to check if all six canisters were there. Yes! "We've got to kill the virus," she said, switching the oven on and twisting the temperature dial. "Heat will do the job—even room temperature, over time. But we don't have time to wait. We need to take a short cut—a couple of minutes at 325 ought to do it." She caught herself tapping the stovetop nervously and willed herself to stop. "We don't want to risk bursting the glass with too high a temp—and who knows if there are weaknesses in any one of the flasks." She seemed to be talking more to herself than to Hank, talking her way through her plan. "When I tell you, start handing me the flasks, one at a time. We'll just cook those bugs to death."

One by one, Hank unscrewed the tops of the canisters, pulled out the flasks and handed them to Angela. She placed them into the now-hot oven, giving each a good couple of minutes to bake the dangerous virus they contained into a harmless state. After the fifth had been done, and it stood with its mate to cool on the counter, she reached back to Hank expectantly.

"What?" he said. "That's all of them." "There were only five. The last canister is empty!"

Angela gaped at him, then rushed back to the refrigerator and tore it open. "That *can't* be! Burns' screed mentioned six!" But the fridge was empty, and even the freezer compartment held nothing but a lone, empty ice tray. They turned to one another, appalled.

It was Hank who broke the silence. "Okay. Burns said six flasks—we've only got five. Where'd the last one go? Is it already out there in the world somewhere? Does that mean we're too late?"

Suddenly Angela was struck with a hopeful thought. "The Yancys! They spilled one. Maybe that's it!" She turned to Hank. "We've got to find out for sure what happened to the flask they spilled. Did it break? Did they put it back? Maybe they didn't and five is all there is! We've got to go ask Luke. He'll know."

Together they ran the flasks lightly under the kitchen faucet so that they could cool them before packing them gently back into the ice chest. Angela then returned the chest to its place in the fridge. Silently they retraced their steps through the bedroom and back down the fire escape until they stood, safe once again, in the alley. Within minutes they were back at the squad car.

*Thursday February 27, 2003 — 10:15 am*
*Temporary FBI Headquarters, Hot Springs, Arkansas*

At last, the phone that Holmes had been watching finally rang. It was the computer forensics lab in Quantico. Holmes' end of the conversation was brief and to the point. "Yeah?" he said expectantly. After a few tense moments, he spoke again. "Right!" he said. "Send the decontamination team. We'll meet them there!" and then he slammed the receiver down.

"We got 'em!" he shouted to the assembled agents as he came out of his office and walked right past them, heading for the door. "Let's move out!" Moving fast, he forced his agents to scramble or be left behind. Rosie caught up with Holmes at his sedan, and eased into the driver's seat. "Where to, Boss?" he asked. "Hammerstone—Yun Luck Restaurant. It's those Kim boys after all," Holmes said. Rosie peeled out of the park-

ing lot and sped toward the highway. The other agents followed close behind.

### Thursday, February 27, 2003 — 10:45 a.m.
### Yun Luck Restaurant, Hammerstone, Arkansas

Hank reached through the window of his car and snaked
up the handset of his radio. "Take 'em, Thelma," he said curtly.
From their vantage point up the street, both Hank and Angela
watched as Vern entered the restaurant. Inside, he and Thelma
quickly encircled the Kim brothers, subduing and cuffing
them with little trouble. Then Vern and Thelma began to herd
the boys out of the restaurant.

As the small party of cops and prisoners exited the building, the dark sedans of Holmes' team of feds shot into the
street, screeching to a halt in front of the restaurant. For a
moment, confusion reigned as the federal agents argued with
the locals over jurisdiction. Holmes watched the road anxiously, but he didn't have long to wait—a big white van roared
into view, and screamed to a stop not a yard from where he
stood. A pair of figures in decontamination suits stepped out,
and Holmes sent them into the building. When they disappeared from view, he turned back to the ongoing argument
between agents and cops, taking personal custody of the two
Koreans. Thelma and her team were left standing at the curbside, empty-handed. Hank looked at Angela with relief. They
both knew now how close they had come to letting the live
virus get into Holmes' hands.

Hank and Angela got into the car, unsure of what to do
next. "We have to get to Luke," Angela said. "Maybe he can
tell us what we need to know." Hank put the car into gear
and took the back way out of the neighborhood. "Let's just

hope Luke's feeling talkative today," he said as he headed for Mountain General Hospital.

*Thursday, February 27, 2003 11:35 a.m.*
*Mountain General Hospital, Hammerstone, Arkansas*

Grimly aware that they were working against the clock, Hank and Angela hurried down the corridor to Luke Yancy's room. Of the two of them, it was Angela who was most likely to get Luke to tell them what they needed to know, so Hank remained outside while Angela moved swiftly to Luke's bedside. When Luke saw his visitor, he beamed his goofy grin.

"How's my buddy?" Angela asked, pitching her voice low and friendly. Luke grinned.

"Okay," he said. She forced herself to smile reassuringly, though her heart was pumping a mile a minute.

"Hey, Luke. We got a puzzle we can't solve, and you're the only one who can tell us the answer." Luke preened at her words. "Luke 'aart," he said, pointing to his head. "That's right," Angela agreed. "Luke's very, very smart. So I bet you can tell me what I need to know." Luke tried to arrange his face in a suitably sage expression, and if Angela hadn't been so acutely aware that time might be running out she would have had to laugh. Instead, she pressed on with her question.

"Luke, remember back when you and Jesse were on Arrowhead Mountain and you spilled the powder?" Luke pooched out his lower lip, his expression immediately becoming guarded. Angela could have kicked herself for having pushed too fast. Like a little kid caught with his hand in the cookie jar, Luke was close to clamming up on her. She had to try a new tack, and fast. "Don't worry, Luke—really. You're not in trouble for it." She leaned in conspiratorially. "I want to win

222

a bet with Hank—he bet me a whole bag of candies that you don't know the answer, but I said you were too smart for that. If you help me win the bet, I'll give you half my candies. What do you say?" Luke's sunny grin resurfaced immediately.

"Right. So about that powder. What did you do about the spilled powder? Did you just hide the bottle? Throw it away, maybe?" Luke giggled. Then he knitted his brows in what he obviously thought was a crafty look and beckoned Angela to lean in closer. "Back."

"Okay, you put it back?" Luke nodded and grinned, waving for Angela to come closer as if he was going to tell her a secret. Angela bent her ear close to his lips. "Foo'd 'em. Jess foo'd 'em," he whispered.

"How, Luke? How did Jesse fool them?" Luke whispered again, barely containing his glee at the great joke his brother had pulled off. "Powder," he said.

"Powder?" Luke nodded his head excitedly. "Donut!" Angela paused. "I'm sorry, Luke, I don't have any donuts. I tell you what, you tell me how Jess fooled them and I'll ask the nurses to get you a donut later." But Luke just persisted. "Powder.... donut," he said again.

Angela smiled at Luke. It appeared that she was not going to get any more out of him today and time was getting short. Besides, she had gotten the information that she came for. She stood up straight and waved goodbye. Luke's face fell when he realized she was going to leave. "Oh, sweetie," she said. "We gotta go now to get the candies… and the donuts. We'll be back real soon. I promise. And then you and I will share." Then Angela left the room.

"So," Hank said as they hurried back to the car, "are we home free, or is there still another bottle out there, somewhere?"

"There's another one. Luke said that they put it back. He was trying to tell me something about how Jess fooled the

Koreans, but I lost him—he got hungry for donuts." When they got back to the squad car, Angela turned to Hank "so where do we go next?"

His anxiety rose again to full force. "We gotta get to Little Rock, 'cause that's where the target's going to be."

Hank hit the gas, heading for the highway. As he drove he fumbled for the radio and thumbed the channel open. "Patch me through to the state police," he told the dispatcher. After a few minutes, he was finally in touch with the State Police Captain Steve Tucker, the man in charge of security for Bo Li Yeung's visit.

"Captain, it's Chief McLain, down Hammerstone way. I have to talk with you about security for Bo Li Yeung's visit." Hank's voice was raw with urgency.

"What's the problem, Chief? I thought you boys had cleared up your trouble. In fact I just now got a call giving the all clear from the feds."

"The feds are wrong." Hank's words fell starkly into the static of the radio. "Say again, the feds are wrong."

"Well," came the reply from Captain Tucker, "seems we got ourselves a problem here then, son." Hank heard papers shuffling in the background and then the captain spoke again. "Orders to stand down came through by fax just a minute ago—got 'em here in my hand." He cleared his throat as he considered his situation. "Tell you what, Chief. I'll just give our boy Holmes a call and see if maybe we can clear this all up." The radio went silent but for the roar of static.

Hank gave Angela an agonized look, then bore down on the car's accelerator. He switched on the siren and flashers as he pulled the car over into the fast lane, then really let his engine's horses loose. The minutes seemed to tick by agonizingly slowly, even as the car sped towards Little Rock. Suddenly the radio crackled back to life and he snatched up the microphone. "McLain here," he barked.

"Well, Chief, it seems you got yourself left out of the loop. I just spoke to the FBI and they told me that they had the Korean fellas in custody already."

"You got to *listen* to me." Hank wanted to scream, but he kept his voice even. "They don't know the whole story. There's at least one more terrorist out there—and he's still got the weapon!"

"Don't know what to tell you. The feds said stand down, and stand down's what we did." The captain remained stubbornly unmoved. The man seemed determined to ignore the catastrophe that even now could be occurring.

"Has the plane landed yet? Is there *anybody* detailed to guard Yeung when he gets here?" Hank was shouting now.

"Don't see no need to get yourself all worked up. We have three men riding shotgun on motorcycles; they'll see your boy safely to his hotel. The plane should be landing just about now, I'd say."

"What route will they take?" Hank said, increasingly desperate for answers, and knowing that he will probably have to take matters into his own hands.

"Well, no special route now. I expect they'll take the fastest one. They'll probably get off at Lafayette."

Hank slammed the transmitter back into its holster on the dashboard, terminating the connection. His mind was moving rapidly now, calculating the likely motorcade route from the Little Rock airport to the Palace Hotel. Speaking more to himself than to Angela, he said, "They're coming from the opposite direction. Seems the best route would be down Sudbury. That way we can bypass the heavy traffic and intercept them by the warehouses." He allowed himself a swift glance at the dashboard clock. Still a half-hour out of Little Rock, with no time to lose. He gunned the engine once more, and the speedometer needle slipped a notch past 100. The scenery beyond the car's windows was just a blur.

"We gotta head 'em off before they hit the main streets." Again, he spoke mostly to himself, but he heard Angela's soft murmur of agreement. "It's all we can do," she said.

Hank's car barely slowed even on the off ramp from the highway, but he had to cut his speed to navigate the city's streets, and he cursed every second lost to traffic. His eyes darted frantically as he swung up one street and down the next. "Be there, be there, be there," he chanted as he drove, praying that his guess as to the motorcade's route was correct.

He made a hard left onto Magnolia Street—this would be their one chance. If the motorcade didn't appear, he'd guessed disastrously wrong. But luck was with him. Even as he was wresting his car out of the turn, he saw the motorcade bearing down on them. He swung the car into an arc and shut the engine down, blocking the street and forcing the motorcade to a stop. The limo swerved out of control, slamming into a utility pole. In a flash Hank was out of the car and running, pulling open the flap of his holster. Before the state cops could dismount from their bikes, he had reached the limousine, his gun drawn, shouting, "Hands where I can see 'em!" As his words left his mouth a shot rang out.

The limo driver lay sprawled across the front seat, a bullet hole in his temple. In the back, a white-faced Bo Li Yeung was splashed with the scarlet blood of the dead driver. Angela had followed Hank and they rushed towards the limo, along with the three motorcycle cops.

Inside the limo, panic reigned. Yeung and his guards came barreling out opposite sides of the car. When Bo Li exited, deeply shaken, he caught sight of his old friend Angela. He rushed to her, staggering into a parody of an embrace, as Angela struggled to hold him up.

Yeung's mouth worked soundlessly for a moment, but at last the words came. "He... he... he threw something into the back seat and then he shot himself."

Angela suddenly froze as she looked into the car and saw a broken flask and a pile of white powder lying on the back seat of the limousine. "Shut the doors!" she yelled to Hank, then quickly checked Bo Li's bloody jacket, just inches from her face. It, too, was covered with a white powder. My God, she thought, she had been exposed to the virus!

Time stood still. In a moment, her life was turned upside down. All her life she'd known good health, but had watched her mother face the slow, steady loss of function as MS took its toll. She'd witnessed her mother's courage with pride, but lived as well with the unacknowledged fear that someday she, too, might face the challenge. And now—now the day had come! She imagined herself in a wheelchair, the object of unwanted pity. She saw herself facing the anguish, the loss, the pain, the panic, the doubt—all those things that her mother and so many others had risen above—and she feared that she would not prove equal to the challenge.

Suddenly, she felt Bo Li's weight sag against her as he passed out in dead faint. Her instincts as a doctor immediately trumped her fear. She let her patient down to the ground, and as she did some of the powder on Bo Li's jacket puffed into the air. Unable to avoid it, Angela breathed it in through her mouth and nose—and was struck by the familiar taste. Her thoughts shot back to Luke's parting words at Mountain General. She took a closer look at the white powder that stood out against Bo Li's black jacket as he lay on the asphalt. Suddenly all the pieces fell into place.

"Sugar!" she cried out. "It's just powdered sugar!"

Hank rushed over to help her with Bo Li as the wail of approaching ambulances could be heard in the background. After a moment, and to the amazement of onlookers, he had to join her in nervous laughter while they marveled at their good fortune; that the flask that Luke had spilled—now filled with powdered sugar—had been the one chosen for the hit on Bo Li.

The scene was soon bustling with emergency workers in gas masks—there still may be some virus left in the flask—as neighboring buildings were evacuated and the National Guard biohazard containment team arrived. But even as this surreal scene unfolded, Angela felt born again. It seemed ironic to her that serendipity had foiled this complicated plot in such an innocuous way. But often answers are found in the simple things, she thought, as she watched the ambulance disappear down Magnolia Street.

And as her odyssey was coming to a close, Special Agent John Holmes' journey was just beginning. Across town, Vince's hand picked decontamination team entered three powder-filled flasks into the evidence log of the Little Rock Field Office of the Federal Bureau of Investigation.

# EPILOGUE

*September 19, 2003*
*Hot Springs Convention Center, Hot Springs, Arkansas*

The Yancys were out of their element, and it showed. Jesse ducked his head apologetically as he helped Luke navigate between the tables full of Hot Springs' notables, his face red with embarrassment. It was hard enough to rub shoulders with all these successful people, but he had hoped that maybe he and Luke could have slipped in without being noticed. Instead, they'd arrived late—after all it wasn't easy getting Luke in and out of the truck—and now they had to make a very public walk to reach their assigned table at the front of the hall. He was acutely aware that everybody else in the room was in fancy dress, while the best that could be said about him and Luke was that their jeans were clean.

Nevertheless they were thrilled to be there. There was no way they were going to miss this, the Hot Springs Chamber of Commerce award ceremony, honoring their all-time favorite doctor, Angela Donatelli.

Jesse helped Luke set aside his crutches and take a seat at the table, then sat himself down. Almost immediately, Marie Donatelli, Linda Tackett, and Jennifer Richmond made a fuss over them. Much to Luke's delighted surprise, Jennifer even leaned across the table to plant a kiss on his forehead, and Marie reached to give Jesse's hand a reassuring squeeze. But there was no time for conversation, for the master of ceremonies, up on the dais, finally came to the end of her long speech and said the name they'd all come to hear: Angela Donatelli.

The announcement of the night's guest of honor touched off loud applause throughout the hall. Angela bowed her head at the tribute, and waited for the noise to subside. When at last the hall was quiet, she raised her eyes to the crowd and began to speak.

"Good evening. For me, tonight is a very special night. I look out and see the faces of my family, my friends, my patients—my community. The people who matter most to me." The audience murmured appreciatively. "I know that most of you came expecting to hear, once again, the story of Dr. Burns's virus and about the bioterrorist attack that was foiled in the nick of time." Again the audience applauded. "But I've told that story many times, and tonight, with your permission, I'd like to take a different tack." The audience grew silent, and Angela looked over to Marie, who nodded silent encouragement.

"You see, I'm fortunate in having a very wise mother." Marie blushed at the unexpected remark. "While everybody was making a big fuss over the terrorists and the bioweapon they created, she reminded me that this story is not just about them. She showed me that the events we've all gone through together have a very human side. Tonight, I want to talk about that side of the story." The audience was hushed.

"For us, this was personal. When these terrorists chose their weapon, they didn't appropriate just any disease. They picked one that we—my mother and I—know all too well. Many of my patients have spent the better part of a lifetime negotiating with this disease, understanding its subtleties and making peace with it when they can. But the voices of people like these—people who struggle daily with chronic disease—are rarely heard. Most of us who are blessed with full health simply don't know what to say to them—or we're inhibited by a kind of guilt, because we're healthy and they are not."

She took a deep breath. "Yet, they came through for all of

us. We could never have foiled the terrorists in their plot without the help of so many people who live their lives dealing with MS. And those people joined our cause because they *understood* the way few others could ever hope to understand. When they learned of all the people coming down with the mysterious disease that hit Hammerstone, these long-time veterans of MS knew immediately the kind of fear and pain their neighbors were facing. That empathy moved them to act. Our story really is their story. It belongs to the people who suffered most from the attack, but still had the fortitude to rise up and fight back." She paused and again the hall erupted in a storm of clapping. Again, Angela waited until the applause died down.

"So what do we do, now that the heroes of our story have been unmasked? Simple. We vow never again to ignore the voices of these courageous folks. We give them a voice, and we listen to what they have to say. They have a lot to teach us—about empathy, about strength, about honor, about integrity. For too many of us, these are just abstract ideas—but for people who live with chronic illness, there's nothing abstract about them. These people get up every morning knowing the struggles that lay before them, and they find the strength to go on anyway! When they lose abilities that we all take for granted, they find the courage to adjust. They build fulfilling lives in the face of hardship." Angela looked searchingly into the crowd. "Who among us can afford to ignore the lessons they can teach us?"

"A patient once told me something that I'll never forget. She said that at first living with MS was almost intolerable, but once she got past the fear, she began to see the lessons. That is what I urge all of you to do. Get past your fear of people with chronic illness, listen to their voices, and learn the lessons that their experiences have to offer. Thank you, and goodnight."

# AUTHORS NOTE:
## YOURMOVIEPROJECT.COM

Angela implores us to listen, and that is just what I did before I sat down to write this book. My plan, several years ago, was to start a company that would provide an effective media voice for patients through entertainment. In particular, I realized that the art of storytelling would allow me to spread the word about MS and chronic illness—what it is and what it means to the people who live with it—to a broad public. After all, stories have been used for centuries as a vehicle for teaching. And if the story's good enough, we may even *enjoy* the process of learning.

But to do the job right, I needed first to learn the truth about what life was like with multiple sclerosis. As a physician who treats people with MS, my understanding of the disease is from the outside, looking in. Even though I understand the clinical and research aspects of the disease, I have never personally lived with MS—and I knew that I was hardly likely to learn the human side of it simply by asking a few questions in the examining room. If I wanted the true, honest voices of MS patients, I had to provide them with a forum in which to speak.

And that's how YourMovieProject.com was born. In conjunction with an MS documentary project I was working on, I created a web site where people with MS could post letters, stories, and essays about their lives. I welcomed similar submissions from the families and friends of MS sufferers as well. The web site was an immediate hit, and I received hundreds of letters from all fifty states and six countries. The letters provided much insight that was useful for my documentary, but that's not all. They inspired me to try my hand at a novel, and it was these letters that gave me the first glimpses of the fictional characters that would fill its pages: Marie, Jennifer, Linda, and the other MS patients in this book are all composites, expressing the voices that struck me so powerfully in the letters that real MS patients sent in.

But even with the completion of *Point Source*, the voices still call out to be heard. As they inspired me, so also they may inspire you. I invite you to listen. In the section that follows, you have the opportunity to hear, first hand, the courage and hope that my new correspondents have offered to share. Thanks for listening.

Richard G. Pellegrino, M.D., Ph.D.
Stonemeadow Rise,
Hot Springs, Arkansas


***


*Anne, Tennessee*

It was mid-afternoon and I was shopping in a large department store near Memphis. I hadn't felt very good that day, but I couldn't pinpoint the problem. I hadn't been diagnosed with MS yet.

As I browsed in the pajama section, a warm feeling trickled down my leg. I looked down and apparently had lost control of my bladder. I stood there in complete horror and confusion watching the light blue jean fabric change to dark denim. I know my head even in its confusion was demanding I take control of my body. I couldn't. Tears ran down my face in such a fury, they too made more dark denim spots. I froze and then suddenly an elderly saleslady came up holding a handful of tissues. She must have seen the terror, the embarrassment, and the confusion on my face. She saw what happened and told me in a very quiet, soothing voice while handing me the crumpled tissues, "Don't worry. Stay here, honey. I'll be right back." It seemed that only seconds had passed when she returned with a big gray T-shirt. "Put this on over your shirt. It should be long enough." I was fumbling for my wallet and she said, "I took care of it. You just get home safely."

I did. I sent flowers the next day to the department store. I only knew her first name and put it on the card. I hope she received them as I have never experienced that kind of love and caring from a stranger.

***

*Mandy, England*

I do not suffer with MS, but I am the only child of a woman who does. She is very fortunate that she is not debilitated by the disease. Her mobility has varied during my lifetime from being stuck in a wheelchair with Home Health coming around to get her up and me to school, to being perfectly fine and competing in my school's sports day parents' race. However, despite all of her problems she is almost always happy and we try to laugh and look at the bright side of things. We have many memories

235

of bad times, but even these have a funny side. There is a story I wish to relate. I must have been about 5 years old at the time. My mother was mobile using sticks, etc. She had been put on a high steroid treatment which had caused her to retain water and balloon out to almost twice her size. She is only 5' tall and we nicknamed her a walking ball. My grandmother had come to visit for a few days and we were both downstairs in the kitchen when we heard a shriek from my mother upstairs. I had followed my grandmother to the first floor landing only to find the call was coming from the WC (bathroom). The room was about the size of a normal public toilet cubicle. When we were able to get the door open, there was my mother squashed between the toilet and the wall. She had tried to manage by herself and lost her balance while going to sit on the seat, having missed it. The extra fluid she was carrying let her slip into the small gap and had wedged her fast. So there we were, the three of us, Mum stuck and all three of us laughing so much we were unable to do anything. We tried water, butter, soap, everything you can think of to free her. To cut a long story short, we don't know if it was the effect of all these things or just that as my mother got colder the swelling subsided, but after about an hour she was free. We really thought we would have to get the fire brigade to release her.

Despite this being a low point in her life, the point is we still laughed and found humor even in the darkest times. It is this that I have found most inspiring in all people who have MS. They do not feel sorry for themselves and go around with a chip on their shoulder like many fully healthy people I know. They just get on with whatever this disease throws at them. The only other point I would like to make is please in your film tell people that just because a person is in a wheelchair they DO exist. They can speak for themselves and they do have a brain. So many people speak to the one pushing the chair and treat the one in it as though they were a child.

\*\*\*

*Gabriella, Arkansas*

I was diagnosed with MS in 1996. … I tried to work for two more months, but I just couldn't get it together…. My accounts were getting behind…. I was now out of a job with three kids, a mortgage, and a new car.

I not only lost my job but I lost my self-esteem. I felt worthless. I couldn't cook a decent meal anymore. My family knew dinner was ready when the smoke alarms in the house went off. It became a family joke. Easter came around and I hid the eggs for my kids. When they went out to find them, I didn't know where they were either. I remembered about six out of twenty-four hiding places. Now we have another family joke. I can hide my own Easter eggs. We also found out that I never had to watch a rerun. I never remembered what I had and had not seen so I could watch a whole movie sometimes and never know that I had just seen it a week ago.

All of the family jokes started to bring me out of my funk. I was still in a wheelchair, but for once in my life I was able to stay home and watch my kids grow up. I always worked so hard that I missed a lot of my two older children's lives. I couldn't pay my bills, but I was spending my time with my family.

I took my youngest son to a martial arts class to see if he would be interested. After his class, the instructor came out and asked me why I wasn't in the class. I looked at him like he was crazy. After all, I was sitting there in a wheelchair. How was I going to protect myself if I couldn't even control my own legs? He took me into the classroom and spent almost two hours with me showing me how to take an attacker out without the use of my legs. I was amazed. I now have a black belt in Tae kwon do and have gained back my self-esteem. I learned to protect myself in a wheelchair and then when I went into remission I learned to use a cane as a weapon. Now I can kick butt with the best of them. I have several national first place trophies and even more second and third place trophies. I also have almost thirty medals. I am whole again. I fight my MS with the same conviction and strength that I would fight any other attacker and I am winning.

***

*Jennifer, Massachusetts*

My mother passed away from complications associated with MS weeks before my tenth birthday…. As I remember her, it is sometimes hard…. A school play she hobbled to or unread stories at bedtime because of visual loss…. It is more often her sense of humor in spite of such a disease that I remember most.

***

*Anonymous*

While there are an infinite number of words in the English language, it would be difficult to find the words that appropriately describe my father. However, one word that does come to mind is "strong." My father is one of the strongest people I know. Never once have I heard him complain or take out his frustration on other people.

My father has been struggling with multiple sclerosis for six years now, since I was about 11 years old. When I first found out about his disease, I was overwhelmed with emotions. I felt pain, anger, confusion, and sadness. I was frightened and extremely frustrated with all of the unanswered questions that remained. I was fearful of not knowing what multiple sclerosis was, but I think that most people are scared of the unknown.... I still wonder, "Why my father?" I guess that is the one question I will never find an answer to.

It is still difficult to express my feelings about my father. My family is unaware of the heartache I feel seeing my father suffer. I cannot help but think about the constant pain he endures and the persistent numbness he feels. We never discuss my father's disease; it is almost as if it is just not there. My father takes his daily injections, goes to physical therapy, and works hard to fight his disabling disease. He presses on through every painful day. I am so proud of him and I love him so much. Not only does he support his family financially, he supports emotionally as well. I take to heart all of his advice more than he will ever know and his opinion is very important to me. He always encourages me to be myself and to do the best that I possibly can.

***

*Stacey, Indiana*

I worried my husband would leave me because I had MS, but he assured me he wouldn't despite the fact we were going through marital strife at the time. I told him to take me out to the field and shoot me. I fell into a deep depression and didn't share my problems with many people. I contemplated suicide. I even thought of all the different ways I was going to do it. I even went to a gun shop to look at guns and after much thought I decided not to do it. I couldn't leave my 3-year-old son motherless.

I had to quit working altogether. I laid on the couch all day. I had painful leg spasms and debilitating fatigue. I couldn't watch TV or read because of my double vision and I was too weak to do anything else so I would just listen to the radio. I began to pray to God to help me feel better and to relieve my devastating depression that kept me down in the pit.

Eventually I started going to church and became interested in Bible study and prayer groups...

Now I facilitate an MS support group and I meet all kinds of people with MS. Faith really makes a difference in people who are ill. One of the outcomes of my faith has been my out-reach to other people with MS. I visit many shut-ins with MS who are worse off than me. Working with the support group is helping keep my focus off myself too. I try to encourage others to do what they can to keep from becoming too self-centered with their own problems and to reach out and help others. It has done a world of good for me.

I could say MS was a blessing for me in a way because it made me look at myself and the way I was living before MS and work to change my life for the better. Life is more REAL now. MS was the entryway for God to come into my life and change me into the person He wanted me to be. I know this may sound hokey, but I know many people are much better off dealing with illness if they have faith in God.

*\*\**

*Karen, Pennsylvania*

I had many flares with MS until July of 1993 when I learned I was pregnant at the age of 42. Having our younger daughter put me into remission with MS.... My estranged husband (of 28 years) wants a divorce after all these years. I don't understand why spouses leave their mates when they come down with MS. I guess they want the better things in life that their spouse can't give them anymore, but to me that is a big cop out. I pray that you will portray the MS as closely as you can to what all of us have gone through to get to this point in our lives, if it is with our eyes, bladder, bowels, marriage, or whatever. Thank you for listening.

*\*\**

*Ralph, England*

A wall of silence has been built.
It wasn't always there.
We had a carefree happy life.
And everything we'd share.

Somewhere back in those happy times
My illness took its grip.

242

Our parameters were changing
As my life began to dip…

Words just ceased as time progressed
But things needed to be aired.
The silence was expanding
And for the first time I was scared.

That silent world we built at home
Was a cold and lonely place.
With silence still expanding
The first tears streaked my face.

Then finally you took the step.
I suppose it had to be.
You found yourself a "proper" man.
Oh, to be rid of me.

We live our separate lives now.
Adrift, alone, bereft.
The silence has expanded
And now there's nothing left.

*** 

*Anonymous*

MS has empowered me intellectually and
emotionally with my ability to deal with life in a

successful and meaningful way. Rather than be bitter, I have chosen to embrace life with love.

\*\*\*

*Julie, Arizona*

I am 37 years old and was diagnosed with relapsing-remitting MS in October of 2001. I am the mother of two children, 10 and 11. I have apparently had MS since probably 1992 and definitely since 1996. Although I am still learning to deal with this condition, our family has found humor to be the greatest healer and laughter makes for good medicine. When my initial neurologist met with my husband and myself, he asked if we had noticed clumsiness, tripping, etc. We laughed and said that I hadn't been nicknamed "Grace" all my life because I was graceful. I always have some unknown bruise or scratch which is always a lot of fun for us to figure out. My husband and children will claim to suffer from mommyitis if they forget what they are going to say or trip over words or forget to do things. MS has opened up opportunities to share with people and to learn about their conditions once they see how I am managing mine (and they didn't even know I had MS).

Good luck on your project. Life is filled with little blessings and maybe dealing with MS is one
of them?

***

*Pamela, Alabama*

I was diagnosed in March of 1998. It took me
a year to accept MS fully. At this same time, I
lost my dad. I think that prolonged it some.
First I was in denial that I even had it and then I
had to deal with it. My family and friends tried
to help me with dealing with MS, but I had to
get it worked out in my own head first. When I
did that, I adjusted to whatever came my way,
and boy, did it come my way. I went through
being paralyzed and told that I would never
walk again to my bladder being so messed up
that I had to have a device surgically implanted
in order to go to the bathroom.

I have been through a lot in my 36 years of
life, but you know what? I'm a better person
from it. I am a very positive, strong, and stubborn woman who thanks God every day for my
waking up. You see, through my determination
and my will to beat this thing called MS, I can
walk and I can help others to see that MS does-
n't always have to be a death sentence. We can
band together and do our best to conquer it the
best way that is right for each of us in our own
way. I believe that we all are very special people and that we can deal with this disease. I
have made some great friends that I cherish

because of this disease called MS. I feel lucky to have them in my life. I have to stay positive.

***

## Anonymous

MS affected me as a sexual being in a huge way. When I had to accept that I had MS, it shattered my view of myself to such a point that I lost all self-esteem for a while. My self-worth had been wrapped up in the physical workouts and shape I was in and how successful I was in my career. When I relapsed and lost all that (lost my job and could no longer work out), I didn't know who I was. I became a sick person and that was devastating. It has taken two years, but I'm finally able to enjoy sex again. It was really hard on my husband that I couldn't have sex very often because of pain, feeling tired, etc., but now that my self-esteem has improved I seem to be able to manage it (more often). Our relationship is far more normal now since we don't talk about MS as much anymore. We don't avoid it, but I'm not talking about it every day.

***

## Krisha, Indiana

There are days when I get very down. Like when I've been trying to do some gardening or decorating, my leg will give way. There then becomes a fear in me that I may fall. In my mind I know that I can do it, but my body doesn't want me to. When I go for a walk in the countryside knowing there is every chance that my leg will drag and I will fall, I just cannot help pushing myself to the limits and when I do I get very fatigued. I get frustrated, agitated, and sometimes angry. At times like these, I prefer to be in my own company so that no one can see my weaknesses. I prefer people to see me as I am, leading a normal life rather than someone who is unwell.

The future is unknown, but right now I am able to retain my independence, which is the one thing I value most. I will never be well again. I have learned to accept my illness and manage my symptoms as best I can.

*\*\**

*Cory, Ontario*

I was 17 the year I graduated from high school, moved out on my own, and found out I had multiple sclerosis... My first relapse in ten years began one night on my way home from a long day at work...

At first I focused on how much I had lost and how much I might have to give up. I was devastated, feeling the full weight of the pain I had been suppressing. Searching for understanding, I began to write it in a journal and it wasn't long before a simple recount of my symptoms transformed into a rich exploration of thoughts and feelings. In little time, writing became my

247

haven, my place to be uninhibited, my place to rant, and eventually my place to recall what I could have done better. With a renewed sense of peace, I began to accept my symptoms and my MS.

When MS was no longer an adversary, I became open to its lessons. I learned the importance of living in the moment knowing that happiness can be chosen rather than merely found. I have discovered that self-esteem is not necessarily preceded by vocational, educational, or physical accomplishment. More importantly, I have learned to embrace difficulty and take advantage of the tremendous opportunities afforded by acceptance.

***

*Beth, Pennsylvania*

I began walking with a cane eleven years after my diagnosis. My family had mixed reactions, but we worked through it together. For example, my sister knew I was feeling awkward about accepting having to use a cane so she came to my house, did some chores, took care of our beagle puppy, and told me to nap for a while. When she saw me lying around and being a hermit, she told me to get up and take a shower and that she would go with me to buy a cane at a local pharmacy. She was trying to motivate me with her companionship. It worked. We were out of the door in an hour to go buy it together. She made it fun for me.

On the other hand, my mother was crying just thinking about it. The next time she came over I told her I would go get the cane and show her how much it helped me walk. Even though she had to accept the cane as a new part of me, we faced it together and now it is not an issue. She always tells me how good it is to see me moving a little faster with the cane.

A dear friend was with me in a restaurant the first day I used the cane. Knowing I was shy about it, she said very loudly to complete strangers, "Look, everyone. Beth's using a cane now." I knew she was trying to get me over my embarrassment and I told her that I would beat her with the cane, but in my heart I knew she was trying to help in her own way. I wasn't embarrassed about it for long.

Mall walks have become shorter, but I remind myself that I am still moving. Good luck with your project and thank you for allowing us to reach out.

***

*Donna, Alabama*

The most difficult thing for me and still is about the disease is knowing I will always have it. There is no end except for my death. My mother was a great help and very understanding. My husband is my rock and if I could I would nominate him for sainthood. My children are wonderful. Other family members and all my friends just don't understand what I am really going through though. That is okay, but sometimes I could scream. My legs won't let me go hiking anymore. I used to dance, but that is over. The things I love more than anything are slowly slipping away and I can't do a damn thing about it. I want to do everything now before I can't do anything at all. Depression and heat are my worst enemies. I will fight this with all my being, but sometimes I get down and think why bother? I like to think that MS stands for "mighty special" and then reality sets in and I realize I don't feel that way. Thanks for listening.

*** 

### Elleni, California

It was three months from graduating college when I found out I had MS. I was returning from a road trip and concert with my roommates. The morning after the concert I got up from my bed and I couldn't feel my legs. My hands had a numb feeling and my chest felt as if it were in a corset. I remember thinking, "Please don't let it be a brain tumor." The moment I stepped outside the room (after seeing the neurologist), the moment I stepped outside to my friends I went and collapsed on them.

At age 23, I was diagnosed with MS. I was devastated. I was on track to go into a career in the media either in front or behind the scenes. The doctor said that would be too stressful and may exaggerate another exacerbation. Five years of college down the drain! I took a year off to figure out what career path I would go into. Today I am a teacher. I am healthier and thinner because a good diet and exercise are part of my regimen. I haven't had another exacerbation, but my secondary symptoms are getting worse. Primarily my sense of balance is deteriorating. I stumble more often. I have to hold onto the rail on the treadmill machine. I can't dance like I used to. I can't even walk in a straight line.

Here I am cute, educated, well mannered, and fun to be around and then I get MS. I question my worth many times. I cherish every day I can still walk. That is frightening. Will I be able to walk down the aisle on my wedding day? Who knows? That's MS. No one does know.

I enjoy teaching. I plan on getting a master's degree. I aspire to become a writer, maybe get married. I don't mind the injections. I wish I could always be animated and vivacious and avoid becoming an emotionless clump.

That is what I thought a year ago. Now I can't feel my left leg or walk without taking baby steps while limping like I have a twisted ankle. With my wedding four months away, I want to be able to walk down that aisle. Everybody said that I was okay as long as I could walk. Well, now what am I supposed to do? I feel like I let everyone down. In many ways, this is worse than dying. It is pitiful and demoralizing to slowly lose your abilities, especially when one was a vibrant, energetic, and social person as I was. I guess being an only child doesn't help either. I mean, my poor parents. What a disappointment this must be to them. But then, hey, at least I got to participate in the MS walk this year and raise some money for research while I can still walk!

*** 

*Mary, Texas*

Living with the uncertainty of what a day or hour may bring forth is one of the maddening maladies of MS. In the beginning days of my diagnosis, I shrank away from making definite social commitments or other agreements. For quite some time, I was unable to attend church and finally did quit my job as an executive assistant. What bothered me the most was that whenever I did make plans I had no guarantee I would feel well enough to carry them out.

Then I decided one day that life had to go on and that whether or not I was able to do what I had planned I would plan things anyway so I rejoined choir at church and tried to continue to have social interactions with friends. My husband and son had a difficult time adjusting to mom not always being there for them to go on fishing trips or to ballgames or things outdoors like we always had done in the past. I told them, "I want you to go ahead and enjoy life. Just realize that I won't be able to come along, but you go ahead."

Since my lifestyle came to a much slower

pace, I embraced solitude and found much to my surprise that I enjoyed the alone times which gave me time to "re-tank," so to speak, spiritually, emotionally, and yes, to rest physically. I told my friends when planning things that I was going to "pencil it in" to feel great on our scheduled time together, making a joke of it but also thinking positively that I would feel great that day. It was a way of breaking the tension that often occurred whenever no one really knew what to say to me, knowing that I could give them no guarantees.

Three things that worried me most would be that I become totally dependent upon my family and/or a nurse, meaning that I become bedridden. That is my worst fear. I do not focus on it a lot, but the reality is that it is always there in the back of my mind. I am concerned also with being more of a burden on my family, especially my husband, who has been such a tremendous support.

Another great concern of mine is that my mind becomes so affected I am no longer coherent. The fear is sparked from the cognitive problems I am experiencing at the present time. I have had greater difficulty this year with my cognitive skills. I know that I have lost some of my IQ level and I can't always think as quickly or as clearly as I am accustomed. Not being able to find words and speaking opposite words than what I am thinking is just intolerable. I'm so afraid of losing my mind. Having enjoyed being able to think on my feet and do quick problem solving plus having a bright mind, it is excruciating to me to suffer this malady. I would rather experience more physical pain or even to be in a wheelchair than have problems with my brain.

At this present moment in time, I am able to walk, talk, speak, see, breathe, and on good days think. For this I am eternally grateful to my God. Implementing a stronger faith walk in my daily life is the best and most important solution I have chosen in coping with this chronic illness. Realizing that I have been much worse than today and having experienced much more pain in the past, I struggle to remain positive and pray to handle the difficulties with grace and some of my dignity. Sometimes I fail miserably at having a good attitude. Depression has often been my shadow.

Allowing myself to go at a slower pace, setting boundaries with friends and family with regard to my limits, and being self-disciplined enough to rest when I am exhausted are strategic solutions which have been implemented for self-preservation. My family and I are in agreement. That is, that I will not ask them to do something for me that I could do for myself. Also, they will not try to do everything for me but will wait for me to ask for their help. Sometimes I have to remind them that when I say I need their help I truly need their help.

Not being involved in my son's education has probably affected his attitudes towards his studies. I have had to let go and allow my son, who will be a senior this year, to flounder and make his own mistakes without much involvement from myself. It would be my desire generally to become involved in activities and parent-teacher meetings at school, but I resigned myself to the truth and reality that I am unable to do so.

Presently I have signed up to be a volunteer in the local community hospital. I have written and facilitated a biweekly support group for women with chronic illness and taken a class on becoming a lay counselor in my church and community. Singing in the church choir is one of my favorite activities, although I know that I may not always be able to meet the criteria of attendance demanded of its members. It is a step of faith for me to become involved in any of these activities. Actually I am now busier than I would really like to be, but I can remember days when I wished that I could do the dishes or cook or even drive the car so right now I am taking one step at a time and enjoying each day that my body and mind decides to function at a tolerable level.

***

*Elizabeth, Tennessee*

I received my MS diagnosis a year and a half ago. I believe with all my heart that people with MS should live their lives exactly how they would without this scary diagnosis. It is very hard to move to that place in your heart of understanding and let go of your fears.

***

*Carrol, Oklahoma*

In 1998, I finally met the man of my dreams and my life was more than I ever thought it would be. We were engaged and making wedding plans. Two weeks from our wedding, the pain in my head got worse. One morning I got up and my right leg was so weak I kept falling. My right hand felt like it was asleep. My fiancé took me to the hospital where they admitted me thinking I had a stroke. All this time, my fiancé never left my side. They took tons of tests and an MRI and I was told I most likely had MS. I was totally in shock, angry, scared, all the emotions out there I had. The doctors told us to go ahead with the wedding and our planned cruise.

At this point, I was thinking that there wouldn't be a wedding. I mean, after all, why would anybody want to marry someone that has a disease that could totally take everything away from them? I know two people with MS, my ex-sister-in-law and my adopted sister. Both are very dependent on others for everything. The thought scared me so bad. I talked to my fiancé and told him he could back out and I would totally understand. He started crying and informed me that no matter what I had we would face it together. The wedding was beautiful as was the cruise. When we returned from the cruise, I got a second opinion and it was MS.

My husband is the most amazing man. He has so much love in his heart even though he himself has suffered a great loss. He lost his oldest daughter in the Value Jet crash in 1996. Luckily I have been very fortunate. I have had only one exacerbation. We finally realized our dream and have bought a ranch in Oklahoma. I pray every day that I never progress any further with the MS than I am right now. I have bad days when my legs or arms want to do something other than what I have planned, when the dizziness won't go away, or I forget things (that is the worst), but I am learning every day to deal with that and just be thankful that I am as good as I am. I know without the love and support of my husband I wouldn't be doing as good. I feel for all the people who are so much worse off than I am and pray that some day soon there will be a cure and we will all be cured.

*\*\**

*Pamela, New Jersey*

I can view my future okay right now. However, I think it is scary to know that it is possible to change from the relapsing-remitting MS which I have been since 1991 to progressive MS. My only child was only 8 months old when I was diagnosed in 1991 and I can honestly say it is the best thing that ever happened to me. Unlike his father who left me, my boy has seen me through thick and thin with the disease. There have been many times I had to explain why mommy can't go to the beach or play outside in the sun or overdo it and cause a relapse, which unfortunately he has seen happen too much. I have prayed he will grow up to be a neurologist who finds a cure for MS. After years of not being able to work because of horrible relapses, I am once again working full time thanks to the new medications. I hope when my boy is old enough to walk down the aisle that I can do so then also and hopefully see him do it. I say no more losing of my eyesight or stiffening of my limbs!

***

*Nicole, New Hampshire*

I was diagnosed with MS one year ago at the age of 25. Of course, when you are young and full of life, the last thing you think of is having a disease and when I was diagnosed it was hard. But after the initial shock of it all, I decided that education would be one of the ways I could prepare myself for any obstacle. I have always been an extremely positive person and I thought that I could use that energy to help others that needed some guidance. I recently met Stephanie, who is only 20, and she started an organization for young people with MS. I am now vice president of this awesome group. On a personal level, I am going to train to become an aerobics instructor not only for my own

health but hopefully for other MS patients.
Thank you for the project and I hope that you
do show all aspects of the disease because there
are a lot of healthy young people who do want
to live a very positive life and they don't want
to give up at all. We are just like the rest of the
beautiful people in the world! Take care and
thanks for listening to my story!!!!

\*\*\*

*Jeannette, New York*

In 1984, within a period of three days, I
became completely paralyzed. In my heart, I felt
this was an MS attack. I remained in the hospital for eight weeks whereby my paralysis began
to recede and I went into total remission. I
resumed work as a psychologist working with
developmentally delayed children and adults.
During this period of hospitalization, I went
from being a proactive, vital, athletic, working
woman and became a terrified, vulnerable,
dependent woman wishing to die. I became
during that period of time the antithesis of who
I really was—an intelligent, independent, vital
human being. In 1986, I became pregnant and
gave birth to my first son, who opened my soul
to the meaning and depths of unconditional
love.

In 1993, I told my husband I would go to a
neurologist to confirm the likelihood of MS. I
was given an MRI which confirmed MS. I was
told this, what I thought to be the end of my

life, in a totally clinical manner devoid of emotion: "Mrs. X, you have multiple sclerosis." I was
devastated and terrified for loss of a word at this
moment to describe my terror. Since my diagnosis, I have gone through the various stages of
the grieving process and have arrived at this
crossroad. I am my best advocate, taking excel-
lent care of myself in terms of exercising, eating
well, and taking the current advised regimen of
medications. I have always tried to be a sensitive and loving person. Little things rarely bother me for I have a long road ahead and I must
be proactive for all who I love and who depend
upon me. Our strength as people lies first in
mothering ourselves and as a result of healthy
self-nurturing we can be powerful (the antithesis to vulnerability) in expressing our drive to
help those that need us. There can be no
greater source of empowerment than giving to
others despite one's physical limitations. In this
life, we all live with the "illusion of power and
control." I have abandoned and relinquished
this illusion.

*** 

*Anonymous*

Life becomes a myopic view of time, much
like B.D. "before diagnosis" and A.D. "after diagnosis." It is the same for anyone who has
endured any sort of trauma such as a car accident or other paralyzing event. Life before diagnosis gradually fades with each passing day but

never, ever goes completely away. I don't want sympathy or seek sympathy. Nope. Leave that for someone who really needs it or wants it. This guy doesn't. A friend once said that he was uncomfortable telling me about his recent trip to Europe. I didn't tell him this, but that remark offended me. No one should apologize for being able to live his or her life. I live my life. It just happens to be different than most.

That's okay. No hard feelings here. I live vicariously through those "normal" lives, those who do not rely on canes or wheelchairs. Those who get up each morning and don't wonder whether they are going to be able to walk to the bathroom or keep hold of the cup of coffee as you lift it to your lips. I live vicariously through those who do not have a blue-and-white crip placard hanging from the mirror in their car. I know it is not PC to call people with handicaps "crips," but I can do that. The humor is not lost on those with handicaps. I saw a shirt one time that said "I'm not drunk. I have MS." I'm looking for that humor. I promise to keep it up as long as you do the same. We have to laugh. Don't take that away.

***

*Rebecca, Massachusetts*

I am 15 years old, I am an actress, and my mother has progressive Multiple Sclerosis. She has had it my entire life. It's been one rough trip, but somewhere in the middle we grew closer to each other. I don't remember much about the disease from when I was younger because she was healthier then. She could do almost anything. We went skiing, skating, played tennis, tag—anything at all. It was almost as if she wasn't sick. Then things really started to turn for the worse. I was about 9. There were lots more trips to the doctor, and more pill bottles in the "pill basket." Her bad days came more often and she fell down more frequently. My chores increased and she needed new items to help her walk like a leg brace, a cane, and eventually a wheelchair.

The worst thing though, was the separation between my mother and my father. I found myself hiding in my room upstairs with my 4-year-old sister listening to them arguing about the situation. Then one day my father was gone. To this day the divorce still is not final, and my father couldn't have made living worse for us. MS didn't only split up my parents but has changed our lives physically and financially. The financial part came mostly from the divorce, but if you trace back, MS was involved. Though we do have a few financial problems my mom does the hardest she can to try and give my sister and I a normal life, and I love her for it. Through all the pain and difficult times she goes through she always seems to pull through for us.

I do have more responsibilities because of the MS, but I don't mind so much. I do all the grocery shopping, and change the sheets from the beds, wash the floors, dust, and clean the shower. Of course sometimes I really don't feel up to doing all these chores, but it's not so bad, and my mom even does her hardest to pay me a little for my work. This is very gracious of her considering her situation. I would have to say that the most frustrating part about MS is the little things, like picking up a glass of water, or writing a letter for my mother. Little things that are the simplest things to other moms that I have to see her struggling with. I forget sometimes that my mom can't do these things and tell her "do it yourself." Then when I realize she can't. We may laugh about it or joke, but it's still sad when you think about it.

Of course I do sometimes get mad at her, and we have our fights. I may not want to do something for her or go with her to an appointment when I could go to a friend's house. But doesn't everyone fight? Our arguments are just a little different, and we always resolve them. It's true that I wish my mom didn't have MS, and that she was like my friends' mothers, but I can't change anything, only help to make it better. MS is bad, and makes me mad and frustrated, but it's the MS, not my mom. My mom is the best person in my life, and I love her, MS and all.

\*\*\*

*Brenda, South Carolina*

This is a story about a true American hero—my son, Andrew. Andrew was diagnosed with a rapidly progressive form of MS when he was 20. I was devastated but Andrew felt quite differently about it. As we were sitting at a traffic light on the way home, Andrew looked at me and said, "I wonder what the advantages are to having MS." I was shocked and replied that I was having a hard time thinking there are any advantages to having MS. He replied that, of course, there were—that the world had been created in a perfect balance and for every negative there was a positive. He added that our responsibility here was to determine just what those positives were and to take advantage of them. A few months later as I was prepared to give him one of his shots which made him very sick, I made the observation that this whole situation was the pits. He just looked at me and said that there was a lesson in this situation somewhere. I laughed a bit and said that it was a lesson I didn't want. Andrew looked at me for a second and then answered, "That is pretty conceited, Ma, thinking the lesson is just for you or for me. It could be for anyone and we may never know who it was for, but you can be sure somebody will learn something very important from this." He continues to meet every challenge that MS or life in general throws his way with the same calm spirit and positive attitude. It may be difficult for most of us to see life this way, but he certainly is proof that with the right outlook on the situation, the human spirit cannot be conquered.

***

*Joan, Florida*

To get right to the point, I think MS is being sugar-coated big-time by the media and the medical profession. You never hear about how millions of people's lives are turned upside down by MS, how people have lost everything they have ever worked for and end up with nothing but maybe a little apartment subsidized by the government. Why don't you show the real truth, like how families are destroyed because the husband can't stand beside his wife because she is sick so he leaves her and the three kids to fend for themselves; a loving mom who is crippled and trying to hold the family together, how she can't drive anymore because she is practically blind and her arms and legs are too crippled up to handle the controls or both, and her child needs to go to the doctor because he is sick and running a temp of 103 degrees, or she needs someone to go to the store for her or take her to her child's first Christmas performance at school or help her with the laundry because she can no longer manage it herself and she is at the mercy of her family members, if they aren't too busy, because that is all she has left. The friends left right after the husband.

Now she has to depend on the children to do things for her and, of course, it is the oldest one taking care of the younger ones. What about how she would love someone to come and make her a pot of coffee and just sit and talk to her or how she wishes for someone to just put their arms around her and let her cry herself to sleep? She can find someone to take her to doctors, but she has to take all three of her children with her because that person can't watch them so because she can't physically handle taking the children with her she doesn't go.

*** 

## Lora, Georgia

Living and learning with MS. Let's see. The story begins on a hot summer's day. I am taking my usual run around the block, which for me is not very long, when I can't seem to get my feet to the pavement just right. My right foot seems to trip me up constantly until I stumble. I eventually give up running. I give up just about everything that has to do with exertion as my energy has completely been stolen by something I know is gnawing at me. I feel as if I know there is something wrong with me, then my doubts creep in and tell me it's all in my head. A few weeks later, my exhaustion sets in and I become so dizzy that I fear I all of a sudden have vertigo. Over the next few days, my vision progresses from blurry to double vision. I visit my eye doctor and he tells me it is allergies. The next day, I wind up in the Emergency Room where a doctor tells my mother I could have a lazy eye. My mother is beyond belief that her daughter of 34 years is being diagnosed with a simple lazy eye. The day following, I am brought in to my primary care doctor who takes one look at me and admits me to the hospital where an assortment of unpleasant and mind boggling tests are run. A day later, I am diagnosed with multiple sclerosis. I am now sinking into a deep dark hole within myself of self-pity and denial.

My mother is strong yet she is so fearful and angry that her daughter was struck with this devastating illness. I receive treatments in the hospital to regain my sight and therapy to help me walk again and was expected to "wheel" out of the hospital within a week. I was determined NOT to be one of the statistics of MSer's (as we MS sufferers say) and "walk" out of the hospital. Well, I didn't exactly walk, but I did have the spirit in me to learn again. When I got home, my boyfriend left me.

It hit me at that point, I hit rock bottom. I sank into a deep, dark, horrible, lonely world and I shut everyone out from me. My mother was desperate to save me before I sank all the way to the bottom, but I was already there. She rushed to my house after a busy hard day at work to care for me, to feed me, and to get me to bed and help me to laugh or cry. I was disabled. I was handicapped. I was nothing. These were things I was so angry about, so "incorrectly obsessed" about inside my own little tiny black life.  I was so angry that it consumed my every move, my every thought, my every breath.

I had a horribly hard time talking about this to my therapist that I was sent to after my diagnosis.  I was "tight lipped" at first with her, but then I got to trust her and began telling her my fears of crippled mannerism and a life in a wheelchair.  She told me a single phrase I will never forget.  "Your anger will keep you alive." That anger got me back on my feet and back to work.  My faith brought me through the darkest of times.  Without my faith in God, I would be nothing, be trapped in that hole.

I began to open back up to life and back into the world as I call it.  "The world of the living." It was difficult from time to time to push away the deep dark thoughts of how I could "end it all" with one quick downing of a handful of any of my many pills needed to survive.  I won't lie. It does seem the easy way out but also the most selfish.  I have a mother who loves me more than life itself and to leave her would be the cruelest thing in the world.  I have many friends and family that would be horrified if I took that route, so I survive.

I slowly began to pull back into reality and only walk with the aid of my trusty cane.  I have the wheelchair and the walker for those times that I have to yield to the MonSter (as we MSer's call it).  However, there is humor with MS.  Like putting your microwave dinner in the cabinet and then staring at the cabinet after you shut the door and can't find where the cook-time button went.  Or putting your keys in your dishwasher and not understanding that that was not the counter. The icing on the cake was when my mother and I went to one of my many doctor visits out of town. I was exhausted and my limbs were shaky and so was my mind. The drive was long and we had finally made it. I jumped into the shower at the hotel starting to feel as if I was fainting. The whole air around me began to fog horribly right in front of my eyes. I thought, "Oh no, not now. I did so well today. I drove a four-hour drive. Not now." I yelled to my mother, "Mom, come quick, Mom." She ran into the bathroom and yelled, "What" with a panic in her voice. "Mom, I can't see! I can't see!" I screamed. "Take off your glasses, then, silly" in a calm, almost relieved voice with a tiny laugh inside. She didn't want to burst out laughing until I had realized the situation. I took my fogged-up glasses off, breathed a sigh of relief, and began to put conditioner on my hair and when the conditioner wouldn't come out I realized I had put hand lotion on my hair.

It's small things like this that happen often to make our families say, "I'm having an MS moment." The laughter and the anger are the only things that keep me alive and fighting. I've come a long way since those dark days wanting everyone in the world to know about MS and the monster we live with. Doesn't everyone live with some monster? Don't we all have some disability to overcome or some fear of imperfection? So I say to your readers, whatever it is, whatever the outcome, get angry and fight. Laugh at yourself just a little and you will feel the healing begin.

***

*Arlys Minnesota*

The biggest ordeal for me was self-doubt. I knew within myself that there was something terribly wrong, but it's pretty hard to convince oneself of this when numerous doctors and specialists and tests come up with nothing. After all, they were the so-called experts and who was I to question this authority? I was told the reason I couldn't do any work (like vacuuming) was because I didn't *want* to do it. One day a friend who knew the ordeal I was going through happened to visit. She noticed me trying to vacuum and said, "Are you trying to kill yourself to prove the doctors wrong? Get away from that thing." From then on, I began to listen to what my system was telling me and found out that being true to yourself really does make a difference. The biggest influence for helping me through this horrible time was having faith in God and above all having a loving, caring husband and children and friends who although not

270

fully understanding were always there for me through thick and thin; and a huge sense of humor.

***

*Danielle, Illinois*

The hardest thing to accept has been the reaction of my family. They love me and I know that, but they suffer from the same syndrome that has afflicted my friends. "You don't look sick. Therefore, you must be a liar when you say that you are sick." The most sickening depth of exhaustion keeps a person with MS from functioning as they did before. Spouses, children, elders in the family, friends all want a part of you. You don't look sick so why don't you participate in our lives? Why can't you cook, clean, baby-sit, run errands, visit, go shopping, make love? It seems that if your skin is not rotting off your body before their eyes, they just can't understand why you can't be a part of their lives as you used to be. It's so frustrating. You feel victimized by this horrible disease and by your own family and friends. Finally, you give up trying to get them to understand what you are going through and become introverted and moody. I didn't invite MS to my life and I don't accept it. I fight it every day of my life.

How do I fight it? By staying on top of all the information about this disease that I can, by drug therapy, by diet and lifestyle. I believe that fighting back at your disease gives you hope. If

271

I resign myself into "acceptance of an uninvited guest," there would be no hope – MS would win. MS may destroy my relationships with those I love or even take my life, but I won't go down without giving it a fight. Healthy people have no idea how thankful they should be. Money is so powerful. It can buy your dreams, but it can't buy your health and all the things that money can buy are not pleasurable when you're sick. Good luck.

*\*\**

### Donna, Missouri

In some ways, I have MS to thank for forcing me to slow down and appreciate my life. I have three wonderful children (18, 16, and 4) and a wonderful husband. I don't know what I would do without them. My husband keeps an eye on me and will tell me to slow down when I go back to my 110-mile-an-hour pace that I have lived for so long. Each day I wake up and I am able to walk without numbness or able to see, I thank God for another "normal" day.

I used to take for granted walking an entire parking lot or up and down a flight of stairs. Now I get excited when I can. I am much more organized (although my husband may not agree). I try to plan ahead and think of how I can or will handle certain situations.

Things are looking okay for me. I try to think of MS as a minor inconvenience and my reality check when I begin to take on too much. I have no control over tomorrow, but I can be thankful for today. The only thing I can control is how I can handle this disease and handle the uncertainty. A positive attitude is the best medicine a person can have and will take one a long way. I choose to wake up each day and thank God because I don't know if I will be able to walk tomorrow, but stop and think. No one is guaranteed a tomorrow, are they? My best advice for whatever that's worth is, "Live life, love your family, and in the words of my husband, have balance." MS in a weird way has forced me to find balance and strength in my faith in God and all that is good. That's my story.

\*\*\*

*Sherry, Texas*

Losing my job and experiencing all that I did (because of MS) gave me the greatest gift I could ever have—the ability to help others.

\*\*\*

*Anonymous*

I was an artist eons ago before MS. I gave it up as a thing of the past now that I don't have the fine motor skills which is a good thing, I guess, because if I had to express my feelings about the disease I would portray it as your body being its own enemy, being eaten from the inside out. The MSAA has been wonderful. They have sent me so much to make my life more normal. It was also depressing. The walker and the scooter didn't upset me, but the little sippy cup they sent me broke me down. I sat and looked at that thing and the whole realization that I was sick came crashing down on my head. I have seen MS take one of my legs and turn it into something I don't recognize due to atrophy, while the other has stayed normal. Being a proud Southern woman, I despise being in a wheelchair and others look at me with pity. I may never be a mother. How can I ask my husband to take care of me and a newborn baby?

I want to dance on New Year's Eve. I have a good support system—my husband, my brother, and my aunt who is more like my mother. They keep me going and motivated and they don't treat me any differently. I am not sure I've helped with this letter, but at the very least I shared who I am with another person.

\*\*\*

*Lois, California*

I was diagnosed with relapsing-remitting MS in July of 2003 after awakening with two numb feet and a numb left leg. This diagnosis has been devastating. I have a 12-year-old son and a 4-year-old daughter. I wonder if I will be able to dance with my son at his wedding. Will I be able to fix my daughter's hair and makeup for her first dance in high school? Will I be strong enough to hold my grandchildren? Will I make it through my daughter's childhood without too many relapses and episodes that affect my walking as this one did, or will I have enough time to work and save for my uncertain future?

***

### Shaunee, Florida

I finally got diagnosed last year, in January 2002. Next month will be my second year. I accepted the fact that I had MS. I think I was glad to know something was wrong with me and I was not crazy after all I went through to finally know.

***

### Christine, Ohio

I used to do ballet. I was in variety shows and have spoken before large crowds. I can either grow bitter or grow better and I have chosen to grow better. I am praying for a cure for MS, not just for me but for all the ones who are hurting. Thank you for listening.

*****

*Larry G, Vermont*

My son is going on 10. He is in fourth grade this year. Last year in March just before the parent-teacher conferences, they were given a "pot of gold" and told to write a paragraph. It was posted outside the classroom. I started reading them from the left side and my son was in the last right column. They were all looking for paying off their parents' mortgages and bills, getting maids or buying a new house, getting every possible toy there was, mostly for themselves or their family. Then I read my son's paper. It gave me pause. He sure was paying attention to everything we were talking about over the year. He wrote, "If I found a pot of gold I would be the luckiest person in the world. I would spend it on the diseases to help my dad so he isn't sick from MS. Then with the rest I would give it to the poor. If I had some left I would buy toys and give them to the orphanage." Not one mention of anything for himself.

# PROJECTS SPONSORED BY YOURMOVIEPROJECT.COM

FILMS

*Documentary on MS (Presently Untitled)*
In production                                    Release date:  Winter 2004

BOOKS

*Point Source*
Published Summer 2004

*Adverse Event*
In progress                                      Release date: 2005

To order more copies of *Point Source*, please call or write Moments of Discovery Press at the address and phone number below, or log onto our website at YourMovieProject.com.

## TAKE THE NEXT STEP

If you enjoyed this book, and want to learn more about Angela Donatelli, be sure to watch for Dr. Pellegrino's next book: Adverse Event, due out in 2005. If you want to reserve an advance copy of the book, signed by the author, write to the address below, or log on to our website at YourMovieProject.com.

Moments of Discovery Press
P.O. Box 20230
Hot Springs, Arkansas 71903
1-866-storyline (786-7954)

# For further information on
# Dr. Pellegrino's Multiple Sclerosis Clinic
# and Rehabilitation Program

Call 501-623-8534

Or write to:
Richard G. Pellegrino, M.D.,Ph.D.
Donatelli Multiple Sclerosis Clinic
and Rehabilitation Program
1 Mercy Lane, Suite 505
Hot Springs, Arkansas 71913

Or visit our web page on:
YourMovieProject.com

\*\*\*

For more information about Multiple Sclerosis
you may contact:

The National Multiple Sclerosis Society
1-800-344-4867
or visit their website at
nmss.org
Or
The Multiple Sclerosis Association of America
1-800-833-4672
or visit their website at
msaa.com

## A Note about the Movie
## in YourMovieProject.com

I am currently busy adapting *Point Source* to a movie script. This, of course, will provide the loudest and most persuasive voice for people with MS. If you like this book, please help us make it a hit. As you know, movies are typically developed from best-seller books, so spread the word and encourage your friends and family to support the project by purchasing a copy. Visit YourMovieProject.com for ideas on how to publicize the project and raise awareness. Help us get the ear of Hollywood by making the project a success!

Thank you for your help.

Dr. Richard G. Pellegrino

To purchase a book, visit YourMovieProject.com or call 1-866-storyline.